the chains of orion

Arc of the Oracles
Book Three

gordon bonnet

Can you loose the bonds of the Pleiades, or break the chains of Orion? Can you lead forth the garland of crowns in their season, or guide the Bear with its children? Do you know the ordinances of heaven? Can you establish their rule on the Earth?
—- Job 38:31-33

part one
the palimpsest

one

. . .

Thurial Keene, the last Patriarch of the Holy See of Klen, stood up, trying not to let the ache in his knees and back show as he straightened his body to face the cameras. He knew he was old, and that his followers would forgive him the weakness and slowness that comes with age, but he was not ready to concede that much to himself.

He had been the Patriarch since he was forty years old, now almost three decades ago. It was hard to fathom that it had been that long. His mind was still sharp, and his memory of the day of his investiture, of accepting the jeweled orb as symbol of his high office, still had the clarity of cut crystal. Since then, he'd done his best to lead his flock and administer to the more practical matters of overseeing the care of Klen and its inhabitants.

Klen was like a country within a country, a tiny autonomous zone within the Kingdom of Cascadia. The Patriarch was not allowed to form any sort of military beyond personal guards for himself and his staff. Technically, the defense of the zone was the responsibility of the King, Lennis Acoca XII. The two men, who were almost exactly the same age and had been (respectively) invested and crowned the same year, lived in an uneasy truce. There were enough adherents of the cult of the Patriarch in Tecoa, capital of Cascadia, that deposing him would foment unrest. On the other hand, the Patriarch himself was grudgingly dependent upon the king—and the rest of Cascadia—to provide Klen not only with defense, but with food and electricity and goods to support its twenty thousand residents.

The King and the Patriarch didn't particularly like each other, and neither would have shed a tear if the other had suddenly dropped dead. But until that happened, there was nothing much to be done about it, not without altering the balance of power and creating an untenable situation.

This was why the Patriarch hadn't told anyone, not even his most trusted advisors, that he knew he would be the last to hold that office—and, in fact, since about five years ago, that one piece of information made up the sum total of his oracular gift, his knowledge of the future.

He'd only become aware of the loss gradually. It was like a river slowly drying up, becoming first a creek, then a shallow rill, then barely a trickle. The transition to a completely dry stream bed must have happened at some point, but he was damned if he could recall when.

It hardly seemed fair. His predecessors, so it was told, had complete knowledge of the past and the future, saw things so clearly they perceived no difference between the two. Seven centuries ago, one of the most famous of the Patriarchs—then called Guardians of the Word—one Kallian Dorn, was renowned not only for his foresight but for his strength, and if the legends were true, had singlehandedly defeated and slain a barbarian king who threatened his people.

Those were the days of renown. Things had been different then in so many ways. It was a harder time, when most people lived in what would now be considered poverty. Even the traditions, as timeless as they seemed, had evolved. For one thing, women had once been invested as Guardians. The shift to a patriarchy had been about two hundred years ago, by edict, ostensibly as a way of consolidating power to meet the growing strength of the king of Cascadia, and to narrow the rules of succession.

Sometimes Thurial Keene wondered if it wasn't simply because the men were afraid of sharing their power with women, but he didn't say it aloud.

And so much along the way had been lost. The Guardians had been respected, even revered. Now, the Patriarch himself was little more than a figurehead. When he was called upon to prophesy, he felt as if he were just mumbling vague words to placate his devoted followers, making it all up as he went along. Thus far, none seemed the wiser, although a couple of his advisors sometimes looked at him with suspicion when his pronouncements sailed too close to the wind.

They should have known. The thought was bitter. The Blessed Perry had said it himself, fifteen hundred years ago, during the Before Time, immediately before the Fall. The oracular gifts had come from the gods because the other means for knowledge were about to be taken away. They would last as long as they were needed, and then—when those paths to knowledge were rediscovered—might well vanish once again.

Who could look around at the cities of Cascadia now, with their FastRails and telescreens and electronic information storage and missions to the Moon, and think that the oracles were anything but a rapidly-fading anachronism?

Seemingly, though, no one did. Everyone still looked to him for guidance, as if he heard the voices of the gods as clearly as the Blessed Perry and the other Founders had.

And all the time, the knowledge burned in his mind. He would be the last Patriarch of Klen. That, and nothing else, was absolutely certain. He wasn't even certain what words he was about to utter to the waiting cameras, words that would be broadcast all over Cascadia, and probably farther still.

Worse, he didn't much care. None of it seemed important, somehow, compared with knowing the end of his entire lineage was nearly upon him.

He tried to settle his face into some semblance of confidence and command, as if he had no doubt that the words he spoke were from the very minds of the gods. He gave a nod to the woman standing behind the nearest camera. Simultaneously there was a volley of clicks as buttons were pressed to begin recording.

"My dear people of Klen, and those of the secular realm of Cascadia who nonetheless look toward us for spiritual guidance and knowledge of the eternal, I greet you. Now, in the thirty-first year of my service as Patriarch of Klen, I have momentous news of a sort that has not been possible for fourteen centuries. Not only before our own time, but before the Black Years, when war and plague and famine nearly ended our entire species. We are on the threshold of a goal last accomplished by our far distant ancestors, in the Before Time of which only a few accounts survive."

He gave a long, dramatic pause. May as well try to stir up some excitement in his audience, even if he felt little for the enterprise himself.

"As you no doubt know, the king of Cascadia has seen fit to take on the challenge of exploring other worlds, and working in cooperation with scientists from his neighboring realms, the Intermontane Empire and the Republic of Darset, manned craft were sent to the Moon five years ago to establish a permanent base there. We have always given our blessing to this effort, as anything that furthers our knowledge of the universe within which we live is to the greater glory of the gods we serve. But now, one of our very own has been chosen to lead a survey mission into the unknown, charting the far-Earth side of the Moon—something we only know of through fragmentary records, of uncertain reliability, from nearly fifteen hundred years ago.

"A young man named Kallman Dorn will be responsible for this history-making venture, leading an intrepid band of young men and women who soon will leave behind the safety of our mother planet for the airless cold of space, coming back only when they have achieved their goal of broadening our scientific understanding. One day, perhaps, reaching the almost godlike levels of sophistication possessed by our distant ancestors, may their memories be blessed. It is perhaps significant that young Kallman is himself a direct descendant of one of our most renowned lineages, and traces his heritage back to the Patriarch Kallian Dorn and his consort, the Lady Challis Mazerine, and further back still to two of the Founders, the redoubtable Colin Dorn and his consort Emily Banfield, who together helped to lead a tiny remnant of our forebears out of the fire and flood and devastation that struck down the old world, and founded Klen, which still stands proudly as a testimony to their courage."

One camera operator made a circular gesture with one hand. *Move it along.* The Patriarch absently wondered if his predecessors would have tolerated being urged to brevity by a commoner, or if they'd have had the offending hand summarily cut off. Certainly King Lennis wouldn't put up with it. The thought made his mouth twist with annoyance, and it took an effort not to grimace. In any case, he couldn't do anything while the cameras were still rolling.

"So I hope you will join with me in a prayer for the brave men and women who are taking part in this expedition, which is scheduled to launch in three weeks' time from the Cascadian National Space Agency's site near Tecoa. And most especially our beloved representative Kallman Dorn. May the gods' hands shield him until he is safely back in Klen."

He bowed his head in what he hoped would look like a gesture of sufficient piety to edify the watchers, as with another fusillade of clicks, the camera operators stopped recording.

Then they all started packing up and chatting with each other, without so much as a by-your-leave. The Patriarch had given his blessing. It was time to go get a quick breakfast and forget he even existed.

As Thurial Keene prepared to return to his office, his mind slipped into darker pathways, ones he'd been treading more and more often recently. Was there *anyone* left who actually believed? Oh, there were the Zealots, of course. There would always be Zealots. But where was the steady, clear-eyed acceptance earlier leaders of Klen had? Then, the belief of the common people in the pronouncements of the Guardian of the Word and the other oracles had been rock-solid and unshakeable. An enviable position. Why couldn't he have been born centuries earlier, when everything was so much simpler?

But, he reflected, back then what the Guardian said actually came from the divine.

What had happened that had separated him so strikingly from the source?

He trod the hallway of the Patriarchal residence, so familiar he could have found his way in the pitch dark, giving a longing look at the closed door of his quarters. How nice it would be to slip inside, turn the lock, spend the day reading in front of a crackling wood fire, letting the warmth seep into his body and chase away the chill he felt even on warm days. And not some theological tome, or even the latest scientific findings.

The science used to excite him. It seemed like new discoveries were being made every day, and that the people of Cascadia were perhaps finally approaching the knowledge humanity had achieved fourteen hundred years ago, before the fall and the flood and the intervening Black Years during which so much was lost. They'd scraped together what they could from fragmentary records that had survived—much of which had come from the Great Library of Tecoa, which had somehow escaped the worst of the destruction—and reassembled the rest through nothing more than dogged determination.

But even that no longer thrilled him the way it once had. Mostly what he wanted was escape. To fall into some cheerful fiction, and forget for a time that his own life had become an exercise in fiction as well, but without the cheer.

No such luck today. Duty called, as it always did.

He continued the long walk past his private quarters to his office, where a pile of paperwork awaited him. Mostly formalities, needing only a cursory read and his signature. Land purchases and sales negotiated with functionaries from the king, trade agreements—same. A pledge to contribute to a joint effort toward scientific exploration of the geology of the region—same. A donation of money to aid people in the western part of Cascadia, near the ruins of the ancient city, whose homes had been damaged in an earthquake three months previous.

One he still had to consider—the possible commutation of a death sentence against a citizen of Klen who had made an attempt on the life of King Lennis. Since the man had been captured within the boundaries of Klen, by a previous treaty his fate was in the Patriarch's hands, not the king's. But still, it was a sticky issue since they were, at least nominally, allies. Even so, it bothered him to execute a man for attempting something when Thurial Keene would have been just as happy had he succeeded.

He opened his office door with a sigh, walked silently across the plush carpet, and dropped into the elaborately-carved chair behind his desk. The chair, an expensive gift from the king three years earlier, was uncomfortable as hell, but his inclination to have it burned was quashed by his Chief Minister, who worried—probably rightly—that word could get back to the royal ears.

At least it discouraged him from falling asleep.

The morning hours ticked away as he worked his way through signing documents, saving the potential commutation for last. He glanced up at the clock, wondering if he could justify breaking early for lunch before making a decision, when the door to his office burst open.

Chief Minister Andres Ballinger. His dark hair was in disarray. He looked as if he'd just gotten out of bed. Impossible, though, knowing the man's habits. Thurial had often wondered if the Minister slept at all. No matter what the time of day, he had the sleek, unruffled composure of a cat.

And he *always* knocked on the door before entering the Patriarch's office, even if he'd been summoned there.

"My lord," Andres gasped out.

"What's wrong?" Only then did Thurial notice that the Minister's sleeve was torn, and his right arm had a bleeding scrape.

The Minister stared at him, his expression somewhere between horror and disbelief. "You don't *know*?"

"I…" Thurial swallowed, their gazes locked. Here it was, then. "I want to hear it from your own mouth."

Andres took a deep breath, nodded, trying to regain some of his usual calm. "I… I bring foul news, my lord. There has been… significant unrest has begun in Cascadia. It is… it is worst in Tecoa, and martial law has been declared for at least parts of the city center. But agitators are active here as well, right in the heart of Klen. I was assaulted coming out of my home this morning. I would have been here for your news conference. I apologize…"

Thurial waved this away. "Why? Who has started this?"

Once again there was a look of incredulity, and dawning understanding, from the Minister. Thurial could read it in his eyes. *He didn't know. He didn't foresee any of this. His gift is gone… and how long has it been this way? How long have I been blind to the fact that the old man has been stumbling around, reaping the privilege of powers he no longer has?*

But the Minister only said, "The Zealots. The same men and women who have been protesting the corruption and wealth of the crown and the scepter for three years now. I did not—*we* did not—recognize how organized they are."

The switch to *we* registered immediately. The office of Patriarch, and before that the Guardian of the Word, had always been held by men and women whose foresight was respected and feared. It was understood that not everything they knew was fit knowledge for everyone, and that having a detailed knowledge of the future brought with it a responsibility to decide what parts of it were necessary to reveal. Everyone took it for granted that the Patriarchs and Guardians would use their foreknowledge and wisdom to protect the people of Klen.

That one word—*we*—told Thurial Keene that the pretense was collapsing around him, just as he'd feared for years. Andres Ballinger had figured out in one blinding flash that the Patriarch was only a quite ordinary doddering old man who loved wealth and ease and was no better equipped to safeguard Klen than anyone else. Whatever gift from the gods earlier Patriarchs had, it was gone, and they both knew it.

And the expression on the Minister's face said something else as well. *But this will be our little secret, because both our lives depend on keeping up the fiction.*

Andres cleared his throat. "My lord." He shifted his feet. "I hate to be the one who delivers such news to you, but… it is my opinion and the opinion of others on your council that you should be conveyed to a different location, for your own safety. Because… your friend and ally, King Lennis Acoca XII, was murdered last night as he slept in his royal residence. He has no heir. The kingdom of Cascadia is without a ruler."

two

. . .

Kallman Dorn woke up slowly, relishing the warmth of the bed and the nearness of Marig's body. Marig was still sleeping peacefully, his chest rising and falling slowly, face completely relaxed.

Kallman closed his eyes and snuggled up. Only three more weeks, then a long, painful separation.

Almost four hundred thousand kilometers, to be exact.

Marig sighed, nuzzled the top of Kallman's head, and went back to sleep.

Kallman, though, couldn't settle back down into slumber. His mind worried at everything that had happened to him in the past years, especially the fact that very little of it had been from well-thought-out choice. He had always been fascinated with flying, and from childhood intended to become a pilot. His goal was to own a small airplane and hire out for cargo runs up and down the Pacific coast, perhaps as far as Darset. In training he'd shown astonishing aptitude, and instructor after instructor pushed him to loftier goals. By the time he graduated, he was licensed to fly jets, the first in his class of nearly a hundred young men and women. It was only a strong pacifist streak that kept him from joining the Cascadian military, but when on a lark he'd put out feelers for entering the Cascadian National Space Academy in Tecoa, he received a handshake acceptance to the program before he'd even completed the application.

He went from being a young, freewheeling guy who had no higher aspirations than to do short-flight cargo runs with his own airplane to a member of a survey crew charged with mapping the far-Earth side of the Moon in something under five years.

Along the way, he'd fallen in love with Marig Kastella, and that wasn't supposed to happen, either.

He'd had flings before, with both men and women, and they'd been mostly about the physical side of things and never lasted long. He met Marig in a bar in Tecoa one night after a grueling day of flight training. Something about the man caught his attention immediately. He was beautiful, there was no doubt about that. A mop of curly auburn hair, fair skin with a splash of freckles across the nose, long-lashed deep blue eyes that radiated kindness and intelligence. A mouth that quirked in a wry smile when he saw Kallman watching him with obvious interest.

"You look lonely," he said, dropping onto the barstool next to Marig. "Can I buy you a drink?"

"I thought I was hiding it better than that. Is it obvious?" He spoke in a low, sweet baritone, warm and mellow, with a hint of melancholy.

Kallman shrugged and laughed. "No. I just thought it might work as a pickup line."

Marig's smile widened into a grin.

Okay, he had great dimples. Always a checkmark in the *plus* column, that was.

"You're not wrong," Marig said. "And sure, I'd love a drink. I'm Marig Kastella."

"That sounds like a Darsetian name."

"My father's from Darset. He's a diplomat, still works at the embassy. My mother's from right here in Tecoa."

"I'm Kallman Dorn. I'm from Klen."

Marig's eyes widened. "With a last name like Dorn, you'd have to be. That goes back a long way."

Kallman's cheeks warmed. Sometimes having a famous last name was more of a burden than a benefit.

"Everyone's families go back exactly the same distance," he said coolly. "Some of us just wrote our names down more, is all. Nothing to brag about."

"I suppose." Marig shifted on his seat. "Sorry to touch a sore point."

"You didn't. In any case, let's get those drinks. Afterward, I might have the courage to ask you to dance, so you should think ahead and get your answer ready."

The answer was yes.

Three months later they were living together. Six months after that, Kallman was offered the opportunity to lead the mission to the far-Earth side of the Moon.

"Doesn't the idea terrify you?" Marig said one night, as he lay with his head resting on Kallman's shoulder.

"I've lost track of the number of hours I've flown."

"That didn't answer the question."

A low chuckle. "Fair enough. I guess what I'm saying is that if flying scared me, I wouldn't still be doing it."

"It's not the flying. It's being out there in the vacuum of space. And I mean... the Moon. No air. 120 degrees in the daytime, 120 degrees below zero at night."

"That's why we have space suits."

Now Marig laughed, but it sounded a little strained. "You know what I mean."

Kallman's arm tightened around his partner's shoulders, pulling him closer. "I'm not trying to make fun. I'd be lying if I said I haven't thought about it. But there have now been twenty manned missions to the Moon, and since five years ago a permanent base. Even so, we've only just begun to explore it. They've found remnants of the bases from the Before Time. From fifteen hundred years ago, can you imagine it? Hell, they're not remnants, they're time capsules. Frozen in stasis. Nothing on the Moon rusts or breaks down. Can you imagine what we'll learn? We're going to Tycho and Cassini—two places where we've done flyovers and verified there are still structures standing. It'll be like taking a time machine back a millennium and a half."

"It's hard for me to imagine."

"I'm feeling just about every emotion there is, shifting from one minute to the next. I spent my entire childhood looking up toward the stars. Now I'm going there, and most days I don't know whether to laugh or cry."

"Crying because you're overwhelmed with awe, because you're sad to leave Earth, or because you're afraid?"

"Probably a combination. Yeah, it's a little scary. It's an unforgiving place. Here, you make a mistake, there's still a good chance you'll survive. On the Moon you can't make mistakes."

"That was supposed to be comforting?"

"Well, here's the comforting part. Twenty manned missions, and we haven't lost a single person."

"Don't you be the first, my love."

"I'm going to try my hardest not to be."

"I'm excited for you. Honestly, I am. I can't help but worry, though. I spent a significant part of my life alone. Now that I have you, I can't face the possibility of losing you."

"I'll be gone for six months. Not a day longer."

"You promise?"

Kallman kissed the top of his head. "I promise."

But as the weeks and months of training went by, Kallman's confidence sagged. Part of this was because the trainer —a gray-haired veteran of four of the twenty Moon flights named Arys Quentra—left nothing to the trainees' imaginations about what would happen if there was an accident.

"If your suit depressurizes, or you're exposed to the interplanetary vacuum for some other reason," she said, her face grim, "you have perhaps thirty seconds of consciousness within which to do something about it. At that point, not only will you have run out of oxygen, the drop in pressure will cause the dissolved gases in your blood to bubble out. If you are not repressurized quickly after that, you're dead from an air embolism."

"Cheerful," the team member next to Kallman whispered.

Arys's head snapped around to face her, and there was a long moment when no one spoke. "I'm not here to cheer you up, Orzen. I'm here to prepare you for what's ahead. I have no interest in soft-pedaling what you're facing, and if you're serious about this mission, you shouldn't have, either. I thus far have a one hundred percent record of getting teams out to the Moon and back safely, and this mission will not be the one where that record is destroyed, not if I can help it." She paused, and her face softened. "I understand the combination of excitement and fear you're all feeling. I know it first-hand. Both emotions are part of why we do this, and in balance, they are a good thing. The problem is when one of them swamps the other. Too much excitement and you take unnecessary risks, endangering your life and the lives of your teammates. Too much fear and you can freeze in situations where you need to act. The key is to keep both right in front of your face. Know where you are, hone your skills so they're all second nature, understand the dangers as well as you can, and be ready for what could happen."

"We can't anticipate everything, Mem," Orzen said in a quiet voice.

"No. You're right. There's always the unexpected, the incalculable. Even the tiny bit of the universe we've explored is mighty huge when you get out into it, and it will always contain surprises. My goal is to minimize the likelihood of surprises of the unpleasant kind."

That, Kallman reflected, hadn't exactly been comforting, either.

The months of training flew by. Each day he'd come back physically and mentally exhausted, able to eat only a few bites of dinner and then falling into bed, often too tired even to make love. Then, the next morning, he'd drag himself back to the Space Academy and do it all again.

"Did you hear the Patriarch's speech?" Marig asked one morning, as Kallman came into the kitchen, fastening the last buttons on the shirt of his uniform.

"No. Was it edifying?"

"Extremely. Of course, he mentioned your famous ancestry."

Kallman gave a deep sigh. "He would. You have no idea how often I've wanted to change my name."

"You've mentioned it once or twice. It's nothing to be ashamed of, Kall. From what I've read, your ancestors were good people. Worth being proud of."

"So I've heard. If you can trust the legends, you know? Who knows how much of it was made up after the fact? Chances are they were all ordinary people, and the Patriarchs spun those tales about them to give them a gloss of being something special." He scowled. "I bet ninety-five percent of the stories are pure fiction."

"You think?"

"Come on. You really think they had knowledge of the future?"

"Some people believe the Patriarch still does."

Kallman gave a scornful laugh. "I'm sorry. He seems like a decent enough old man, but I flatly refuse to believe he knows what's going to happen, any more than you or I do. Mostly what he's good at is coming up with pious-sounding words."

"Never thought of you as the heretical type."

"It's not heresy any more. Hardly anyone believes that stuff. It's a mystery to me why they don't force him into retirement and abolish the office completely."

"People need someone to look to for inspiration."

Kallman tugged on his shirt to straighten it. "As long as they don't look my way. I'm just a guy, whatever my name is."

Marig leaned over and kissed him. "You're my guy, and you inspire me."

"That will always be enough for me."

They said their goodbyes, and Kallman left the apartment for the three-block walk to the FastRail station.

He'd only gone a block when he realized something wasn't right. The quiet neighborhood he and Marig lived in wasn't quiet—it was silent. Despite the sunny, clear, mild weather, there were no cars or bicycles, no one out for a walk, no children playing in front yards. The only sound was the light rustle of the breeze moving amongst the leaves. The feeling of dreamy surreality grew—enough that he almost turned back toward home to see if Marig had any idea what was going on—but with some effort he continued his walk to the station.

When he arrived, there were only two other people waiting for the next train, instead of the ordinary dozens.

Both of the other commuters stood near one of the large telescreens, watching a newscaster whose face was the color of whey. Kallman walked over to join them, frowning in perplexity.

"… riots in downtown Tecoa," the newscaster was saying. "Everyone is cautioned to avoid the southern and western parts of the city, especially near the palace and the central administrative offices. Some FastRail routes are still running, but expect delays until police get the situation in hand. Many businesses are closed today, so call ahead before you venture out. It is recommended that if you don't have essential business, stay home."

One of the commuters looked over at Kallman, his eyes wide. "I think I'm going to take his advice."

"Might not be a bad idea. I missed the beginning of the broadcast. What's happened?"

His expression became incredulous. "You didn't hear?"

"No."

"Someone assassinated the king."

Kallman gaped at him.

"Why?"

The other man shrugged. "No one's quite sure. You've seen the protests by the Zealots over the last few months, right? Probably one of the same crowd."

Kallman shook his head, trying to dispel the persistent feeling that this must be a dream. "I never thought they'd get violent. They mostly seemed like ultra-religious crazies objecting to the fact that they don't have as much power as they used to. Weren't they negotiating with the king's people to enact some kind of legislation protecting their beliefs?"

This elicited a snort of laughter. "You think so? The king's negotiators weren't listening. They never were. They were paying about as much attention as my wife is when she nods after I say something and says, 'Yes, dear.' It was obvious from the beginning they were only pretending to listen, to get the other side to quiet down and accept the status quo the same as they always have. Besides, the Zealots don't want legislation protecting their beliefs. They want legislation forcing everyone to believe what they do." He gave Kallman an up-and-down glance. "You military?"

"No. Space Academy."

"Figured if you were military, it'd explain why you accepted that the king's people were negotiating in good faith. Gotta accept the party line." Another evaluative look. "But I thought Academy folks would be smarter."

Kallman felt a little stung by the man's scorn. "I'm not saying I disagree with you."

This got a nod. "Anyhow, lucky thing for you you're Academy. If you were military, you'd probably be getting a call-up today. The king's people aren't going to accept this. They've already called for martial law in the worst-affected parts of the city. You can bet there'll be retaliation." He paused. "You think the Academy's going to still be running?"

"Guess I'll find out. It's twenty kilometers from the city, so maybe the riots won't have affected it."

"Hope not. That rocket you people are sending to the Moon in three weeks, I was looking forward to watching it go up."

Kallman nodded solemnly. "Yeah," he said. "Me too."

three

. . .

Reysa Sahin, Director of Antiquities at the Historical Museum of Klen, closed and locked the laboratory she leased from the Library in Tecoa and walked toward the massive front doors, her footsteps echoing on the polished marble floor. She carried a cloth-wrapped bundle underneath one arm, cradling it with her other hand as if it were an infant.

The words *You are carrying something priceless* passed through her mind. In, of course, the creaking voice of the Head Librarian of Tecoa, a gaunt old woman who looked as ancient as the Library was itself. *Their care is your personal responsibility. If they are damaged, the loss would be incalculable.*

Which Reysa knew. She had discovered what it was, so none knew better. Before her research uncovered it, no one thought they were anything more than five very old notebooks with records of accounts, detailing the sales and purchases made by a Tecoan merchant during the reign of King Lennis Acoca II, four hundred years ago. Something that would be of interest only to a scholar curious about the minutiae of economics in a nation at that point only beginning to emerge from the shadow of the Black Years.

Reysa was the one who figured out that the notebooks were a great deal more than that.

The first hint that she was studying something considerably more important than a set of four-century-old accounting books came only a week ago, while she was trying to decipher the marks on a page that had faded badly. She hunched over the manuscript, magnifiers in front of her eyes, touching the fragile paper gently with one gloved finger, and it struck her that the reason she couldn't quite make out the script was that there were other marks there as well.

They were fainter than the writing she'd been poring over, and at first she thought it was weathering, tendrils of mold, or possibly just the grain of the paper. But then, in the space between two columns of numbers, she made out what could only be letters.

...ansa...

The rest of the word, if indeed it was a word, ran under the next line of figures, and was indecipherable. But when she found a second set of letters—these even clearer—in what should have been a blank space on the following page, she was sure.

Even so, she didn't rush to tell anyone until she had found a half-dozen other examples. Caution was a reflex. Once she was certain, she tidied everything up in the lab, putting away all five volumes in a locked drawer in her desk. Only then did she go to the Librarian, after having arranged her face into some semblance of impassivity.

She gave a quiet knock on the Librarian's office door, and a dry, throaty voice responded, "Come."

Only the Head Librarian of Tecoa, Mem Andreen Veris, could pack so much meaning into a single syllable. Annoyance, superiority, exasperation, impatience, disapproval at being interrupted. Undaunted, Reysa opened the door, which swung soundlessly on well-oiled hinges.

"Mem Veris," she said, deliberately emphasizing the

honorific, and keeping her voice level with an effort. It wouldn't do for the Librarian to know she was excited about something, nor to show the older woman intimidated her. Best to act deferential but unflustered, even if she didn't feel it.

"Yes?"

"I've found something I believe you'll consider worth investigating."

This generated nothing more than a lift of one of Andreen Veris's thin gray eyebrows.

"As you know, I've been studying records from the Early Rebirth Era, during the reign of King Lennis II and his successors. In the archives there were notebooks dating from that time, catalogued as accounting books."

"Yes."

"I believe that at least some of them are more than that. It appears whoever created the accounting records, four hundred years ago, reused paper that had previously recorded something quite different. Something… much, much older."

A flicker of interest came into the Librarian's eyes. "What you're saying is that you believe they are palimpsests."

"Precisely."

"How old is the older text?"

"I am not certain, not yet. Little of it is decipherable with the naked eye. What I've seen, however, appears to be in an archaic script, but the language is clearly the Common Speech. If we can uncover the marks, it should be quite readable." She paused. "But there is one thing that especially piqued my interest. On the very first page of the first notebook, there is a name near the top of the page. I can't be sure, of course, but from the position on the page I believe it to be the name of the person who wrote the original text." She swallowed. "Julia Lowell."

The Librarian's eyes flew open wide. Reysa had to stop

herself from smiling. She'd anticipated this would get a reaction.

"You're sure of this?"

"Yes, I'm certain that's what it says. Under magnification, and in proper light, it's quite legible."

"Why has this not been discovered before now?"

"Three reasons, I think. First, the writing is quite faint. In ordinary light, it's difficult even to see. Second, I don't believe anyone thought to look. Ledger books aren't what most scholars are searching for when they come to the Library, so it's unlikely these have been pulled off the shelf in decades, possibly centuries. And third, even if someone did open them at some point—well, there's the problem that people so often tend not to see what they're looking at. If you glance at a page, and what you expect to see is a column of numbers and lists of goods for sale, then that's all you *do* see. Our expectations create a remarkably efficient set of blinders."

"Not for you, though." Mem Veris's voice and expression were wry.

Reysa shrugged. "I'm no different. It just happened that I *was* interested in Early Rebirth Era economic records, so I looked carefully, and noticed something more. There was a good measure of luck to it. I could easily have missed it myself."

The Librarian gave a nod of approval, the first one Reysa could remember getting in a long while. Modesty was always a good choice when dealing with her.

"What of the original text have you deciphered thus far?"

"Not much. The only parts that are readable are where spaces between the words and figures of the later writing left blank areas, and it's obvious the person who used these notebooks as ledgers wanted to conserve paper as much as possible. He, or she, filled just about every available blank area."

"Paper was a precious commodity back then."

"Yes. Thus the reuse. But here are a few of the fragments I've been able to make out. This is tentative, you understand, pending further scrutiny. I wanted to inform you of the discovery before pursuing a deeper analysis of the manuscripts."

She set a sheet of paper down on Mem Veris's desk, and the older woman frowned at it, reading.

...f Julia Lowell, rec...

...ecords of the set...

...ansa...

...lood as fores...

...lled Klen, as...

...one of th...

...die...

"Fascinating," Mem Veris said in a husky whisper.

"I thought it was."

"Whom have you told?"

"No one. As the Head Librarian, you needed to be informed first."

This got another nod. Time to capitalize on her thus-far positive response before the opportunity passed.

"I would like to make a proposal," Reysa said. "We have, at the Museum in Klen, devices able to perform multispectral imaging. I, and others at the Museum, have studied other palimpsests, although none dating from the First Settlement Era..."

"It's a surmise the manuscript is that old," Mem Veris interjected.

"Certainly. But even if this wasn't written *by* Julia Lowell, but *about* her, it's still well worth scrutiny. We have cameras that take multiple images of the manuscript, using different frequencies of light, and superimpose them. Then digital analyzers combine the images, allowing marks too faint to see —or hidden behind more recent writing—to be read. You have nothing of the sort here in Tecoa, do you?"

Reysa knew the answer, but might as well follow the protocols.

"No," Mem Veris admitted. "I believe that there are antiquities departments in research facilities in Darset that have something of the kind. But no, nothing here."

"I would like to request permission to take the notebooks back to my laboratory at the Museum, where they will be thoroughly analyzed. When we are done, they will be returned here."

"And the procedure does no harm to the manuscripts themselves?"

"Of course not."

The slight note of annoyance in Reysa's voice was enough to cause a perceptible stiffening in Mem Veris's posture, but it was obvious the older woman's curiosity had been engaged enough to overcome this.

"These notebooks—if you are correct, they are beyond price. You must understand that my caution stems from a desire to protect them."

"I do understand, and agree completely. We will treat them as such. Keep in mind that not only the notebooks themselves, but the information they may contain, may uncover knowledge that has lain hidden for fifteen hundred years. While I understand your concern about my taking them, the other option—leaving artifacts of the First Settlement here, unread—seems to me to be passing up an opportunity of incalculable value."

This time, Mem Veris didn't caution her against making assumptions about the manuscripts' antiquity.

"How long do you think the analysis will take?"

"It's hard to say. Months, I suspect. But rest assured that I will stay in constant communication with you. Whatever I and my assistants uncover, you will know about immediately. The notebooks are yours, after all."

"Yes. They are."

"The partnership between the Museum and the Library has proven of tremendous value to both our facilities in the past. This venture could lead to a new level of cooperation and scholarship."

Now Mem Veris's mouth quivered, which was as close to a smile as those thin lips ever got. Okay, maybe that had been laying it on a bit thick.

"Very well, Reysa, you've made your case. I understand the situation completely and will consider it. Come back tomorrow, and you will have your answer."

As she returned to her lab, Reysa congratulated herself—it could hardly have gone better. Knowing Mem Veris's prickly disposition, and her tendency to act as if everything in the Library was her own personal property, a categorical *no* had not been outside the realm of possibility. While a positive decision wasn't a certainty, there was no doubt she'd played the Librarian's intellectual curiosity skillfully. Now, just give it a day to settle in, so Mem Veris would lay claim to the idea as if she'd come up with it herself—this was always a necessity—and before long Reysa would be bringing the precious notebooks back to her own laboratory in the Museum in Klen.

It had played out almost exactly as she hoped. Two days later, she made a presentation to the Library's Board of Directors. She chose her words carefully, leaving it ambiguous whether she had discovered the secret of the notebooks or Mem Veris had. Reysa had no problem letting the Librarian have an undeserved share in the discovery, especially since the decipherment of the palimpsests was going to be entirely Reysa's doing.

Even Mem Veris couldn't justify laying claim to any hand in that, given that the equipment wasn't in Tecoa.

So a week, almost to the minute, after her first shocked realization of what she had laid out on her desk, Reysa Sahin walked with the cloth-wrapped bundle of notebooks out of the Library and toward the FastRail station that would take her back to her home in Klen. The old woman's final stern words still rang in her ears.

"Remember. You are carrying something priceless. Their care is your personal responsibility. If they are damaged, the loss would be incalculable."

Reysa smiled. No more nonsense about *we don't really know how old they are.* It had only taken the Librarian a few days to go from a doubter to full acceptance that here were fifteen-hundred-year-old documents from the First Settlement Era, a time that was so lost in the deep waters of history that many thought every piece of information known about it was nothing more than mythology.

Now, if luck stayed with her, soon she would have evidence that the five slim volumes she had tucked under her arm were written by one of the founders herself—someone the Patriarch himself occasionally referred to as *Saint Julia.*

Reysa boarded the train in such a profound reverie that it was only once she was seated that she stopped to wonder why she was the only passenger in the car.

four

. . .

"**B**ut, my lord…"

Thurial Keene cut off the words of his Chief Minister, Andres Ballinger, with a wave of the hand and a quick shake of his head. "Absolutely not."

"We cannot guarantee your safety if you stay here in the Patriarch's residence. The violence in Tecoa…"

"Does not involve us," the Patriarch said. "It is a revolt against the secular leadership, not the spiritual. The Zealots are true believers. They would not harm the people who represent their faith."

"My lord, I think you are wrong about that." Ballinger met his eyes for a moment, then looked down, as if ashamed that he so blatantly contradicted someone whose knowledge of both past and future was supposed to be absolute. "The Zealots lump us in with the king and his people. They don't want to support the faith, they want to purify it. With fire, if need be. They believe we've been corrupted by wealth, and that we traded our belief for money and power. At its heart, it is a conflict between those who have privilege and those who do not." He gestured toward the Patriarch with both hands. "It is undeniable what side of that equation you lie on."

The Patriarch looked around at his richly-decorated office, and decided there was no arguing that point.

"I fail to see how barricading myself into the guest house at Falcon Lake will accomplish anything."

"It is high up in the mountains. The road to it goes through Wind Ridge Pass, which is narrow and easily guarded. It is in territory that was ceded to Klen, so we have jurisdiction there if any attack should occur. The guest house is amply provisioned, with supplies for eight weeks or more. So in the unlikely event that we were cut off..."

The Patriarch smiled. "We?"

Ballinger's sallow cheeks reddened. "I naturally assumed, my lord, that if you were to move your administrative office to the guest house, that as your advisor, I..."

The Patriarch waved him off again. "Naturally," he said, his tone gently mocking. Ballinger's choice of words had left no doubt—he was badly scared, not just for the Patriarch's safety, but for his own.

For good reason. The history of Tecoa gave ample evidence that when a ruler was assassinated, his cronies usually were eliminated in short order.

The Chief Minister swallowed hard. "I would only accompany you if you wish, my lord. I merely urge you to consider moving to Falcon Lake because here, in the middle of Klen, open to all who come... your residence here would be much harder to defend should the need arise."

"You know that was a choice. My predecessors wished the Patriarch and his staff to be accessible to the people."

Ballinger's lips tightened with annoyance. "I know that, my lord, but in this situation..."

"This situation is no different than any other. I have no desire whatsoever to leave here."

This, in fact, was a lie. The truth was the thought of escape had never been far from the Patriarch's mind in the last months. The difference was that he didn't simply want to retreat, tail between his legs, to his fancy guest house, where he would still have to attend to his duties and deal with signing never-ending paperwork and keep up the pretense that he actually had the authority and knowledge his devotees believed he had.

No, he would only leave if he could get out of Klen entirely. Go into retirement. Maybe head south to one of the sunny seaside towns in Darset.

Would they grant him asylum, allow him to spend his final years there? A tranquil little house with a small garden, no duties or responsibilities other than doing what he wanted, no one looking up to him in undeserved awe. Quiet, faceless, nameless anonymity was what he craved, not a temporary change of venue.

Unless he could get that, he was staying right here in his residence, where at least he had the comfort of his own bed at night.

And if the Zealots broke in and killed him, what then? He wasn't fond enough of this life that the thought frightened him. Six hundred years ago, a woman who was being forced into exile had made a prophecy that the last of the Guardians of the Word would live to see the Royal House of Acoca come to an end. When the Patriarch came to the knowledge that he was, in fact, the last of the Guardians, he wondered idly if it would prove true, or if the woman had merely been screeching her anger at the king and his cronies. The claim, like much of the old lore, seemed like nothing more than idle storytelling, as likely to be false as true.

A heretical position, certainly, and one he didn't speak of to anyone.

But sure enough, he'd outlived old King Lennis. The prophecy had been right after all, thanks to some assassin. If the Patriarch himself died now, it was only fitting that the whole ridiculous superstructure of government and faith came to an end simultaneously.

But Ballinger was speaking again.

"My lord, you know best. I simply fear for your safety. Our intelligence shows that the Zealots are targeting people all over Cascadia, not only in the capital. It simply seems prudent to move your residence for a time, until this violence can be contained."

"No. Categorically no." He met his Chief Minister's eyes steadily. "This conversation is over. But you mentioned there was someone else who desired to speak with me this morning?"

Ballinger clearly recognized a lost argument, and gave a small sigh of resignation. "Yes, my lord. The Director of Antiquities at the Museum, Reysa Sahin. She claims to have made a remarkable discovery, something she believes will be of great interest to you."

The Minister himself sounded anything but interested.

"Oh? What is it about?"

"It concerns a manuscript she found in the Library in Tecoa. I don't know the details. Shall I bring her in?"

"Yes, please do."

Ballinger nodded and left the office, the displeasure rolling off him in waves.

A moment later he returned leading a small, slim young woman with wavy dark hair in a trim cut and intelligent hazel eyes. In her hands she clasped a sheaf of papers.

Ballinger gestured toward her. "My lord Patriarch, Reysa Sahin, Director of Antiquities at the Historical Museum of Klen."

"A pleasure," Thurial said. "I don't believe we've met?"

"No, my lord. I've only been in the position for eight months, and prior to that I did archaeological field work in the ruins of the ancient city. It's only been recently I've spent much time in Klen."

"But with a name like Sahin, you must be from here." He smiled at her in what he hoped was an encouraging fashion.

She shifted her weight slightly, and the papers rustled, but her eyes never left his. Not intimidated, the Patriarch could see that. Good. He appreciated someone strong enough to meet him on equal footing.

"Yes, my lord," she said. "My mother and father both come from old lineages of Klen."

"And my Chief Minister tells me you have made some sort of a new discovery."

"I have. I have been interested in finding documents from the Black Years, and spent time in the Library in Tecoa searching the Archives for records that might have been stored there."

"I don't believe many records of any kind were kept during the Black Years."

"No, my lord, indeed not. But I found notebooks that appeared on first glance to be the accounting records of a merchant from about four hundred years ago, and that turned out to be something far older."

"How much older?"

"Before the Black Years. It is a palimpsest, my lord. Pages that were overwritten during a time when paper was a rare and precious commodity. We have begun to decipher the older writing, and found that it is from the time of the First Settlement."

The Patriarch's heart gave an uneven gallop. All right, this was interesting after all. A welcome diversion from the unpleasantries that had occupied his mind for the past week.

"You're sure about this?"

"Quite sure. I and my team have done a multispectral analysis of the first ten pages of the first notebook, and it is evident that the document is a record book written as an account of the founding of Klen." She paused. "It was written by the Blessed Julia Lowell."

There was dead silence in the Patriarch's office for nearly a minute. Even the Chief Minister seemed to have forgotten his pressing concern about the Patriarch's safety, and was staring at the young Director of Antiquities with undisguised astonishment.

"Am I understanding you correctly?" The Patriarch stopped and cleared his throat. "Did you say the writing is *about* the Blessed Julia, or actually written *by* her?"

"The evidence is incontrovertible. It was written by her."

"No records survived that directly chronicle the First Settlement," the Chief Minister said quietly.

"No records that we knew of," Reysa said, without turning to look at Ballinger directly, but continuing to address the Patriarch. "You undoubtedly know that there are many books in the Library that date to the Before Time. During the time of the flood and the earthquake, and the years of plague and famine that followed, the ability to keep written records was lost in many places, including in Klen. Your own predecessors, my lord, entrusted all knowledge to their memories because there was no other way to maintain it from generation to generation. The very capacity for reading and writing were lost."

"Yes."

"When your honored forebear Kallian Dorn and his consort, Challis Mazerine, brought back the knowledge of writing to Klen, records began to be kept once again. Histories began to be written, some of them chronicling the Black Years, but all of them were writing down what were then only distant memories of the Lackland Wars and the horrible times that followed. We thought that between the destruction of the ancient city in the earthquake and flood, and Kallian Dorn's time, there were no primary records whatsoever that had survived." She paused, and those intense eyes never left his. "This understanding was wrong."

"Might I... might I see some of what you've uncovered?" He could hear the tremor of excitement in his own voice.

When was the last time something had affected him emotionally like this? It felt like decades.

"Of course, my lord. That is the reason I came here today." She placed the sheaf of papers on the desk in front of him.

He began to read.

This is the account of Julia Lowell, recording how, guided by oracles whose knowledge came from the mind of God, a few were spared from the devastation wrought upon this land only three years ago by earthquake and flood. I will tell how we fortunate men, women, and children came here to this place of refuge, in the month of July during the Year of Our Lord 2035.

Without looking up, the Patriarch breathed the words, "I can hardly believe this."

"I feel the same way, my lord."

The document continued:

I wish not only to record here the doings of the people of Klen, but to set down what came before as a caution to anyone who might read this. The old city of Seattle, and the rest of the modern world, did not collapse through some kind of accident. Destruction was wrought by the hand of God, yes, but more than that, our nation and the others like it brought it upon themselves. We of the old world were undone by our own arrogance. Wealth and justice were only available to the few, and those few used their positions of power to gather more and more riches, thinking that they were secure in their mansions and palaces. But desperate men and women can only be crushed underfoot for so long before they will realize they have nothing to lose by acting.

Perhaps by recording these events here, our descendants can stop themselves from repeating the mistakes that destroyed the world we knew and left us ragged few banding together just to survive. My wish is that you take this not only as a history but as a warning.

"It's..." The Patriarch stopped, licked his lips, and met the gaze of the Chief Minister. "She could almost be describing our own time."

Ballinger's face was ashen, and he did not respond.

"My lord," Reysa said. "When I saw this, I knew I had to bring it directly to you. The fact that this document came to light right now, considering what is happening in Tecoa—it is not a coincidence."

"I… I don't know." The excitement had winked out, and what rose in him was a bleak horror at what the document contained. What had he expected? That it would be filled with the kind of bland platitudes his own speeches were composed of? As little as was known for certain about the First Settlement, and the Black Years that followed not long after, no one doubted that they must have been terrible to live through.

He had hoped the discovery would be an interesting diversion from the worries about what was happening in the world outside. All it had done was put the current situation under an even sharper lens.

"You need to tell everyone about this," Reysa said quietly. "Bring the Blessed Julia's warning to the people who are sowing division and violence in Cascadia before it's too late."

"Who would listen to words from a fifteen-hundred-year-old document?" He almost added, *or anything I have to say about it*, but that was too self-pitying to voice aloud to this earnest young woman.

"My lord," she said, "the message in the manuscript speaks directly to what is happening. If you brought this to light, people would listen, I know they would."

"I fail to see how the Blessed Julia's words would stop the violence, when the efforts of the authorities have been insufficient to do so."

"The Zealots—don't you see, my lord? This might be the only sort of message they *would* listen to. The words of one of the first generation of oracles. The woman whose memory has been revered for a millennium and a half, who is looked upon almost as a god. What would happen if you, the leader of the faith on Earth, were to give them the words of the Blessed Julia herself, saying, *You must stop this, this is wrong?* That it had been tried before, and created something very like hell?"

He didn't answer, and for a moment, there was silence in the room.

"Don't you believe this document was discovered for this very purpose?"

The Patriarch gave a weary sigh. "I don't know," he said again.

A flicker of doubt came into the young woman's eyes. Doubt, he sensed, not about the discovery she claimed to have made, but doubt that he had any faith at all left in his own authority.

Something the Patriarch was beginning to recognize all too well. He'd seen it in the face his Chief Minister. With Ballinger, though, it had carried a different message. *You and I both know, but there's no reason anyone else has to find out.* Here, what he saw in the young researcher's expression was more *You really are nothing more than an old fraud, aren't you? And a bit of a coward as well?*

"My lord," she said, and appeared to be exerting some effort to keep her voice level. "Before you decide, perhaps you should read the passage on the last page. When I saw this, I knew I needed to see you, to speak to you about what I'd found."

He stifled another sigh, and turned to the last page in the stack.

Do not misunderstand. We did not fail as a society because we were wicked. Ours was a sin of omission, not of commission. Yes, evil people did evil things, but none of us asked the question of why these men and women chose evil in the first place. Middle-class citizens, leading their middle-class lives, became so comfortable that we neglected our duty of care toward those who labored and toiled on our behalf. We willfully turned away from the needs of our brothers and sisters, and have paid the price.

The purveyors of chaos who destroyed the world we knew did not come from hell. They were not created by Satan. Once, I would have found that easy to believe myself. All too easy—because if evil is created by some powerful supernatural being, we can put our hands together and say, "I will pray for God to intervene," or worse, throw our hands up and say, "Nothing I do will make a difference." The truth is far more ordinary, and far more devastating. Extreme beliefs of any kind are born of a desperate need to find meaning and justice in a world that seems to have neither. The anger of the terrorist and the fire of the zealot come from the same sources: the desire to make sense of suffering, and the terrifying reality that the only cure for it is the leap of faith that is love.

We failed because we were blind. Blind and afraid. Blind to the suffering of our brothers and sisters, and afraid to see reality, afraid to admit that we'd been wrong to shrug our shoulders and leave the care of others in the hands of God. We were complacent when we should have been fierce, and resigned when we should have fought with everything we had.

Listen, I am just an ordinary old woman, and all too soon I will be gone. But I see the young people here in Klen growing up and having children of their own, and I know the world will rebuild itself. Perhaps it will take centuries, but it will happen. I write this down not because I am some kind of authority making pronouncements from on high, but because I have been a witness to events that will haunt my dreams until the day I die. If this document survives, and is read by someone years hence—I beg you, listen to these words and don't make the same mistakes we did. So many were lost, and so much. Humanity should never have to endure this again.

Temper yourselves with love, not with fire. Reach out your hand instead of striking out with the sword. Care for the knowledge you have, care for the land, and most of all, care for each other.

In the end, nothing else really matters.

Reysa stared at the Patriarch.

The Patriarch stared back.

"At least tell the people what she wrote," Reysa finally said.

"What if they don't believe it?"

"What if they do?" Reysa's words, quick and sharp as a struck bell, were nothing short of a challenge.

The Patriarch shook his head.

"All you can do is try." She tipped her head toward Andres Ballinger, still standing to one side, silent. "Talk it over with your Chief Minister. I will leave this transcription with you. I have another copy. You will do what you think best." She paused, and a determined look came into her eyes. "However, if you don't make this public, I will."

five

. . .

Dain Sarkos swept an imperious gaze across the crowd in the dimly-lit hall.

"It's been done before." His intense voice hardly needed amplification, and the room was deathly silent, as his devotees waited breathlessly for his next pronouncement. "Let the secular so-called leaders tremble to think of it. Two thousand years ago a man named Martin Luther dared to stand up to the corrupt men of his time and say to his followers, 'Be confident of entering into heaven through many tribulations rather than through the false security of peace.' He wrote out his words of challenge and nailed them to the door of the place of worship, despite the risk to himself."

Someone in the crowd said "Amen," in a quiet voice.

"And fifteen hundred years ago, Saint Julia stood up to the evil ones of her own day, the corrupt and iniquitous, and said, 'Leave everything you have behind, and follow me.' And some few did, the blessed ones of memory, but many more did not. They ridiculed her words and stood firm in their foolishness and wickedness—and the hands of the gods struck them down with fire and flood, with plague and earthquake and famine. See how the sinful are met with swift justice."

Louder shouts of "Amen."

"Every generation has its people of courage and its cowards. The pure and the corrupt. Just a week ago the king himself was struck down by a man of such pure heart." He swept his gaze over the upturned faces, meeting one pair of eyes after another, as if saying, *I see you. I look into your very soul.* "It may be that some of the king's party are here in this room right now, waiting to hear what I say so they may silence me. And to that I say—I welcome you to try. Like Martin Luther, like Saint Julia, the virtuous will not be silenced. Why do you think the one who killed the king has yet to be found? The gods guided his hand, and they are protecting him now. Saint Julia herself looks down at him with approval. Against such righteousness as this, the secular powers will quail and slink back into the darkness where they were born."

He paused, letting his words sink in, letting silence settle back over the crowd.

"Look at what the secularists have done to us. Turned our eyes away from the spiritual, kept us focused on the foolish and the mundane. Made us believe that knowledge can be found in books. Why are books necessary when true knowledge comes from revelation? Books fall into two categories. Either they agree with revealed truth, in which case they are superfluous, or they contradict revealed truth, in which case they are heretical. In either case, they should be banned, or destroyed outright.

"Despite this, we have allowed the words in books to take over our schools. To endanger our children's very souls. Even our sacred language, given by the gods to the Blessed Quaice, is only taught as a curiosity, studied like some fossil instead of revered as a living language, as the very language of the gods.

If I said to you, *'Magzome lóga,'* which even of you would understand and be able to respond, *'Kles, lémba bak^?"*

Many of the crowd shifted uneasily in their seats. Sarkos allowed the moment to hang suspended. When he spoke, it was nearly in a whisper.

"'The darkness is coming.' 'Yes, so let it be.'" He gazed around at the upturned faces, spectral in the dim light. "I tell you, even the secularists know in their hearts what they have done, and understand the judgment that awaits. Why do you think they turn your focus onto such diversions as traveling into space? They think by breaking the bonds of Earth, they can escape the justice of the gods. Or do perhaps they think that out there amongst the stars, they will find the abode of the gods and become gods themselves? Such pride cannot be tolerated. The men and women who have raised science to a false idol, who try to turn your faces away from piety and propriety, must be stopped. They and the secular powers are in league to have dominion over the Earth, but they shall not triumph."

An even longer pause. No one in the audience dared to move. Some seemed to be holding their breath.

"Do not be afraid," Sarkos thundered. The explosive violence of his voice made a number of people startle. "Let *them* be afraid. Be certain that the feeble and aged Patriarch is shivering in fear right now in his palace in Klen. His false piety is vile. His days, too, are numbered, and he knows it. Whether it is one of us who strikes him down, or the hammer of the gods themselves, the time of corruption is nearing its end. The worship of wealth, the elevation of opulence and ease and frivolity—all of it will be burned by the purifying fires. From those ashes shall come a society where the only thing to fear will be the righteous wrath of the gods toward those who embrace evil."

He stopped, closed his eyes, and bowed his head, putting his hands together.

There was nearly a full minute of silence, then one by one, people started to clap. At first it was only a few, but soon everyone was on their feet, bathing Sarkos in a whirlwind of applause and shouts of acclamation. Many were screaming. Some were weeping, hands raised over their heads, inviting Saint Julia and the gods to rain down their blessings on this prophet who stood before them.

Sarkos held himself completely still, letting the noise wash over him.

All would be well, he said to himself. Perhaps he would be arrested as soon as he set foot outside the hall, but even so, all would be well. Tonight, the avalanche he had worked so hard to create over the past few months had reached a size and speed that could not be stopped.

Let them arrest him. Kill him, even, for all the good that would do them.

The gods, and the blessed Saint Julia, were watching.

He left the stage, the crowd still in a near frenzy, into the waiting hands of his aides.

"You think that was wise?" one of them said, handing him a handkerchief to mop the sweat from his face. "Explicitly promoting violence against the Patriarch?"

Sarkos gave a grim laugh. "You think anyone here in Tecoa honestly cares about that old fool? He's not even a figurehead any more. The ones who claim to follow him are no better than the seculars."

"I know, but to state publicly you want him assassinated…"

"Let them arrest me, then. They'll have a riot on their hands." He jerked his head toward the room where the crowd was still in tumult. "I stated nothing more or less than the truth. The king's cronies might have stopped us, had they acted earlier. But now? It hardly matters if I live or die. Our people will purify society, or else burn it to the ground." He gave the aide a brittle smile. "That's the difference between me and the Patriarch, you see. I actually believe what I'm telling people."

"I know," the aide said again, a hint of exasperation slipping into his voice. "I merely fear for your safety."

Sarkos gave the man a long look. Perhaps it was time to reevaluate which of his followers he chose to surround himself with. This one—what was his name, Latimer? He couldn't recall for certain—didn't seem to have the fervor and certainty he required.

To judge by the reaction of the crowd, there were plenty of other men and women who would be honored and delighted to step into his role.

Maybe a house-cleaning was in order.

"There is no need to fear for me. If I am harmed, even killed, what of it? My place in the Afterworld is assured. As for my enemies, they may seem to triumph for a time, but they will ultimately fall into ruin." He paused, and their gazes locked. "If you feel that your spirit is wavering…"

"No, no, not at all," Latimer said, his eyes growing wide with alarm. "You are our leader, is all. I wish no harm to come to you. But you are right. Our sacred cause can never fail."

Sarkos let the moment hang there, then gave the aide a reassuring pat on the upper arm. "I appreciate your devotion. You and the others, see to it that the hall is cleared and locked. Give it no more than a half hour." Another chilly smile. "If there is damage to be wrought, let it be against a more deserving target than our own meeting hall."

Sarkos donned his light jacket, trotted down the stairs, and exited into the alleyway at the back of the building.

It was only a three-block walk to the run-down apartment he rented for a nominal fee from one of his devotees. He lived off gifts from his followers, but most of them were in no positions of wealth themselves. It was enough to buy food, but hardly enough for any luxuries, including a nicer dwelling place.

Oh, well. The twinges of envy he felt sometimes toward people like the King and the Patriarch, in their opulent palaces eating the finest food and sleeping under down blankets, had to be balanced against the knowledge that Saint Julia and the others of her time had endured hardships the likes of which he was yet to experience. That time might well come—if what he had planned worked, it *would* come—but until now, his life had been one of comparative ease.

A light rain hissed down from the overcast night sky. It swirled in gauzy curtains against the glow of the street lamps, and rivulets of water snickered and chuckled as they ran down the gutters and into the storm sewers. Despite his confidence, there was no denying he was tired. The first goal—assassinating the king—had been achieved. Targeting his ministers, who aided and abetted the secularization of the entire society, was next. Then, to breach Klen, and go after the Patriarch and his party, who as the nominal leader of the faith, should—of all people—have known better.

O ye of little faith. It was a line Sarkos had read in one of the books of lore from the Before Time. He'd found it in the Library of Tecoa as a child, and never forgotten it. And the other passage, burned into his mind indelibly.

Woe unto you, scribes and Pharisees, hypocrites! For ye shut up the kingdom of heaven against men: for ye neither go in yourselves, neither suffer ye them that are entering to go in. Woe unto you, scribes and Pharisees, hypocrites! For ye devour widows' houses, and for a pretense make long prayer: therefore ye shall receive greater damnation. Woe unto you, scribes and Pharisees, hypocrites! For ye compass sea and land to make one proselyte, and when he is made ye make him twofold more the child of hell than yourselves.

The ancients knew. They understood. Did the Patriarch even read the books of knowledge they'd had in the Before

Time? Few enough of them had survived, but the ones that had were priceless. Chances were, if he did, he picked and chose the bits that justified his hypocrisy and allowed him to continue amassing wealth.

All very well. It would end soon. He would see.

For now, though, to a well-earned bed…

He reached out for his doorknob, but at the same time a firm hand clamped across his wrist.

"Dain Sarkos?" The voice was a deep rumble. Its owner's face was unrecognizable, obscured by the shadow from a hat.

"I'm Dain Sarkos."

"You are under arrest for fomenting violence and rebellion."

His arm was pulled roughly behind his back, the other seized and treated the same way, and a pair of handcuffs snapped across both wrists.

Sarkos laughed. "You think this is necessary? I have no interest in fighting back against you."

"Standard procedure," the man growled, and put one hand on Sarkos's upper arm.

"I wonder what sort of standard procedures the dead king's soul is enduring in hell right now?"

This elicited a grunt of anger, and his captor jerked his arm and forced him to walk back to the street, where half a block away, a car waited.

It amused Sarkos that they'd parked far enough away that he wouldn't know they were waiting for him. They really did misjudge him if they thought this kind of thing could make him afraid.

The ride to the headquarters of the Tecoa Police Force took only ten minutes, and no one spoke. Just as well. He had nothing to say to them, nor, he suspected, they to him.

Once there, he was pulled out of the car and propelled into the building. After one particularly vicious shove, Sarkos said, his voice full of cheer, "Was that part of standard procedure, too?"

"Shut up."

Down a well-lit hall, up a flight of stairs, and into a corridor with multiple doors. Finally, near the end, into a small windowless room with a table and a pair of chairs. He was forced to sit, and the cuffs unlocked temporarily so they could be looped through the chair back. Then the man who had arrested him scowled at him, and Sarkos stared back, unperturbed. The policeman was a big man, well over two meters tall, with a fleshy face and heavy eyebrows.

"They'll be here to question you soon."

Sarkos shrugged. "Saint Julia sees everything you do."

The officer snorted in derision, but didn't respond. He exited the room, locking the door behind him.

They left him waiting for nearly an hour. All, he knew, part of the plan. Leave him there for a while to contemplate his fate, hoping it would make him more willing to talk when the time came. He sat perfectly still in the chair. The only sound was, for a time, the slow drip of rainwater from his jacket onto the floor, but finally even that stopped.

Eventually there was the sound of the door lock turning, and it opened to admit a tall, slender man with a weather-worn face, thinning hair, and a close-cropped mustache and beard. Their eyes met, and he seemed to be evaluating his prisoner. His expression was keen, perceptive, intelligent. Eyes that noticed everything, a mind that forgot nothing.

"Dain Sarkos?"

"I am Sarkos."

"I'm Davit Kelway. I'm the Chief Investigator for the Police Force of Tecoa."

"I would offer to shake your hand, but I seem to be indisposed."

This did not elicit a smile, not that he expected it to.

"Before we begin, I need to inform you that we are

currently being recorded, so anything you say could be used as part of the prosecution, should this case come to trial."

"I am aware of that."

"You know why you were arrested?"

"Yes."

"The officer arresting you explained the charges?"

"Yes."

"Do you have anything to say in response?"

"In response to my being accused of encouraging violent revolt?"

"Yes." Kelway's voice betrayed a hint of annoyance. "That's what we're discussing, isn't it?"

"Indeed. In that case, my only response is that I have done exactly that. The abandonment of the faith by the people in power has left me and my followers with no choice."

"So you're admitting to what you've been accused of."

"Exactly."

"You realize that this will make it impossible for there to be any defense, or indeed, a trial. When the judge receives this recording, you will proceed directly to the sentencing phase."

"Of course I'm aware of that."

Kelway frowned. He seemed to be trying to determine if there was something more to the man's words than was apparent.

"Very well," he finally said. "But there are other matters about which I have questions. The king's assassination was carried out by a member of your cult, was it not?"

"I object to your referring to it as a cult, but otherwise, that is an accurate statement."

"The name of the assassin is Bennit Oswill."

"Are you telling me that, or is it a question?"

"I am asking for your confirmation of the fact."

"I will not bear witness against someone of whose actions I approve. Whoever killed the king, I would not lift a finger against him. And I will neither confirm nor deny his identity. That is up to you to determine."

Kelway nodded. "That's what I expected you to say."

Sarkos gave him a smile. "I'm glad to have confirmed your expectations."

"What about the Patriarch?"

"What about him?"

"Did you incite your followers to violence against the Patriarch?"

"I have no doubt you have agents of the police present at my meetings, and therefore know exactly what my words were. But no matter. If you wish to hear them again, what I said was that his time on Earth is nearing its end, and that whether I, or one of my followers, or the hand of the gods is what strikes him down hardly matters. The time of his false piety and corruption is almost over. What will come afterward will be purification. The choice will be to burn, or to be burned. Which will you choose, Mr. Kelway?"

"Are you threatening me?"

Sarkos laughed, and pulled at his handcuffs. "I am hardly in a position to make threats personally. But"—he fixed Kelway with a fierce gaze—"perhaps I am not the one you should be concerned about."

Through the solid walls of the building, there came from the outside the noise of raised voices. Screams, shouts, clashes of metal against metal. Then the unmistakable report of gunshots.

Kelway and Sarkos stared at each other for a long moment.

"Perhaps, Chief Investigator," he said in a completely calm voice, "you might want to consider repentance right now, while you still have time."

six

. . .

One week until launch.

The violence plaguing Tecoa in the last weeks had, thus far, spared both Kallman Dorn's neighborhood and the Space Academy. For those who didn't work downtown, fairly quickly most people shrugged their shoulders and accepted that the overall risk was probably low, and in any case, they couldn't stay home from their jobs forever. The FastRail lines were mostly still running, although—in the words of the chairperson—"delays will sometimes be inevitable," a statement that was as unhelpful as it was vague. Kallman's daily rides to the Space Academy were back to about half the crowds there'd been before the riots started in earnest, and the riders he spoke to mostly had the attitude, "It all seems to be calming down, things'll be fine."

So each day, Kallman dressed in his uniform and headed off to the Academy, nestled in the wooded hills twenty miles east of the city center, ready for the last bit of training detail before he'd be on the rocket that even now sat on its launch pad, waiting to pierce the vacuum of space on its way to the Moon.

That morning, Kallman came into the living room to find

Marig sitting on the sofa, staring at the telescreen, eyes wide, jaw slightly open. His expression of astonishment would have been comical if he hadn't seemed so completely serious.

"What?" Kallman said, straightening his tie, then giving Marig a kiss, which he reciprocated in an abstracted sort of way.

"Do you have a moment before you have to go? Because you *definitely* need to listen to this."

Kallman nodded. "I have a minute or two." He turned his eyes to the telescreen.

The Patriarch sat behind a desk holding perhaps a dozen microphones. Kallman recalled the old man's benedictory speech from two weeks earlier, and frowned. Then, his face had been filled with the same bland piety his words carried. Now? He looked terrified. He had the frozen expression of a fox cornered by a pack of hounds, knowing it was trapped, that there was nowhere to run, and its destruction was mere moments away.

"… may seem beyond belief to my listeners," he was saying. "I know I found it amazing as well. But the Director of Antiquities at the Museum has found unequivocal proof. The passage I read to you was written by the Blessed Julia herself, shortly after the Fall. In other words, during the time of the First Settlement, when she and the other men and women of renown—Soren, and Finn, and Quaice, and Brandon—were living, breathing human beings.

"The Blessed Julia goes on to write:

"'If you think this could not happen again, that the harshness and inequity and hatred that brought down our civilization could not once again be unleashed upon humanity, think again. I have been an oracle, yes, and privileged to receive messages from the mind of God, but all who lived through the horrors of the last few years know it, whether they hear God's voice or not. It doesn't take divine knowledge to see why we fell. Nor was it divine retribution that caused it.

What started the avalanche that very nearly buried all of humanity was triggered by our own rejection of love, and embrace of violence as a solution. Know this: it may seem as if desperate times call for desperate action. But that is a lie. If you are tempted to take up arms against your fellow men and women, there is always another way. If you think that the fire of self-righteousness can bring about God's kingdom on Earth, you have been lied to. Taking up arms and wielding fire only accomplish one thing—inflicting pain and death on the innocent and the guilty alike.'"

The Patriarch looked up, but his eyelids still drooped half closed. He looked as if he'd aged ten years in two weeks.

"If any of the Zealots who are currently waging war in the city of Tecoa, who are advocating violence as a means to control, are listening to this, I beg of you to heed the Blessed Julia's words. She is central to our faith, and the resurfacing of a document she herself wrote fifteen hundred years ago is a sign. Therefore, I don't ask you to listen to me.

"Listen to *her*."

He set down his notes with a weary gesture, and nodded to the cameras as a volley of questions began from the unseen reporters in the room.

The Patriarch stood, straightening his back and legs slowly, and said in a flat, uninflected voice, "I will not be taking questions at this time."

He exited the stage, and the interview was over, to be replaced by a panel of five newscasters who seemed as stunned as their listeners undoubtedly were, but at the same time, eager to comment upon what was surely the biggest news story in the past five years. They began yapping to each other immediately.

A pack of hounds indeed.

Marig turned the volume down as Kallman said, in a quiet voice, "I'll be damned."

"Yeah."

"What do you think the Zealots are going to do with *that*?"

"Don't see that they have much choice. It comes from Julia herself. The only thing that would be more direct is if the gods themselves descended and spoke to them."

Kallman frowned. "That's if they believe it, of course."

"With the Patriarch and the Director of Antiquities behind it, both saying it's real…" Marig trailed off and shrugged.

"Doubt it'll make a difference, honestly. People call them *Zealots* for a reason. They didn't get where they are because of logic and evidence."

"So they hear the actual words of someone they revere as a saint, and reject it when she says 'Stop what you're doing, it's wrong.'"

"Exactly." Kallman paused. "Maybe that's why the cult of the Founders arose, you know? So little was known about them—known for sure—that people were free not only to interpret any way they liked what little was remembered of their words, but to make things up to fill in the gaps. Up till now, if they wanted to portray Julia as some kind of sword-bearing warrior preaching fire and destruction, who was going to step up and say, 'No, that's not who she was and that's not what she said.'"

"But now they have her actual *words*…" Marig said.

"Which is why I predict they will reject them out of hand. Which would be easier—for them to say, 'Oh, I guess we were wrong, then. Put down your weapons,' or 'The Patriarch is lying because he's on the side of the secular government and is afraid for his life. Julia never actually wrote all that, the Patriarch and the Director made it all up.'?"

"Doesn't it ever occur to them to wonder why the wishes of the gods always seem to coincide with their own personal desires?"

"No. I don't think it does."

"So they receive the truth, and deny it rather than change their minds."

"Precisely. The last thing they want to do is stand down. These people *need* something to be angry about. Rage is their life's blood."

"I can't imagine that. Why would anyone want to feel angry?"

"You ask that, my love, because you are a gentle and caring person." Kallman leaned over and kissed him, and it was returned with more vigor this time. "I don't really understand it, either."

"I wish you didn't have to go."

"To training, or on the mission?"

"Both."

"It's not going to be easy, missing you. Last night…" He reached out and stroked Marig's jawline.

Marig made a noise a little like a purr. "I'm ready for a second round. I don't suppose you could… you know, take a later FastRail…?"

Kallman laughed. "Tempting, but I can't. I have a briefing this morning with the rest of the crew, and Arys will skin me if I miss it."

"I'll tackle you when you get home, then."

"No argument."

"What am I going to do without you for six months?"

Kallman gave him a wicked smile. "Become really good friends with your right hand, I'd imagine."

"Oof. But yeah, I suppose there are no conjugal visits on the Moon."

"Not unless you want to do five years of training and become an astronaut yourself."

"You're not going to hook up with some handsome member of the flight crew, are you? Six months is a long time."

"Never. You're it, my sweetheart. Even if we're four

hundred thousand kilometers apart, you're my lover. Now and always." He glanced at his watch. "But now, I really do have to go, or I'll miss the train." He gave Marig another quick kiss on the mouth, picked up his backpack, and headed for the door at a light jog.

On the three-block walk to the train station, his mind returned to the Patriarch's words.

A message from Julia Lowell herself. It'd be interesting to see if his prediction of the Zealots either ignoring it completely, or else claiming that the Patriarch was lying, would turn out to be accurate.

He frowned. What if the Patriarch *was* lying? Kallman's parents had raised him as a nominal believer in the faith of his ancestors, revering the memory of the Founders, never referring to any of them without the honorific "Blessed." But it all had seemed perfunctory. Growing up, they taught him and his two brothers all the stories and legends about the founding of Klen, but he had responded with nothing more than mild interest. It was neither "belief" nor "faith," it was merely "knowledge." The legends of the Founders were no more plausible than the books of fairy tales he had when he was a child, no more to be believed than "There once were three brothers, and a witch gave each of them a magical gift…"

Did the Patriarch make up the message from the Blessed Julia as a way of pacifying the Zealots? It seemed all too likely —words from one of the Founders saying *stop this* was about all they *might* listen to—but then he remembered the expression on the Patriarch's face.

The old man looked like he was in the extremity of fear. If this was some cool calculation to pull the Zealots' sting, wouldn't he be more confident about it?

It was possible, of course, that one of his ministers was coercing him. Someone in the shadows operating him like a marionette. Kallman had long suspected the Patriarch was losing his edge. He could remember listening to the old man's speeches on his parents' telescreen when he was a child, and they always seemed like a bunch of nice-sounding words that didn't mean much. He recalled his father once commenting, to the *tsk*-ing disapproval of his mother, that trying to get anything worthwhile from one of the Patriarch's sermons was like trying to nail pudding to the wall.

Lately, even that was a generous description of the regular speeches Kallman sometimes watched on the telescreen, speeches after which he'd have been hard pressed to recall one definite point the Patriarch had made.

The talk this morning, though, had been different. And the more Kallman thought about it, the more convinced he became that the Patriarch wasn't lying. His expression was not that of a con man. These really were the words of the Blessed Julia, or at least he believed fervently they were.

And the whole thing scared the absolute hell out of him.

Kallman got to the station just as his train was pulling in. He showed his pass to the ticket collector—it was hardly necessary, they saw each other every day—and went through the gate and into the spotlessly-clean interior of the FastRail.

As it was pulling away from the station five minutes later, his mind returned one more time to what he'd heard. The Zealots—especially their leader in Tecoa, some lunatic named Dain Sarkos—constantly claimed they knew what the gods and the Founders wanted them to do, that they were delivering the Blessed Ones' wishes directly to the ears of their followers. And they believed him. Just a week ago, Sarkos had been arrested, but then freed when rioters assailed the police station, intent on setting him loose themselves, and probably tearing the station down for good measure. The police spokesperson said ,"Sarkos was not directly charged, and was ultimately released on his own recognizance, but will continue to be monitored."

Which sounded like bullshit. If he hadn't been charged,

"on his own recognizance" was nonsense. He would simply have been released. The truth was, they'd charged him, or intended to, and caved in when it looked like the police station was going to be stormed. The police were scared of the guy and his followers, there was no doubt about it. The Zealots clearly had the upper hand.

Would the Patriarch's revelation change things? Surely Sarkos couldn't simply ignore it. How would the Zealot leader respond now that one of the Founders had herself said, *No, you've been misleading them, that's not at all what I wanted?*

But the reason zealots of all kinds are so dangerous is that it honestly never occurs to them that they could be wrong.

Maybe at least it would give them pause, and quell some of the violence. So far, the direct impact to Kallman had been little more than an inconvenience, slowing down the trains and closing some businesses. He knew he'd feel differently if he worked or lived in downtown Tecoa, where there'd been a lot of damage and even a few deaths.

Nice if a message from the Blessed Julia came along just in time to calm everyone down.

Perhaps his earlier pessimism was unwarranted, and Sarkos and his followers would turn out to be more reasonable than they'd appeared. Certainly it'd be easier to leave Marig knowing that Tecoa was back to its previous tranquility.

Otherwise, he'd spend the entire six months worrying about him.

seven

. . .

The protestors were waiting for Reysa Sahin as soon as she stepped off the train.

She tried not to look up, just concentrate on putting one foot in front of the other. Let the personal security guard the board of the Museum had hired to protect her do their job. But knowing she'd regret it, she still couldn't stop herself from glancing upward.

Signs everywhere. "Stop LYING." "Saint Julia sees what you are doing!" "Down with the Patriarch!" "False scripture will never break our resolve."

A woman, her mouth twisted with anger, got past the guard, grabbed Reysa by the upper arm, and snarled right into her face, "You and the Patriarch will be in hell soon!", before she was pried away and pushed back into the tumult of the crowd.

Other epithets and obscenities were hurled in her direction, but the noise made most of them impossible to understand.

Fortunately.

Finally it was over, and they escorted her up the stairs and into the Museum, then locked the door behind them.

Locking the Museum doors during daylight hours was also a new thing.

Most of the security detail was grimly silent as they walked her into the cool, shadowed front hall of the museum, but one of them—a young man who looked like he couldn't have been more than twenty-five—gazed at her with sympathy in his eyes.

"I'm sorry you had to go through that."

"Don't use past tense," Reysa said. "I still have to get home tonight. Then do it all again tomorrow."

"Maybe…" He paused, shrugged. "Maybe you should just, you know. Take a vacation until things simmer down."

"No." She met his eyes steadily. "I'm not going to back down when I did nothing wrong. What I reported finding on those manuscripts—it is word for word what was there. In places where it was illegible, I simply left the transcript blank. I didn't make up anything to fill in gaps. And I most certainly didn't invent some sort of message from Julia Lowell to undermine the Zealots' faith."

"I believe you," he said, obviously trying to introduce a soothing note into his voice. "I'm not one of them."

"I know." She gave a harsh sigh. "It's just maddening. If what they believe runs afoul of the facts, that's not my fault. Nor is it my problem."

The corner of the man's mouth quirked, but he didn't respond. It was clear what he was thinking.

It'll be your problem if you go out alone and those crazies kill you.

"I'll be fine from here," she said, now addressing all of the security detail. "There's no reason for me to leave the building until I'm on my way home this evening. I'll let you know if I need you before that. Thank you for your assistance."

The guards mumbled their responses and turned back

toward the foyer, leaving her to make her way to her office on the second floor alone.

Reysa's window overlooked the front courtyard, so she was able to watch as the protestors continued to mill about, chanting and waving their signs, and—when it became clear she wasn't coming back out—gradually dispersed.

Such vicious anger. Where had it all come from? A lot of it, she knew, came from inequity. The same thing, Julia wrote, that had felled the civilization of the Before Time. Surely at least that much resonated with everyone.

The Zealots did have a legitimate grievance against the ruling class, there was no doubt about that. Just like the zealots of fifteen hundred years ago had. Did people learn nothing from the errors of the past? Were they doomed to repeat the same mistakes over and over and over again, like some evil wheel spinning out of control that no one knew how to stop?

She'd been naïve to think it'd be easy. The anger had been there for years, ready to boil over. Her efforts to quell it had backfired spectacularly. One person telling the truth about an ancient book, expecting the message to calm everything down, had instead whipped the rage into a frenzy, given it a focal point.

Reysa turned away from the window with a sigh, sat at her desk, and angled her personal telescreen toward her, then entered the number for the Head Librarian in Tecoa.

Mem Andreen Veris knew she would be calling. Unless it was some kind of unprecedented emergency, Reysa never would have disturbed the old woman with a call without some sort of prior warning. Besides being a stickler for decorum, Mem Veris was notorious in her dislike for technology, despite its obvious convenience in not only communication but in information storage. As she would tell anyone willing to listen, she remembered when the entire contents of the

Library had been kept in handwritten notebooks, and the subtext of her diatribe was always that it'd been better that way.

Probably because then, she had been critical. Mem Veris had an encyclopedic knowledge of what was in those notebooks, as remarkable in its own way as the knowledge of the Guardians hundreds of years ago, before Kallian Dorn's time and the rediscovery of the written word. Now, neither was needed. With the information interfaces everywhere in the Library—everywhere in the world, really—anyone could find whatever they wanted, unassisted.

Understandable, perhaps, that the old woman felt some resentment.

There was a low blip, and the eternally pinched visage of the Head Librarian appeared on the screen. There was no greeting, no questions about Reysa's wellbeing.

"Are the documents safe?"

"Yes, Mem. They are locked up. Even if the building is breached, they are out of harm's way."

Mem Veris nodded. "I've seen what's happening in Klen."

"It's everywhere in Cascadia, apparently."

"Klen is the epicenter. It's shifted from Tecoa now that they succeeded in assassinating the king."

"You and the Library are safe, though, I hope?"

Mem Veris gave a dismissive wave of the hand. "Safe enough. Safe as anyone is. You, on the other hand—you've heard what they're saying about you and the Patriarch? It was on the news last night."

"I've heard," Reysa said dryly.

"You really think the Patriarch was wise to broadcast the Blessed Julia's message? Without any preparation, without any warning?"

"I doubt prior notice would have made any difference. And yes—despite what has happened, I still think it was the right thing to do. Even considering the risk to my own personal safety."

Mem Veris's lips tightened. "We don't need to give the Zealots anything more to riot about."

"If their faith is threatened by facts, maybe they need to reconsider that faith."

"You know they're not going to."

"Then they're fools. Any belief that can be destroyed by the truth deserves to be."

Mem Veris shook her head. "When I was young and idealistic, as you are…"

Reysa made a frustrated gesture with one hand. "It has nothing to do with my being young. Haven't we spent enough time placating the Zealots? When Dain Sarkos was arrested, the police in Tecoa let him go because they were afraid. If we don't stand up to the Zealots, they've won." She paused. "It's exactly what the Blessed Julia warned us about."

The old Librarian glared back at Reysa through the telescreen for a long moment. "You've uncovered more of the records?"

Reysa took a deep breath. A change of topic was about the closest she'd ever get to an admission that she was right.

"Yes. So far, nothing as incendiary as the first part, where Julia outlined what caused the collapse in the Before Time." Her face relaxed into a smile—when had she last truly smiled? "I did find the birth record of Mary Sahin, the eldest child of the Blessed Brandon and Blessed Caria. I trace my lineage back to her. She's my direct forebear."

"The people of Klen are fortunate to have such complete knowledge of their ancestry," Mem Veris said. "Few of us can trace our families back more than two hundred years, if that." The tone of her voice sounded as if the comment had needled her. Not, of course, that it took much.

"We had the Guardians to keep that knowledge intact

through the Black Years. Then, when Kallian Dorn and Challis Mazerine rediscovered written language, they began to write all the lineages down. It's a good thing. Considering how mobile everyone's become in the past hundred years, and how the population has grown, it's doubtful even the Guardians would be able to remember everyone's genealogy now."

"Do you have any other updates?" It was clear the Librarian's tolerance for telescreen conversations was nearing its end.

"I'm meeting with the Patriarch tomorrow to discuss what more from the manuscript should be made public. If anything. I don't think there's any urgent need for him to broadcast the most recent transcriptions."

"Yes, I doubt the people of Cascadia have a pressing need to find out about the birth records of your ancestors."

Reysa let the sarcasm roll off her, as she had so often done before.

"If there's anything urgent, I'll send you a text. Otherwise, I'll speak with you next week?"

Mem Veris nodded, and without so much as a *goodbye* shut off the video.

Reysa murmured, "Poisonous old vulture," then in a panic looked to verify that the telescreen was no longer transmitting.

It wasn't. She gave a deep sigh of relief. She didn't like Mem Veris, but keeping a decent working relationship with her was absolutely critical.

The rest of the morning was spent in the lab, working on the manuscript. She was still only about halfway into the first of the five notebooks, and the thought of what information might be concealed in the others was enough to distract her from the chaos surrounding her. It was a tendency she'd had since childhood—when she was stressed, intellectual pursuits provided a much-needed escape.

It wasn't so easy to tune out completely, however. One of the technicians had the lab telescreen running, showing a news broadcast. The reporters were focusing on the Zealots' protests not only against the Patriarch and the manuscripts from Julia, but against the launch of the Moon mission, now only three days away.

Reysa considered asking him to shut it off, but decided that was tantamount to an admission that the protestors had unnerved her.

Better to pretend she was unconcerned. Maybe eventually she'd convince herself.

"Why do they object to the Moon launch?" one of the technicians said.

"They hate anything that isn't about the faith and the gods and the saints," another responded, without looking up from her scanner. "It's all part of the 'secular poison.' That's what they call it. I passed one of those crazies on the street yesterday, and he was shouting about how it's all a big conspiracy. Sending people up into space, pretending the answers are there, instead of keeping them down here and, you know, getting them to buy into the nonsense about repentance and leading a pure life and so on. They want a true theocracy, not any kind of secular rule."

"The Patriarch's not enough?"

She laughed. "You think the Patriarch actually believes what he's saying?"

"How could you tell if he did or didn't?" He rolled his eyes. "It's not like he ever says anything of substance."

"All I know is if I was going up on the Moon launch, I'd be concerned. I wouldn't put it past them to try to storm the Academy and stop it."

"Good luck to them. Don't they know there are armed guards?"

"Logical thinking isn't their strong suit. Besides, if you're convinced that a blissful afterlife awaits you, you probably don't give a damn if you live or die."

"Do you ever worry that we'll be targets?"

She frowned. "Sometimes. I don't know. We're pretty anonymous. It's not like we're the public face of the Museum, or anything." She suddenly seemed to realize that the Director of Antiquities was sitting there in the room with them, and gave a sheepish glance over at Reysa. "Oh, Reysa, I'm sorry, we shouldn't be discussing this…"

"Why not?" Reysa's response was clipped. She was aware that it sounded like annoyance, then decided she didn't care. "It's not like the thought hasn't occurred to me."

"I'm sure," the technician said. "You've been okay so far?"

"I've been screamed at. Nothing worse than that."

"Maybe you should, you know… come in the back entrance of the Museum. Try to avoid notice. Walking into the front door, with your security guards—it's almost like you're taunting them."

"No!" Now the sharpness was unmistakable. "I'm not going to let the Zealots think they frighten me. Maybe the police in Tecoa are scared of them. I am not."

That halted the conversation, and after a short time, one of the technicians got up and switched off the telescreen.

Reysa's declaration, of course, wasn't true. As a historian, she was all too aware of what a mob could potentially do. She had only to look at the short and disastrous reign of King Sweyn Acoca VIII—understandably, the last of that name— whose insolent arrogance had even exceeded that of his legendary father. The corpulent Sweyn VII had finally died of a long-overdue heart attack, a little over seven hundred years ago, and his son became king at the age of about thirty. He'd only had the crown for two years before his excesses, and his love for the whipping post and the headsman's block, inspired a rebellion. Cocksure until the end, he'd gone out of the palace against the urging of his counsellors, sure that his royal presence was all it'd take to put down the revolt.

The mob had torn him limb from limb, stormed the palace, and captured his mother Pavona. Everyone knew Sweyn himself wasn't very bright and that she was the power behind the throne, and as a result she was hated even more than her son was.

Her last words were, allegedly, "You *dare* to lay a hand on me, you dogs?"

They dared. The rioters dragged Pavona, screaming and thrashing, up to the highest parapet in the palace and flung her over the edge onto the flagstone courtyard below. Her body, and her son's, were eventually dragged off and thrown into the Waterway.

The throne passed to Sweyn's five-year-old son Alun. The royal advisors—what was left of them after a great many decided, correctly, that Tecoa might not be safe for them—arranged a summit between the nobility and the commoners. It didn't take long for the nobility to realize they were cornered, and had no choice but to make concessions. When King Alun IV reached his majority, it was with drastically reduced powers.

Encouraging that here, talking had worked to stand down a revolt. Not that it was much of a comfort to Sweyn VIII and his mother. At least Alun's reign was more peaceful than his predecessors. He died in his bed at the age of seventy.

So Reysa knew what mob violence could do to its victims, whether deserving or not. Her statement to the technician that she wasn't afraid for her safety had been a lie.

But what she'd told Mem Veris earlier, that considerations of risk had to be set aside for honoring the truth, hadn't been a lie at all.

This situation, right here and right now, was what the Blessed Julia had written about. If they weren't going to take her words to heart, what was the point of transcribing the palimpsest? Ignoring the wisdom in books was hardly better than Sarkos's demand that they be banned or destroyed. To have Julia's words, written in the Blessed Founder's own hand, and then to dismiss what she said, to claim it was all a lie?

It was better to have no faith at all than to espouse a belief like that.

eight

· · ·

The Patriarch blinked twice at the sunlight angling into his bedroom window. A beautiful day. Mild, a light breeze, birds singing. Peaceful.

Ironic, really.

What would happen if he just stayed in bed? Waited until Andres Ballinger or one of his other counselors came in to see where he was—and when they did, if he refused to leave his quarters? They wouldn't drag him out, he knew that. Summon a doctor, perhaps, all the while making sure that it was kept quiet and out of the public view, and that even the staff of the Patriarch's residence didn't know he was ill. Such rumors spread fast, and as precarious as the situation already was, there was no way they'd want it made public that the Patriarch was bedridden.

Or, worse, had undergone some kind of mental collapse.

He took a long, deep breath. No sense even thinking about all that. Because, of course, that wasn't what happened. He frowned and shook his head. No—it wouldn't be what was *going* to happen. For this one event, he experienced the peculiar, disorienting forward-and-backward memory that his predecessors, all the way back to Blessed Mary of the Bridge, had enjoyed. They'd apparently had that knowledge about everything, and from the sound of it, the ability had made them damn near omniscient.

Must have been nice.

But about this one single event, he knew what was going to happen for certain. He wouldn't wait for Ballinger to show up and make anxious inquiries about what was wrong. He wouldn't lie in bed and let the doctors fawn over him. He would drag himself from underneath the comfort of the blankets, wash and dress, and go out to his office, where he would meet with the pleasant young Director of Antiquities at the Museum.

Who, despite her good intentions and pure heart, was the one who had set all of this in motion. It took a great effort not to let himself sink into anger at her naïveté, but that was pointless. Her path was constrained as much as his was.

So as he knew he would, he dragged himself from underneath the comfort of the blankets, and set about washing and dressing.

It was like following a script in a theater performance. The actors know what is going to happen. They're merely reciting lines they memorized weeks earlier, performing actions as tightly choreographed as a dance. Only the audience, watching from their seats, is surprised by anything. The actors' job is to keep that pretense intact, to make it look like the character in the play has an actual choice about what they are doing.

That was what he had to do here. Let the charade play out.

An hour later, he sat behind his desk in his office, flipping through the stack of that day's paperwork. More pointless formalities and details he didn't care about. Signatures on papers he barely even read.

What, after all, did it matter?

He'd almost reached the bottom of the stack when there was a soft knock on the door.

"Come."

The door opened, and Ballinger poked his head inside, his face as usual set in an expression of apologetic deference.

"My lord, Reysa Sahin is here to see you."

"Very good. Send her in."

He gave a quick signature on the last three forms without even seeing what they were about, and had worked his face into a passable semblance of a smile when she entered.

"My lord," she said, giving a respectful nod of her head. "Thank you for taking the time to see me this morning."

"It is my pleasure."

She shifted her weight from foot to foot. "First, my lord, I wish to apologize. Your concern about the Zealots' reaction to the Blessed Julia's message… it appears to have been justified. I should have listened to you."

"It is hardly you who needs to apologize, my dear. You couldn't know how they would react."

"No, but you had concerns, which turned out to be all too accurate. I didn't think…" She shook her head. "Mem Veris told me I am too much of an idealist."

"Did she? Well, there are worse things to be. Better an idealist than a cynic. Which, I fear, in my experience of the Head Librarian…" He held both hands palms-upward, and smiled a little.

"I just… I hope that I have not put you at risk."

"I was already a target. That has not changed. The Zealots wish to purify the faith, and I, apparently, am insufficiently pure. If the manuscript you found has intensified their rage toward me, then so be it." He paused. "You have not been threatened, I hope?"

"I've been harassed coming into the Museum and leaving it in the evening. The Museum board has appointed security guards who accompany me when I go out. I don't know how long it will be necessary."

He shook his head. "I am sorry you must deal with this.

Your only sin, you know, was speaking the truth." He smiled at her. "Or, more accurately, inducing me to."

Reysa blushed and looked down. "I truly didn't know what the outcome of my actions would be."

The Patriarch didn't respond for a moment. When she brought her gaze back up, his eyes locked onto hers. Finally he said, in a quiet voice, "No one does. And no one should."

"Sir, isn't that an odd thing to say? Coming from you? I mean no disrespect…"

"None taken. It's simply that I've come to see that my own slim knowledge has done little but set me apart. It is an odd thing, that. Because what the oracles of old could do, and what I can as well in a much more limited way, is nothing that special. We all swim in a sea of knowledge. It is around us, all the time, but most of us have closed our eyes to it. The words of the Blessed Perry say it best, passed down to us from the earliest times. He said, 'They have closed their minds, and cannot hear the voice because they don't think it's real. Some things have to be believed to be seen.'"

"*Do* you believe?" Reysa asked. "Truly believe?"

"Yes." He smiled at her. "I do now."

There was a sharp report, and the glass in the window behind his desk exploded inward, scattering sparkling shards across the floor. The Patriarch's body jerked forward, his forehead thudding against the desk. Reysa gave a strangled scream, dropped the papers she held, and ran around to the other side.

There was a spreading scarlet stain on the back of the Patriarch's shirt. He turned his head toward her, his mouth moving soundlessly for a moment, then with some difficulty, gasped out, "Duck. He has more than one bullet in his gun."

Reysa dropped to her knees, and instantly, there was a second gunshot. A large and expensive-looking vase on the bookcase near the door shattered. From the angle, the bullet had evidently been intended for her.

"I have to get help," she gasped out.

"No. No point in it." He took a deep, painful breath and partly lifted his head. "Get yourself to safety. And keep working on the Blessed Julia's manuscript." The corners of his mouth turned upward in a weak smile. "Odd. Only now do I finally comprehend."

As his consciousness dissolved, he was aware of a great many things, but none of them made much of an emotional impact. It all seemed distant, like the action on a stage he'd contemplated earlier, only now he was no longer an actor but one of the audience. Reysa sobbing, kneeling next to him, her arm around his shoulders. The door bursting open and a whey-faced Andres Ballinger taking in what had happened, then rushing out and shouting orders. A tumult outside, as his assassin was seen and pursued. The sense that now, finally, he understood the oracles, and no longer envied them their knowledge, but pitied them. What a horrific burden to bear throughout your life, to see what was and what would be, and to be unable to change any of it.

His own meager gift—the knowledge of his own death, and that he would be the last of the Patriarchs of the Holy See of Klen—was more than sufficient. Even if his oracular ability was a mere shadow of what the earlier Guardians had, it was enough of a weight.

And his lifelong carrying of that weight meant he was still one of them.

He'd kept the lineage intact, all the way back to the valiant Kallian Dorn and even earlier, to the Blessed Mary of the Bridge herself. Despite his weakness and cowardice, perhaps they would still welcome him to join their exalted company now.

Let the Zealots try to overturn things, and good luck to them. The future was all one piece, now and forever locked in place, and them within it. For all their talk about revolt and purification and change, they could no more alter the path they walked than anyone.

The world would be okay. It would undergo trials and turbulence, joy and tragedy, victories and defeats, but ultimately, all would be well, and the people who lived in it would manage the mystery of this strange and incomprehensible universe as they always had.

As last thoughts before dying, he reflected, he could have done far worse.

nine

. . .

When Marig Kastella woke up on the morning of the launch, his first thought was that he was honestly surprised he'd slept at all.

He rolled toward Kallman, still peacefully asleep on his side, and for a time simply gazed at him, soaking in how sheerly beautiful he was. The copper skin and curly black hair common in Klen, but finely-cut features, long-lashed eyes, high cheekbones.

Hard to fathom that after today, he wouldn't see that face except via telescreen for six long months.

The transport rocket would take a little over four days to go into lunar orbit, then the survey team would leave in the lander for Tranquility Base, the largest permanently-staffed settlement on the Moon. A week to acclimate to the reduced gravity, and the rest of the time would be at Schickard Base. The crew would take turns making mapping runs, crisscrossing the poorly-studied far-Earth side, gathering as much data as possible.

Then six months from now, repeat the whole thing in reverse.

Made it all sound simple.

To Marig's heart, though, it was an eternity. He was honestly happy for Kallman—the mission was the culmination of a dream—but Marig looked at the countdown to the liftoff like a man watching the clock before his execution. The night before, they'd had a celebration with some friends where he'd pretended to be fine with it all. Afterward they'd gone out to the Academy lodging provided for the astronauts and their families, headed up to their room, and made love. Kallman, exhausted, dropped off to sleep almost instantly afterward, nestled in Marig's arms.

Marig, on the other hand, didn't sleep until long after midnight.

It wasn't, he reflected as he lay there that morning, that he didn't know how to be alone. He was the youngest child and only son of Galmon Kastella, the assistant to the Ambassador of Darset, and Nyssa Soliveen of Tecoa. Galmon was a cool, distant man who seldom spent much time at home. Nyssa, a secondary school teacher, was always far closer to Marig's three older sisters. Growing up, Marig had desperately wanted friendships, but always felt clueless about how to gain them. When, at age sixteen, he'd informed his parents that he was gay, it was another barrier between them. Despite the fact that by and large, both Cascadia and Darset were accepting of same-sex relationships, the disappointment was clear in his father's face. They'd followed the tradition, borrowed from Klen, of the female children carrying their mother's surname and the male child carrying their father's, and the elder Kastella hardly had to say aloud what he was thinking.

There goes any chance of having a grandchild to carry on my family name.

All through school, Marig had been a loner, not from choice but from circumstance. He'd followed in his mother's footsteps and become a mathematics teacher, and along the way had a few short-lived relationships, but nothing of substance.

Then, one evening in a bar, he met Kallman Dorn.

He'd been attracted immediately—how could he not be? —but it was only after they spent their first night together, six weeks after they met, that Marig realized how deeply he'd already fallen in love. Kallman was kind, smart, funny, sexy, and a sensitive and passionate lover. His bold, carefree energy was like sunshine to the shadows of Marig's hesitancy and self-doubt. Marig had the sense that he'd been drowning and hadn't even realized it was happening. Meeting Kallman was a lifeline, a strong hand back onto dry land.

He was always cautious, however, not to overwhelm him with his neediness. So now he held back from doing what his mind and body wanted—to wrap Kallman in a tight embrace and never let go.

The result was that Kallman didn't know how much the absence was affecting him. And, hopefully, never would. He made a silent promise to keep himself together until the rocket was aloft. If he dissolved into weeping afterward, that was okay. But nothing should diminish Kallman's excitement about the voyage, where he would lead the exploration of a place that hadn't been seen close-up by humans in almost fifteen hundred years.

Kallman's eyes fluttered open, and he gave Marig a drowsy smile.

"Hi."

"Hi, beautiful."

Marig leaned over and gave him a kiss.

"How long have you been watching me?"

"Not long. And not long enough."

Kallman moved toward him, slipping one arm around his middle and pulling him close, and for a time there was no talking in the little room.

Afterward, as they showered and dressed, Marig said, trying to make it sound offhand, "Are you nervous?"

"I'm about to be strapped onto the front end of a long skinny bomb. Of course I'm nervous."

"But excited?"

Kallman grinned. "Oh, yeah. Excited as hell." He paused, pulling on the inner shirt of his flight suit and zipping it up. "You're going to be okay?"

"I'm going to be okay."

Marig turned away, not wanting to continue that conversation, and switched on the small telescreen hanging on the wall across from the bed. It was set to a news channel, and the moment the reporter's face appeared, he knew something was badly wrong.

"… a dozen or more attacks," she said, and seemed to be keeping her voice level with an effort. "The sniper who assassinated the Patriarch only a half-hour ago has been apprehended, and is thought to be the same person who fatally shot King Lennis three weeks ago. There have been other attacks in downtown Tecoa, resulting in an unknown number of casualties. Also of concern—two known Zealots were apprehended at the Space Academy in the middle of the night, where they appeared to be attempting sabotage of some of the equipment being loaded onto the transport rocket scheduled to leave for the Moon today. Officials at the Academy have stated that the equipment was checked and found to be undamaged, and the launch countdown has not been paused. The alleged perpetrators are in police custody, and we have word from Chief Investigator Davit Kelway, of the Tecoan Police Force, that this morning there have been mass arrests of known members of the Zealots…"

Marig sat down heavily on the bed, his skin suddenly clammy with cold sweat.

Kallman sat next to him, put one arm around his shoulder.

"It's okay. Breathe. They'd halt the launch if there'd been any damage, you know that. They are all about caution."

All Marig could do was nod.

"I've worked with these people for five years. If they thought anything was wrong—anything at all—we wouldn't go up. They must have caught them before they did anything."

"You don't know that."

"I'm as sure about it as I can be about anything. My love, don't let this get to you."

"How can it not?"

Kallman kissed his forehead. "I understand. Deep breath. Come on, do it for me."

Marig met his gaze, and obliged.

"Good. Center. All shall be well."

He fought down the panicked desire to drag Kallman back to the FastRail and then to their apartment, close and lock the door behind them, and shut out the world. The world was just too damned dangerous.

Kallman shook his head. "But gods above. They killed the Patriarch? Poor old guy. He didn't deserve that."

"The Zealots are insane," Marig choked out. "Why? Why would they do all this? It's so… it's so *fucking* pointless. I… I wish I could go with you. Get off this idiotic planet."

Another soft kiss. "So do I, my love. So do I. But since you can't do that, I need you to be here, waiting for me, until I return. And you heard what they said—they've arrested a bunch of them. Hopefully they got, what's-his-name?— Sarkos?—along with the rest, and will keep him in jail this time. If they break up the nucleus of the movement, what's left might not be able to accomplish much."

"I hope so." Marig could hear the bleakness in his own voice.

"So do I." Kallman took a deep breath. "But we need to head to the cafeteria, then I have to get down to the launch site. I've got my final checks to go through." He tried for a smile. "And we need enough time for a proper goodbye."

———

The cafeteria was abuzz with conversation—mostly not excited talk about the launch, now in four hours' time, but about the death of the Patriarch and the attempted sabotage of the mission.

Marig tried his best to tune it all out. His anxiety over Kallman's departure was already wound so tight he felt like he was about to pop a mainspring. But it was impossible to ignore. One woman in a flight suit had obviously been crying, but there was no certainty which of the outrages of that morning had upset her so badly. Several people seemed more angry than grieved. Marig caught a fragment of conversation —"Where in the *fuck* were the security guards?" followed by "I heard they had technicians' uniforms and IDs, so no one knew till they were already in the staging room"—but he finally with some difficulty turned his attention back to Kallman.

"Is this getting to you?" Marig asked quietly.

Kallman took a sip of apple juice. "I'd be lying if I said *no, not at all*. I'm glad we're not delaying, though. It'd just give the crazies another shot at stopping us. As far as the Patriarch and the other attacks—it's awful. Like you said, it won't accomplish anything. And it sounds selfish, but... the timing is horrible. Going to the Moon, you know? It's supposed to be a celebration. A victory. And here these lunatics picked today to do their damage."

"I doubt it's a coincidence. They've been railing against the space program for weeks."

"I know. I just wanted—I *want*—this all to go off smoothly. Both for myself and the rest of the crew, but also for you and the families of the team members. It angers me that they're trying to ruin this."

Shortly after breakfast, the call came for the crew to say their goodbyes to family and friends.

Marig held Kallman close for as long as he could. Tears welled up no matter how hard he tried to force them back.

"Keep the home place safe for my return," Kallman whispered in his ear. "I will be thinking about you every moment."

There was a finality to their kiss, and as Kallman turned away, Marig couldn't stop a sob that shook him like a dog shaking a rat.

But Kallman kept walking, and along with the survey and transport crews, filed away down the corridor for their pre-flight checks before boarding.

It was only when the last of them disappeared that Marig broke down completely.

He had never felt so alone in his life, an island of utter solitude in a sea of nameless, faceless humanity. But as he stood there, weeping helplessly, one hand over his eyes, someone clasped his shoulder. He looked up through eyes bleared with tears to see an older man, balding and round-faced, giving him a sympathetic smile.

"I understand." His voice was warm. "My daughter is going up, too. But don't worry. They'll be all right. The Academy flights haven't lost a single person yet. Not even a serious injury. He'll be back safe and sound, don't you fret. They all will."

Marig nodded, but wasn't able to get any words out.

"I won't tell you all sorts of platitudes about keeping yourself busy, how you should distract yourself and the time will fly. It's just not true, and if it was, it wouldn't say much about your relationship. You'll miss him dearly, but when he gets back, you'll value what you have all the more. It's what happens when your lover, or your child, or your friend, is an astronaut. It's all part of the picture. Doesn't make it any easier, maybe, but at least you know you're not going through this alone."

"Thanks," Marig choked out.

The man responded with a gentle smile and a pat on the shoulder, then turned and walked toward the exit to the observation area, where they would all watch the rocket go up.

After a short time, Marig did the same. The man's words had been a strange mix of solace and commiseration, but still, Marig did feel better.

It would be hard, but it would be okay.

It was a beautiful day, mild and breezy, the sun shining in a cornflower-blue sky. Marig squinted against the brightness, and looked around at the assembled crowd, and in the distance, the rocket that in two hours would take Kallman and the others up into the cold vacuum of space.

The time crept by, and the crowd slowly grew as others came in to watch the historic launch. Marig scanned the sea of faces—some solemn, some smiling—and was shocked when one gave him a nod of recognition. A long, narrow face, with cool gray eyes, arching, ironic eyebrows, lips that seemed unsuited to smiling.

His father, Galmon Kastella.

The older man maneuvered his way toward his son, moving with the cool dignity and grace of a sailing ship, and finally stood facing Marig.

"You came," Marig said.

"It's an important event. The Ambassador himself suggested I go." He paused, and for a fraction of a second, a flash of discomfort crossed his face. "Also, I know it's important to you."

Marig nodded. "Thank you."

"It's quite an honor, Kallman heading the survey team. You must be proud of him."

It was one of the only times his father had ever acknowledged how much his relationship with Kallman meant, and as measured as the comment was, it brought the emotion back full-force. "I'm incredibly proud. But I'm going to miss him more than I can say."

Galmon inclined his head. "I'm sure." He paused. "Your mother would have been here, but she couldn't get time off from the school. She's watching the launch with her classes via telescreen."

The conversation devolved into awkwardness.

But as the clock continued to tick away the countdown, Marig couldn't let the rest of the time pass in silence.

"How am I going to manage without him?" His voice was quiet, reluctant... but intense.

His father met his gaze for some moments before responding. "Like you always have. Marig, you have far more strength and courage than you believe you do. Do you think Kallman would have left you if he honestly thought you couldn't cope? If he thought you would fall apart the moment he was gone? He trusts you because he knows you are strong enough to make it. Not just to make it, but to thrive."

Marig looked at his father in astonishment.

Galmon tugged at his collar, a nervous gesture. "I know I haven't... I haven't told you that very much. I should have. It's not how I was raised, so it wasn't how I raised you. I see now that was a mistake." He shook his head and his thin lips quirked in a rueful smile. "I thought if I didn't coddle you, if I let you figure things out, you'd toughen up. Maybe it wasn't you who needed to toughen. It was me who needed to soften."

"I probably did need some toughening, too."

Galmon shrugged. "Maybe. But you've got an inner strength that's always been there. I didn't create that in you, and I didn't help it by leaving you to raise yourself." He took a deep breath, and straightened his shirt. "I'm glad you found Kallman. You're good for each other."

"What brought this on?"

Another shrug and a faint smile. "Just the sense that it was overdue."

Anything Marig could have responded was interrupted by an automated voice over the loudspeaker saying, "Ten minutes until launch. All systems are go."

Marig looked out at the rocket, sitting on its launch pad. By this time, the entire crew would be strapped into their seats, ready for the explosive liftoff that would carry them into space. The rocket looked so small at this distance. Hard to believe that it contained not only the crew but the landing module and several tons of new equipment, including the sleek survey craft Kallman and his team would fly out onto the far-Earth side of the Moon.

Five minutes. Then three. Marig gave a quick glance around at the rest of the crowd, and noticed something strange. All of the faces were turned toward the rocket except for one. One person, dressed in a heavy sweatshirt with the hood pulled up, stood only a few meters away, and was looking with a fierce intensity not at the launch pad, but at the people assembled there.

And suddenly, Marig knew who it was. He'd seen that face several times on the telescreen. It was a fervent face, one with a grim, unyielding intensity, eyes that burned with the wrath and fire of hell.

"Father," Marig said in an intense whisper. "Sarkos. That's Dain Sarkos. What in the hell is he doing here?"

Frowning, he followed his son's pointing finger toward the man as the clock reached zero and the ignition started with a fearsome roar. Galmon's shout of "That's Sarkos! Someone get security!" was nearly drowned in the noise.

But Sarkos heard him. He turned toward the older man with a broad smile of triumph as he reached beneath his shirt and flipped a switch that was only visible for a fraction of a second.

Galmon flung his arms out to shield his son. Too late. The explosion, like the punch of a giant fist, struck them from the side, flinging Marig helplessly through the air. There was a sudden blinding flash of light, brighter than the glowing exhaust of the rocket, brighter than the sun itself.

Afterward was nothing but darkness.

part two
the garland of crowns

ten

· · ·

Kallman Dorn worked steadily and patiently through the inventory list, noting the location of all the equipment he would have to oversee transferring to the lunar base once the lander separated from the transport. Here, in a small cargo hold with no windows, it was easy enough to forget where he was—in a rocket hurtling its way through the vacuum of space toward the Moon.

Right now, the forward acceleration of the rocket was enough to simulate Earth's gravity, or close enough as to make no difference. In a little less than a day, they'd start to decelerate—and everything in the habitable part of the ship would have to flip, floors becoming ceilings and ceilings floors, during the hour of constant velocity and resultant weightlessness before the slowdown started.

Despite the cramped quarters, he didn't hear his crewmate and copilot Orzen Saxena until she said, "Need any help?"

"No, thanks, I'm nearly done. It's already been checked, of course, but I wanted to make sure I went through it myself."

"Understandable. Quentra's lectures about taking nothing for granted out here must have sunk in."

"Definitely did."

"Kilmaris just told me there's still no telescreen link back to Earth."

"Dammit. What's the problem? I figured they'd have contact established by now. It's been a day and a half."

She shook her head. "Technical problems on the ground. Nothing to be concerned about, and they're working to fix it. That's all they're saying."

"Marig's got to be beside himself. I told him I'd talk to him as soon as we were out of Earth's atmosphere."

"Bit of a worrier?"

"Just a bit."

"Well, don't *you* worry."

"He worries enough to take care of it for the both of us."

"You know how it is. They're probably keeping everybody down there better informed than they are us." She laughed. "And if they think they can keep a secret from my dad, they're going to find out different fast. He's a master of the harangue. He won't leave them alone until it's fixed."

There was a pause, and he gave her a sidewise smile. "Have you taken a look at the new survey craft?"

"Yeah." Her voice registered awe. "It's a thing of beauty, isn't it? I can't wait to fly it. A lot better than the beat-up shuttles we trained on. Shiny and brand new."

He grinned. "Sorry, Saxena, but I get the first flight. Survey team leader's privilege."

"I call second."

"It's all yours."

"How many shuttles are already up there at Schickard?"

"Five. Serviceable, but none of them have the range this one does. We'll all take turns on the old ones and the new one."

"Glad you're not greedy."

"It's tempting, but I'll keep things fair, I promise."

Orzen gave him a grin. "You'd better. Okay, if you've got

things in hand here, I'm heading off to get some food. See you, Dorn."

"Later."

After finishing the inventory, Kallman signed off on the inventory and gave one last look around the hold before returning to his quarters for eight hours of rest.

In the hallway, he crossed paths with Tevin Kilmaris, the commander of the transport crew. Kilmaris was fifty-ish, powerfully built, with close-cropped iron-gray hair and a direct, honest, no-nonsense style that earned him the respect of both his superiors and crew. After a quick exchange of greetings, Kilmaris gave Kallman a scowl.

"What do you think of the radio silence?"

"Don't know what to think of it. Hard to come to a conclusion when you have no information."

The older man shook his head. "And I'm not buying what they *are* telling us. This is more than some kind of technical problem. After all, the voice link to the Control Center is working just fine, so they've still got satellite contact with us and with Tranquility. If they really *had* lost the link completely, we'd be flying silent, you know? But no, they're monitoring us and giving us little course corrections and whatnot, same as always. But then we ask for a general telescreen link so we can talk to our families, and—*no, sorry, there's a technical glitch.* We ask the people on the voicelink to at least give us *some* information, *any* information, and we get, *I'm sorry, sir, I'm only authorized to discuss flight information.* I told them, 'Okay, so put someone on the voicelink who *is* fucking authorized,' and all I'm told is that my request will be communicated to their superiors. Then nothing." He gave a frustrated gesture with one hand. "How hard is it to say, *Everything is fine*? The only reason for the subterfuge is if it's something bad they're not wanting to tell us."

"Didn't think about that."

"No reason you would have, Dorn. You're not the one in

the pilot's seat yet, so you haven't heard first-hand how evasive they're being. Once you and your people get to Tranquility, and then to Schickard, you'll be the one in charge. At that point you'd have realized something isn't right."

"What do *you* think is happening?"

Kilmaris didn't respond for a moment, his weathered features creasing into a frown. "I had to guess, something went down back on Earth, probably around the time of the launch. You heard those lunatics killed the Patriarch?"

"How could I not have? It was all over the news that morning."

"Maybe they bombed the telecom center. I suppose they could have damaged the equipment badly enough that the Academy people couldn't provide good links for nonessential communication. The first priority would be to keep the voice links stable and keep contact with the satellites and with us."

"Why wouldn't they just tell us that, then?"

"Good question. Seems simple enough, but whenever I press them for details, they get mighty vague. You see what else it could be, though, don't you?"

A sense of unease began to well up in Kallman's belly, and he became aware in that moment that it had been there, waiting, ever since he'd first found out about the "technical problems" and resulting inability of the crew to talk to their families on Earth.

"Something worse has happened."

Kilmaris nodded grimly. "Something a lot worse. Something they don't want to tell us about because if we find out, we'll be upset enough to jeopardize the mission. Maybe even scrub the whole thing and demand to return to Earth right away."

"If that's true, at some point, they're going to have to tell us. Saying *sorry, technical glitch* will only work so long before people start demanding. And before everyone gets worried enough that the anxiety itself starts to cause problems."

"Exactly. So for now, I'm downplaying it with my own crew, you know? I don't want to play games with their emotions, and it bothers the hell out of me to pretend I haven't figured out the Academy people aren't being honest with us. If they don't get a link re-established, at some point I'm going to start making some noise myself, and I'll come clean with everyone. I don't keep secrets for no good reason, you know? But for now, I'll parrot the message we're getting. I'd recommend your doing the same with your crew, but it's your decision, of course."

The acknowledgement that a grizzled veteran like Kilmaris considered them to be of equal rank was a nice sop to his vanity. Technically, until the survey ship and the transport separated, and the survey crew got underway to Tranquility, everyone on the ship was under Kilmaris's command, so his nod to Kallman was little more than a kindness, but it was still nice.

However, it didn't assuage the worry the older man's words had produced in him. If something bad had happened back on Earth, he wanted to know what it was. Then he could deal with it.

But contending with a complete unknown—and the possibilities his brain could dredge up as to what might be the cause of the lost link—was much, much worse.

A day later, there was still no new information about the "technical glitch" and when it might be fixed, but the whole crew had their minds taken off it by the upcoming gravity flip.

There'd only be an hour of weightlessness in which to turn everything around—unbolt furniture from floors and rebolt them to ceilings, make sure all small items were secured, check all fluid containers to make sure there were no leaks that might become apparent once the direction of gravity changed. They'd all heard the horror story about a twenty-liter plastic jug of fruit juice with a loose lid. It was clamped securely to a wall, and no one noticed the slight leak during the hour's zero-g. The drip turned into a sticky waterfall once deceleration started—saturating the floor and several crates full of supplies, and resulting in a single-handed cleanup effort by the unfortunate crew member responsible.

The crew member, it was related, afterwards became such a stickler for triple-checking everything that he was put in charge of overseeing the flip during the next three missions.

"Ten minutes to zero-g," came a disembodied female voice over the intercom.

The crew quarters were flipped by their occupants, four per bedroom, but the beds were built to be reversible so the process didn't take long. Teams of three were responsible for small rooms like storage closets, bathrooms, and galleys. Bigger rooms such as the bridge, engineering, and large equipment storage got between five and ten crew members to deal with reversing the positions of movable objects and making certain anything too big to shift was securely strapped down into a position that wouldn't be a problem when the world suddenly turned on its head.

"One minute to zero-g." She added, with a smile in her voice, "Grab a strap or a handle. If there's none nearby, grab your neighbor's ass."

Kallman was still laughing when there was the eerie silence of the engines cutting out.

He'd been in weightlessness before—they all had—but he still was never quite ready for the bizarre feeling of every organ in his body rising. The familiar downward drag was so taken for granted that when it was gone, there was a sudden feeling of falling, like he was plummeting feet-first toward the ground even though he could still see the floor right there beneath him.

Some, of course, couldn't handle the sensation. Half of the people who applied to the Academy for flight positions washed out because their body simply couldn't deal with weightlessness. Many of them got dizzy or violently sick. Some experienced instantaneous migraines or panic attacks. A handful of these stuck with it and eventually coped well enough to fly, but most of the ones who got these physical symptoms decided to switch to the ground crew, or left the Academy entirely to pursue other careers.

Kallman had been one of the lucky ones. Other than a bit of lightheadedness, and an acute awareness of the peculiar bodily sensations, he had no problem with weightlessness.

He and his team, charged with one of the large equipment storage rooms, launched into action, gliding around the space to check straps and bolts, and to move anything that was reversible into its new position on the ceiling. At this point, of course, there *was* no ceiling and floor—all six walls were equivalent. They were in a cubical box with no directionality, where *up* and *down* had no definition.

All of them worked quickly and efficiently, and long before the hour was up, they had everything in their charge secured into its new place.

Once done, Kallman kicked off a nearby wall to glide through the open door into a hallway. He'd loved the opportunity to move effortlessly in three directions ever since he'd first experienced it, and was determined to take full advantage now. Motivated more by a sense of play than any real concern he was needed, he slipped through the air down the hall and inquired at three other rooms if they wanted his help.

None did.

All too soon came the voice again. "Three minutes to reestablishment of gravitation. Make sure you know which direction will be down, or you'll be in for a surprise and no small amount of ridicule when you land on your head. I repeat, deceleration will commence in three minutes."

The one-minute announcement came, then the ten-second countdown.

The engines rumbled back to life, and there was a low groaning noise as the ship and its contents adjusted to the reassertion of the direction *down.*

After the flip was completed, the crew settled back into another day and a half's flight before the lander separated from the transport, bringing him and the rest of the survey team to Tranquility Base. During the lull in activity, Kallman checked the telescreen to see if there was an active link back to Earth.

Once again, there was the message, *Due to technical issues, no active video or audio link is available. Technicians are currently at work to remedy the problem. You will be notified when a link is re-established. We apologize for any inconvenience this may cause.*

He stared at the words for some minutes, pondering what Kilmaris had told him.

Something a lot worse. Something they don't want to tell us about because if we find out, we'll be upset enough to jeopardize the mission. Maybe even scrub the whole thing and demand to return to Earth right away.

But he pushed that away, forcing his attention to return to preparing for the survey mission ahead.

Thirty-six hours later, the transport crew had the ship in stable orbit around the Moon, so it was back to weightlessness again.

The time had come to split the craft in half—part would drop to the surface, carrying the members of the survey team to land at Tranquility Base, and the other half would slingshot around through the lunar gravitational field to gain speed for their return to Earth.

Kilmaris shook Kallman's hand, and wished him and his crew good luck on the survey mission.

"I'll be honest with you, Dorn," the older man said. "This time I'll be glad enough to be back on Earth. I enjoy flying, even quick transport runs, but I've spent this entire trip fighting my tendency to catastrophize."

"Same. Don't see how you could help it. We're all feeling it. Half of my crew has asked me what's going on, and *I don't know, either* is beginning to sound a little lame."

"I hear you. I'll tell you, though. I'll be back in five days, and one way or the other I'm going to get to the bottom of this. I don't give a damn if some paper-pushing administrator gives me a direct order not to say anything. If it's humanly possible, I'll get information to you. It's not fair that they're keeping us all in the dark."

"Thanks."

"We'll get it sorted." He clapped Kallman on the shoulder. "Good luck with your survey mission. Exciting stuff. Wonder what you'll find over there. I've seen the far-Earth side, of course, on high orbit, but there's a difference between that and zooming through the hills and craters. That shiny new survey ship looks like it'll be fun as hell to fly."

Despite his concerns, Kallman grinned. "I can't believe I'm here."

"You and your team are making history, my friend. Good luck."

"Thanks."

Kilmaris gave him a long look, then an approving nod.

"Try not to worry. I'll be in touch as soon as I can."

eleven

. . .

Reysa Sahin pinched the bridge of her nose between her thumb and forefinger for a moment, then peered back at the screen.

The words were still a blur.

The sun had long set, the bit of sky she could see through the laboratory window darkening from azure to ultramarine to black. The lights in the room were dimmed, the screen of the multispectral imager casting an eerie greenish glow on her face, clothing, the furniture, the walls. But she had to keep going despite her fatigue and eyestrain. There was something in this message that she needed to see, needed to understand, and she wouldn't leave the Museum until that happened.

Deciphering the writing on the manuscript was slow and tiring work. Parts of it had simply been too faded to read, even with the aid of the imager. They'd reached the end of the first notebook, and that only because Reysa continued struggling over it long after everyone else had gone home. At least since the disaster at the launch, the screaming crowds had stopped showing up. Whether this was from fear of the police now that a multiple murder had taken place and large numbers of the Zealots arrested, or simply satisfaction that they'd accomplished their goal of killing the Patriarch and attacking the Academy, was anyone's guess.

Not requiring a police escort to and from home was nice. That it had been necessary in the first place was less so.

She forced her eyes to focus on the screen, and the image of the last two pages of the first of Julia Lowell's notebooks.

"Speak to me, Blessed Julia," she said under her breath.

She would never have spoken those words if anyone else had been in the room. Even alone, she felt vaguely embarrassed to say it. Reysa had never been devout. Few of her generation were. Her beliefs—not that she felt the need to announce them to the world—were that the Founders, and the oracles after them, were undoubtedly fine and wise people, but the vast majority of the miracle stories attributed to them were later inventions to give them the veneer of deity. How easy it would be to turn Soren from a powerful leader figure into a full-fledged hero, to cast Mary of the Bridge's death not as an unfortunate accident but an act of self-sacrificial, redemptive magic. Reysa had read many books of lore from the Library in Tecoa, both for entertainment when she was young and as a course of study when she was at the University, and they had been full of that sort of thing. Superhuman men and women, accomplishing their goals and smiting their enemies through power that was nothing short of godlike.

Those stories couldn't *all* be true. And, she had reasoned, if some were false, wasn't it that much more likely that they all were?

But now, reading the words of the actual Julia Lowell—and she had no real doubts that was what they were—she was no longer feeling so certain.

For one thing, Julia apparently took her own abilities as an oracle as a simple matter of fact. She spoke of her knowledge of the future, in some cases of the distant future, like it was no odder than recounting yesterday's news.

There will come a time when these words will be unreadable, when the people have forgotten how to make paper and pencils, will have forgotten that these marks even have meaning. Even if our written knowledge survives, who will know how to decipher it? I am given to know that some of it will endure—not which knowledge in particular, but it is still good to know it won't all be lost. I am also given to know that there will come one of us, an oracle like me although not of my lineage, who will resurrect the understanding of the written word to the people, and so open their minds to the lives we lived before the flood, the lives that are no more. It is he and his beloved who will, in a sense, bring us all back to life.

And that, of course, was exactly what had happened. According to legend, Kallian Dorn of Klen and Challis Mazerine of Tecoa had been the ones to find the Great Library, and somehow, comprehended that the curious marks on the pages of the books had meaning.

It was hard to understand how they could have done that without divine help, and despite her recent misgivings, Reysa wasn't ready to attribute it to the gods. Perhaps they *had* accomplished what the legends said, but it couldn't have simply been a magical revelation, as the true believers claimed. There must be more to the story.

Her training in scientific skepticism wasn't so easily set aside.

Still. Julia knew about it ahead of time. There had to be something to that.

The second thing about Julia's writings that had unnerved Reysa, however, was how often she seemed to be speaking to her directly. She'd tried to talk herself out of it, convince herself that it was nothing more than fanciful thinking brought on by the trauma she had experienced, but the sensation wouldn't leave her.

She forced herself to read the last pages of the notebook for the third time, the ones she had left up on the imager to revisit once her assistants left.

We'd been so fortunate. In the three years since Mary Hansard fell on the bridge, we hadn't lost a single person. Nearly miraculous, when I think about it. The first months were hard, trying to figure out how to feed ourselves, with little access to medicines (very quickly none, as the meager supply we were able to find from the abandoned pharmacies and clinics ran out). While there was some sickness that first winter, none perished, and all of the ones who made it across the bridge were still alive and well.

[This was followed by a space of about a paragraph that was indecipherable, even using the imager.]

…No one lives forever. Still, the luck we had must have led us to believe our little band of survivors would never change, never face loss.

Dear Trevor Keene and his partner, Josie Alleman, are mourning the death of their little girl, Maris. She was born almost a year to the day [indecipherable] *here, and was such a bright little thing, pretty as a flower, and seemingly healthy. But she became ill two weeks ago. Despite my background as a nurse, I'm not sure what it was—some respiratory virus, is my best guess—one of those things that with adequate medical care would probably have been survivable. But it went deeper into her chest, and after lingering for days, barely conscious, yesterday she died.*

The parents are distraught, as [indecipherable]. *I am in the way of knowing they will have other children, but I have not told them that. It would be little consolation, and in any case they will find out in the course of things. I have found since discovering my own oracular knowledge that many times, this sort of wisdom must be dispensed with caution. Sometimes the most difficult part has been in determining what I should not divulge. With God's help, I think I have made the right decision more often than not.*

But Maris's death has brought us headlong into facing our own ultimate mortality. When no one in your little community has died in two years, it is easy enough to push aside, to subscribe to the fiction that we will all last forever. Even I, God forgive me, old woman that I am, act like I will still be here tomorrow, and the next day, and the next after that.

The truth is both harder and more comforting, and I am not just talking about us oracles, who after all have access to knowledge about our own fates. But we all must become friends with our own deaths [indecipherable] ...In the old world, I belonged to a group of believers who thought that the important thing was to be devout now, to pray now, so that after death we would be rewarded with eternal life. Now I see that the reality is more complex than that. My friend Soren says that our lives are all inextricably linked, like a web floating on an infinite ocean. A wave rises and falls, carrying the web with it—but when the wave subsides, the net still remains, and so does the ocean. That, he says, is what our lives are like. Soon begun and just as quickly over, but the substance and the connections are eternal.

I am not sure I understand it. I still said my old familiar prayers as Trevor and Josie buried their little girl this morning. Even if Soren is right, it still hurts, and we still weep for the ones we know we will never see again. The mystery of our lives and deaths has perplexed humankind ever since they were able to ponder such things, and I guess it always will.

So to whoever reads these words—if anyone ever does—I will say to you: if you are troubled, if you are mourning, be comforted. Try to find meaning and understanding, even if what you have endured threatens to break your heart. I won't say "There's a reason for everything," or "God knows what He is doing," as I perhaps once would have. I am only one foolish old woman, gifted perhaps with knowledge beyond my ability to comprehend, but still seeing things through dimmed eyes. I do not pretend to be able to parse the mind of God. What I understand now is so little, really. It seems the closer I get to death, the less sure I am of anything.

But what I do know is that we cannot give up trying to find out —and giving comfort to the other people who walk beside us on our path.

Reysa read it again, trying to bring to mind her own

mental image of Julia Lowell, the real flesh-and-blood Julia Lowell who had lived and died so long ago. She'd seen the wooden statues that once stood in the Hall of Images in the center of Klen, and now resided in sealed, nitrogen-filled glass display cases in a room of the Museum. All of them were cracked and splintered with age, the pigments that had once brightened their faces and clothing dulled and worn away. Julia's was nearly faceless, the eyes hollow sockets, the curly hair showing only traces of the lustrous black paint that had once colored it.

Even so, there was in that weathered wooden visage a deep, almost otherworldly tranquility. Her mental picture of Julia was a fiction, probably nowhere near what the real woman had looked like. The statue somehow came far closer to capturing her spirit, the voice that Reysa could hear speaking as she read Julia's words on the manuscript.

It was hard to escape the feeling those words had been meant for her personally.

She had spent the past three days trying to understand what had happened to the Patriarch, what had happened at the launch, and what her own connection to it was. Reliving the horrifying report of the gunshot, her own panic when she realized what had happened, remembering what were almost the old man's final words to her, right before the assassin struck.

We all swim in a sea of knowledge. It is around us, all the time, but most of us have closed our eyes to it. The words of the Blessed Perry say it best. He said, "They have closed their minds, and cannot hear the voice because they don't think it's real. Some things have to be believed to be seen."

Was Reysa one of those who had become willfully blind?

Both the Patriarch and Julia had spoken of their own gifts in terms of the deepest humility, as if what they could do was nothing unusual. As if they were both just fellow travelers— not leaders, not near-demigods deserving of reverence and worship. Merely two more humans trying, like everyone, to figure it all out.

But Julia had said she believed it *was* knowable, or perhaps even if final answers were unreachable, there still was value in trying to understand. Maybe there *was* something Reysa herself could do, something more than reading the words of the palimpsest over and over in the hopes that the next time, there would be concrete explanations there instead of deeper and more complex questions.

She could talk to the people who had been at the launch. The ones who had been injured, the families and friends of the ones who had died. Give them what comfort she could, perhaps see if there was a path to healing together. Even if the world was a chaotic and cruel place, there was value in seeing the good, and bringing that knowledge to whomever she could.

She shut off the imager's screen, and for a time, sat there in the dark and the silence, recalling another conversation with the Patriarch—the one which had begun their connection that ended so tragically three days ago. More words from the Blessed Julia, which at the time Reysa had thought were directed to the Patriarch and the Zealots, but now she recognized were spoken to her, as well.

If evil is created by some powerful supernatural being, we can put our hands together and say, "I will pray for God to intervene," or worse, throw our hands up and say, "Nothing I do will make a difference." The truth is far more ordinary, and far more devastating. Extreme beliefs of any kind are born of a desperate need to find meaning and justice in a world that seems to have neither. The anger of the terrorist and the fire of the zealot come from the same sources: the desire to make sense of suffering, and the terrifying reality that the only cure for it is the leap of faith that is love.

twelve

. . .

Arys Quentra had never been so angry in her entire life. Strong emotions of any kind were a rare occurrence for her. She had a reputation for being completely unflappable. It was a necessity, a skill she'd developed first as an astronaut, then as the head of the training program at the Academy. Her former students—who now numbered in the hundreds—knew her to be serious but fair, and nearly impossible to rattle. Her phlegmatic disposition became something of a legend when, on a training flight a few years earlier, the valve on a small pressurized oxygen cylinder blew off with a bang, sending the thing careening around the cabin like a miniature rocket.

Unlike everyone else on the flight, she didn't flinch or jump. It was almost as if she'd been expecting it. She reached out and caught it, one-handed, let it sputter its way to empty, and tossed it into a waste receptacle. Then she turned to the students and said, "To return to the point I was making…"

So her reputation for having ice water for blood was well-deserved. Which was why even she was shocked at her current desire, which was to scream at the top of her lungs.

"You cannot keep the crew in the dark about this." Her

voice had the edge of barely-contained fury. "You are treating them like pawns. Like your personal property."

The Academy Board of Directors returned her gaze stolidly.

"Commander Quentra," said the chair, a man of about Arys's age named Denian Stiles. "Are you aware of how much in the way of money and resources has been put into this mission?"

"Of course I am. You know as well as I do how long I've been employed by the Academy. Don't talk to me as if I were a child. Money and resources be damned. The crew have lost friends and family. Many more were injured. You cannot—you *will* not—leave them up there for six months, ignorant of the fact that people they love have died."

"The transport crew will be back in three days," said another member of the Board, whose name she could not offhand recall. His voice was slow and hoarse, but whether with illness, old age, reluctance, or something else was impossible to tell. "They will find out…"

Arys gave an angry gesture with one hand, cutting him off. "I'm not talking about the transport crew, and you know it. Although they should have been told, too, as soon as it happened. How are you going to explain yourself when some crew member asks why he wasn't told for a week that his wife had been killed in a terrorist attack?"

"You are an astronaut yourself," Stiles said. "Think of the missions you were on, and the people you served with. What would have happened if half the crew had been prostrated with grief?"

"We are professionals!" Arys shouted. "As are the crew of the current mission. I trained these people. I know them. They would be devastated, of course. Anyone would be. But then they'd have put the safety and security of their crewmates first, and completed the mission to the best of their very high ability."

"What if the survey crew demands to return to Earth?"

Arys locked her gaze on Stiles's. "Maybe they should have that option."

An amused chuckle ran through the entire Board.

"And then what?" the hoarse-voiced man said. "When they've had the funerals and cried their fill, are you asking us to put them all back on the rocket and return them to the Moon? We have a responsibility to the crew, yes, but also to the Kingdom of Cascadia and the Holy See of Klen, which provided the resources for this mission. Which fund the Academy and everything it does. Which, allow me to remind you, also pay your own salary."

Arys's rage boiled over. "No amount of money is worth treating the crew of this mission like tools." Her voice was a snarl. "Maybe if you told them what happened, they would ask to come back. You could then discuss it with them like adults. But you can't even be bothered to do that much. What do you think, that they'll mutiny, commandeer the ship, and return it to Earth?" She took a deep breath, and her mouth twisted with fury. "You're so used to dealing with spreadsheets and expenditures and meetings that you've forgotten you're working with people."

Stiles shook his head. "You need to understand that we regret deeply what happened, and its impact on everyone. But we could not have prevented it, and now that it has occurred, we have to give thought to the security of this mission…"

"The assistant to the Ambassador from Darset *died*," Arys shouted. "I looked at the list of victims. Five members of the survey crew, and three from the transport crew, lost family members, and those are just the ones whose names I recognized. You think you'll be able to keep how you've handled this quiet? When the transport crew gets back three days from now, and they find out what you did—and that you *still* haven't told the survey crew—it will be you five on people's telescreens, trying to explain why you hid the truth from national heroes."

Stiles regarded Arys with a tight-lipped expression. "We will forbid the transport crew from speaking to reporters."

Arys laughed. "Have you *met* Tevin Kilmaris? Good luck with that."

"Commander Kilmaris will not risk being slapped with a charge of insubordination."

"Commander Kilmaris will tell you to take your charge of insubordination and stick it up your ass. Which, in fact, is precisely what I am doing. When he gets back, I will talk to him and find out precisely what he and the rest of the mission crew have been told. Which, unless I misunderstand the situation, is basically nothing. You have until then to make the right decision, or he and I will take the matter out of your hands." Once again she met Stiles's stare steadily. "Do we understand each other?"

"Perfectly," Stiles said. His voice was icy, hostile, heavy with implicit threat.

Arys turned on her heel and walked out of the room.

As soon as Arys heard the announcement that the transport had returned safely after delivering Kallman Dorn and the survey crew to the Moon, she made a beeline to the reception room in the Academy. She'd wondered if the Board would try to keep the time of their arrival quiet, and at least delay her ability to talk with Commander Kilmaris, but they evidently decided it was inevitable, and the best approach was to pretend that nothing was amiss. The notification came right when expected, and she immediately dropped what she was doing and went to meet the returning crew.

Tevin Kilmaris was the first to enter. Reporters had been excluded from the reception room—itself a new thing—and his brow creased with a frown as he gazed around the area. Then he saw Arys, and gave her a long, evaluative look, his shaggy gray eyebrows rising.

"I think I know what this is about."

She nodded. "I take it they haven't told you what happened."

"You take it correctly. We should find somewhere private to talk."

"I should give you some time to decompress first."

Kilmaris shook his head. "No. This takes priority. I'm fine, and so is the rest of my crew. There's no need to wait."

She led the way in silence to one of the small meeting rooms on the second floor, usually used as a classroom, closed the door behind them, and they sat down in two of the chairs, facing each other.

She gave a gesture toward a speaker hanging from the wall above the door. "Is this okay? There's an intercom, they could be listening in."

He gave her a smile with little mirth in it. "Do you care if someone overhears?"

"Not really."

"All right, then." He cleared his throat. "Neither do I. If they're listening, let them. Now, do I guess correctly that something big happened the day of the launch? They've told us nothing, and refused to answer any questions. It's the only explanation I can think of."

"That's it exactly. There was a terrorist attack by the Zealots the morning of the launch. Fifteen people killed, dozens more injured."

"Trying to stop the launch? Destroy the rocket?"

"Doesn't seem that way. The attack was at the observation area, so too far away to do any damage to the transport itself. As far as stopping the launch, that's probably not it, either. They timed it to coincide with the moment the transport took off. Their reasoning, though—if you can call it that—can only be guessed at, since the bomber died as well."

"I guessed it must be something like that."

She gave him a grim nod. "You know about the attempted sabotage by the Zealots of the equipment on the transport. That happened before you boarded."

"Yes."

"The perpetrators were captured by security, so that part failed."

"Everything on board ship worked perfectly," Kilmaris said.

"Good. I assumed so, because if something had gone badly wrong, I doubt even the Board would have been able to keep that quiet."

"But the attempted sabotage wasn't the end of it."

"No. After that happened, and then the Patriarch was assassinated, the police finally decided to take action. Dozens of the leaders were arrested that morning."

Kilmaris made a scoffing noise. "Did they just release them again?"

"Not this time. I guess the Chief Investigator learned his lesson from when he released Sarkos last month. Not that it'll help him—he and the rest of the leadership of the Tecoan Police Force are under investigation for how afraid they've been to bring the hammer down. Even after King Lennis was assassinated, they still wouldn't hold Sarkos and his cronies in jail. They let him go. There are allegations that half the police leadership is sympathetic to the Zealots, which is probably an exaggeration, but even a few are too many. Chances are, there'll be investigations into that for months. Especially considering…" She took a deep breath. It was hard even to speak the next part out loud. "Since the Zealots failed in their attempt to destroy the rocket, they planned an attack on the people who came to observe the launch. It turns out one of the security guards was secretly one of Sarkos's followers. That's how they got access. He let Sarkos himself into the Academy on the morning of the launch."

"I thought you said he'd been arrested?"

"No. A lot of the Zealot leadership were, but Sarkos himself couldn't be found. We now know why. He apparently decided that if the police were finally going to take action to break his cult's back, and he was going to be arrested or killed, he'd destroy whatever he could on the way down. He got into the Academy observation area, and was standing in the crowd when the rocket took off."

She stopped, suddenly overcome with emotion, then took a long breath, mastered herself, and continued.

"Sarkos had strapped explosives onto his body. When the rocket launched, he detonated the bomb."

There was silence in the room for nearly a minute. Arys's gaze locked with Kilmaris, and she could see the deep shock in his eyes.

"How many died?" he finally said, in a low voice.

"Twelve were killed immediately, not counting Sarkos himself. One of them was the assistant to the ambassador from Darset. Three more died later of their injuries."

"Gods above."

She nodded. "It's horrifying. But what angers me the most is that the Board of Directors for the Academy decided not to tell anyone on the mission what had happened, even though it was the friends and loved ones of the crew who were killed or injured in the attack."

"Do they know you're telling me?"

"Yes. I told them I would. In any case, they have to be aware that once you were back, you'd find out soon enough."

"Do you have a list of the victims?"

She reached into her jacket pocket and pulled out a folded piece of paper. "Right here. I've also listed the ones who were injured. At this point, no one on that list is in critical condition, although some of the injuries were severe. All of them are expected to survive."

Kilmaris unfolded the paper and scanned down the list. "I'll need to meet with my crew. There are names on this list I recognize."

"I understand." She shifted uneasily in her seat. "They may already have been told by now. I don't know how, or if, the Board was planning on briefing them." A flicker of a wry smile crossed her face, there and gone in an instant. "It's not as if I'm in their confidence at the moment."

"Doesn't matter. Given what you've told me about how the Board has handled this, I don't believe they'll give my crew straight answers even if they do decide to brief them. Put simply, I trust you more than I trust the Board."

"Thanks. And I'm sorry to have to tell you all this."

"It's never pleasant to deliver bad news. But I was prepared. I didn't know any details, but I figured it had to be something like this. I asked them over and over what was going on, if something terrible had happened, and all I got was 'You'll be briefed on recent events when you return.' I know everything has to be kept official, but still, when no one said, 'Everything down here is fine, why do you keep asking?', it was suspicious to say the least. And the fact that we had a perfectly good audio link to the Control Center at the Academy, but for some reason no link to anyone else, made me certain they were hiding something bad. It was obvious they didn't want us talking to anyone back home except the drones in Control. I've been thinking about it pretty much continuously the entire time we were away. All you've done is confirm what I already suspected."

"I'll let you go meet with your crew."

He rose, and a hard glint came into his eyes. "After that, though, you and I need to figure something out."

"I know."

"I expected that you already thought of it."

She nodded. "I told the Board I'd find a way to let Kallman Dorn and the rest of the survey crew know what happened whether they approved of it or not. Dorn and his people can't be up there for six months not knowing they've lost loved ones. I'd like to give the Board one more chance to be honest with the survey team, but after that, if they don't— it's time for you and me to get in contact with Tranquility Base ourselves."

thirteen

. . .

Marig Kastella came back to consciousness slowly, like a bubble rising in a still pond. He slowly lifted one hand and touched the right side of his face. There was a bandage swathing it from forehead to jawline, covering a deep ache. His left eye fluttered open, and after a moment's squinting against the sunlight coming in through the window, he recognized his surroundings.

He was lying on his back in a hospital bed.

"Marig, you're awake." The voice was familiar, although heavy with worry.

"Mother." His throat was sore, his speech hoarse, almost alien in his own ears. In a moment, a straw was put to his lips and he took a swallow of cool water. Eased for the time being, he turned toward where she sat in an uncomfortable-looking metal-framed chair. The movement made his neck twinge, and he wondered how long he'd been lying in the same position. "What happened?"

"You were hurt. You're in the hospital in Tecoa."

"I know." He cleared his throat and went on in a stronger voice. "I figured that much out. I mean, how did I get hurt? What happened at the launch?"

Her lips tightened. "That lunatic Sarkos. He blew himself up. You were lucky to survive."

"Father…?"

Nyssa Soliveen shook her head, and tears spilled down her cheeks, but her voice never wavered. "Your father tried to shield you. He… he didn't survive. He and fourteen others."

"Gods above." An ache of a different kind formed in his chest, one that desired the release of weeping, but he was too weak to cry, too weak to do anything but lie there.

"I'm so glad you're awake." Nyssa took his hand, giving it a gentle squeeze. "They said you would be soon. I've been here with you all morning."

"How badly… how badly am I injured?"

She shook her head. "Maybe you should wait till the doctor comes… or when you're feeling stronger."

"Tell me."

She didn't respond.

"Mother, tell me."

The silence hung suspended, and finally she said, "You were hit by shrapnel from the explosion. He must have had— I don't know, metal objects of some sort—strapped to himself. You were struck in the face and the right side. You've been through surgery to repair the damage, but… they weren't able to save your right eye."

It was like a punch in the gut, and for a moment, he just lay there. When he spoke, it was almost in a whisper. "My eye is… gone?"

"The doctors tried, but the damage was too bad. Everything else they said will heal with time. You'll have scars. But your eye…" She shook her head again, and looked down.

"How can it just be gone? Just… gone?"

She simply looked at him, her face twisted with grief.

"I need to talk to Kallman."

"You can't." She gave a helpless shrug. "That's another

thing. The Control Center hasn't been able to keep a tele-screen link with the ship."

He struggled to sit up, failed, and fell back with a strangled cry of horror. The anguish morphed into panic. "They've lost contact? Was the ship damaged by the explosion? Do they know if the crew is okay?"

"No, no, it's nothing like that. The Control Center is still in contact for navigation purposes, and they've confirmed everyone's fine. The mission is proceeding as it should. It's just that they don't have a stable telescreen link for family and friends to talk to the crew. They don't know why, but they said it's nothing to do with the terrorist attack, and they're working to repair it."

"I need to talk to Kallman," Marig said again.

She stroked his hand. "I know. Soon. They've told us it'll be soon."

His breathing gave a painful hitch. If he'd been stronger, he'd have been sobbing. "How long have I been in the hospital?"

"Two days. You were in surgery all afternoon the day of the… the day it happened. Since then, they've kept you sedated."

"I want to go home."

"You will. The doctor said that once you could walk unaided, you could be discharged, but you'd need physical therapy. The muscle in your right shoulder was injured, but they were able to repair it, and said it would be okay with time." She paused. "They suggested… and I thought, too, maybe you should come live with me until you're well enough to be on your own. I know we haven't been close, but now…" She gave a fluttering gesture with one hand.

He nodded. "How are you handling this?"

"It's not easy." She cleared her throat. "Your father and I, we… we weren't doing well. As partners. Honestly, we both knew we were headed toward separating, but taking that final step just hadn't happened yet. He spent barely any time at home, really. But this…" She took a long breath. "Galmon and I didn't dislike each other. I didn't want him to…" She stopped, her mouth quivering, and drew the back of her hand across her eyes. "It wasn't supposed to happen this way. It wasn't supposed to end this way."

"Nothing the Zealots have done has made sense."

"The day of the launch, apparently the police went after them, rounded up a lot of the leaders. High time, but too late. The ones they didn't catch decided to cause as much grief as they could before they were captured or killed." She gave his hand another squeeze. "But we shouldn't be talking about this right now. You will come home, won't you? Until you're better?"

He nodded.

"Good. I think it would be best for… for both of us."

"Does Kallman know about what happened?"

"Oh, I'm sure they've told him and the rest of the crew. The representative from the Control Center at the Academy said they have an audio link for technical purposes, so they must have let them know. You don't need to worry."

"I'm more concerned with how worried he must be. He's always been protective of me."

"He knows you're strong and capable. He wouldn't have left you if he thought you couldn't handle it."

"That's… that's what father said. Before…" His throat tightened, and he was unable to get another word out. And now he did cry, his body shaking, the spasms of the sobs making his bruised frame ache.

His mother, moving as if the gesture was unfamiliar, haltingly put one hand on her son's shoulder. Marig responded by putting his left hand over hers and pressing it to him, and for a while they just stayed there, motionless, deriving what small comfort they could from each other.

Marig was released from the hospital two days later.

He dreaded the removal of the bandages from his face, and his first glimpse in the mirror of what the explosion had done to him. It was bad, but not as horrifying as his maimed visage in dreams, dripping blood, with the white of exposed bone showing. The skin was purpled with bruises, and there was a long line of sutures running from his temple down his right cheek. They'd stitched his right eyelid shut. Beneath was a sunken cavity that highlighted the dreadful loss he'd suffered. Those injuries, and the ones to his right shoulder and upper arm, had all closed up well, so a lighter bandage was reapplied, and the doctors told him it would be another two weeks before he could get the stitches removed—and at that point, progress to an eyepatch.

For the rest of his life.

As he stood in the bathroom dressing, donning the clothes his mother had retrieved from his apartment—the ones he'd worn the day of the launch were beyond salvaging—he thought about how Kallman would react to seeing him for the first time. There still was no working video link for family and friends to communicate with the astronauts, so that event, however it would turn out, was still in the future.

The thought, honestly, had never been far from his mind since the day he'd awakened. He pulled on his t-shirt and gave himself another long, evaluative look in the mirror, his expression solemn.

Kallman had been physically attracted to him from the start. It was obvious, right from the first time their gazes met in the pub. In that friendly expression had been interest, curiosity—and a fair amount of raw desire. Since then, Kallman had complimented him on his beauty more times than he could recall.

But now?

He reached up and touched his right cheek through the bandage. It was still tender, but the pain was growing less day by day as his body healed. Would Kallman still want him now that he was damaged goods?

His rational mind knew Kallman wasn't that shallow, and that there was far more than physical attraction to their relationship. Kallman truly loved him, that was certain. But what he was dreading was that first moment, the video link on the telescreen clicking on, and Kallman's horrified expression at seeing his partner's scarred face.

When that would happen, though, was anyone's guess. His mother still insisted that the Control Center must have told the crew about the disaster at the launch, and that surely Kallman knew Marig had been injured but survived. Probably, she said, they had even told him the extent of the injuries, so he'd be prepared for their eventual face-to-face conversation.

But something in Marig's heart told him this simply wasn't true.

She responded to his doubt by recounting to him the conversations she'd had with Control. As the widow of the assistant to the Ambassador of Darset—who had, after all, been the highest-profile victim of the attack—she had no problem calling through to the higher-ups at the Academy. They'd assured her that everything was fine with the mission, and the crew had been briefed. Nothing was amiss but the persistent technical problem that was preventing a stable video link.

When would that be solved?

"Soon." It was always *soon*. But it had been nearly a week since the launch—the transport was already on its way back to Earth, the survey crew at that moment heading toward Tranquility Base on the Moon—and there was still no contact.

Soon was beginning to ring hollow.

Something felt wrong about the whole situation. But there

seemed to be no easy way to figure out what it was, as long as Control was stonewalling everyone. His mother still believed them—or was unwilling to admit the possibility they were lying.

The thought of what *else* they might be covering up was too terrifying to think about. He pushed that from his mind, and finished dressing.

Five minutes later, there was a low knock on the door of his room as he sat on the edge of the bed, lacing up his shoes.

"Come in?"

He was expecting his mother, there to pick him up and bring him home, but it turned out to be someone he'd never seen before—a slim woman, about his age, with neatly-cut curly dark hair and intelligent deep brown eyes. She gave him an apologetic smile.

"I'm sorry, I hope I'm not disturbing you."

"Not at all." He could hear the question in his own voice.

She stepped toward him, and grasped his hand in a brisk handshake. "My name is Reysa Sahin. I'm the Director of Antiquities at the Museum in Klen."

"Nice to meet you. I'm Marig Kastella, but I'm guessing you know that?"

She nodded. "I'm… I'm on a pilgrimage, you might say. I want to talk to all of the people who were injured in the attack, and the families of the victims. I want to… to apologize."

"To apologize? For what?"

She took a deep breath. "I'm the reason it happened."

Marig looked at her in mute shock. Finally he said, "I beg your pardon?"

"I'm not a Zealot. I'm not responsible that way. But in another, I am. I'm the one who discovered the manuscript from the Blessed Julia. The one that triggered the Zealots to attack."

"I heard about that. The manuscript."

"Yes. Most people have. It's been all over the news. And the Zealots—they rejected it. They thought it was some kind of falsehood we dreamed up to discredit them. It's why they assassinated the Patriarch." She paused, and added, in a quiet voice, "I was with him when he was killed."

"That must have been awful."

"It was."

"But the fact that you discovered the manuscript doesn't make it your fault he was killed."

She shrugged in a bemused sort of fashion. "It's a funny thing, cause and effect, isn't it? When something bad happens, it's always because of a confluence of events. Some of them deliberate, some completely random. If one of them had happened differently, or not happened at all, it would change everything. Suppose I hadn't found the document until six months from now. Maybe by that time Sarkos would have been arrested or killed. The Patriarch might still be alive. And you… you wouldn't have been hurt."

"We never know that sort of thing until afterward."

"I know. Did you know that hundreds of years ago, there were people who did? There were oracles who saw their own futures. They knew exactly what would happen—and therefore, what each of their actions would lead to. The whole web of reality, every cause and every effect, laid out before them."

Kallman was descended from one of them, but he didn't say that. "I don't think I'd want to have that much knowledge about my own future. Or anyone else's."

She gave him a faint smile. "No. It comes at a cost, doesn't it? But is what we do any better? Blundering around, trying our best not to ruin things, and still somehow ruining them anyway?"

"This doesn't make what happened your fault."

For a moment, there was silence in the hospital room.

"I'm honestly not sure why I'm doing this," she finally said. "Visiting all the victims. It's not for absolution, you know? I mean, I hope you'll forgive me for my part in this, but that's not why I'm here. I'm more trying to understand."

"Maybe what you're trying to understand is beyond human comprehension."

"Maybe." She paused. "It's like a book I read when I was young—about seventeen years old, I think. It was from the Library in Tecoa, which has always been one of my favorite places. It was written in the Before Time by an author named Thornton Wilder. It's called *The Bridge of San Luis Rey*."

Marig shook his head. "I don't know it."

"It's about a religious man named Brother Juniper. He lived in a place called Peru. While he was there, a bridge over a canyon collapsed, and five people died. His belief was that the gods always have a reason for what they do, so he set about tracing the lives of each of the five victims to determine how they, and no one else, had been on the bridge that day. Why they died, and no one else did. There had to be some common thread, something that gave their deaths meaning."

"What did he find?"

"After studying their lives, he came to the conclusion that either the minds of the gods are so inscrutable that humans can't parse their motives—or else there is no reason. Things simply happen because they happen."

"That's kind of what I've always thought."

"The authorities of the time disagreed. They burned Brother Juniper at the stake, along with his manuscript."

Marig stared at her, horrified.

"So it looks like the Zealots have always been with us," Reysa said. "Sarkos and his followers are just the latest incarnation. I don't know, maybe they always will be. People who think they know the answers, and are willing to kill the ones who question."

"Don't let it stop you from questioning, though. That's letting the Zealots win."

"Even though you got injured because of it?"

"Even so." He paused, and when he went on, it was in a low, quiet voice. "I lost an eye. My father was one of the ones who was killed."

She looked down, shook her head. "I saw the names. I thought you must be father and son. I'm so sorry."

"So am I. It's horrible. And maybe, like Brother Juniper decided, there's no reason for it. There are a thousand things that could have changed the outcome. My father and I could have been standing a little farther away. The switch on Sarkos's bomb could have malfunctioned, or the security guards could have stopped him before he got to the observation site. Any number of things could have gone differently. But they didn't."

"And we don't know why."

"I certainly don't."

"Neither do I. I guess it's the human condition. Which is a non-answer, but maybe it's the only one we've got."

"We just have to take what comes, and start where we are. Work with what happens to us." He took a deep breath, and felt something shift in him, like a knot loosening. "And know that the important things—the people who love us—will still be there regardless. That love and kindness and friendship will triumph over hatred and bigotry."

"You still believe that? Even after what happened?"

"Yes. I do."

Her smile returned, and seemed more certain this time. "Well, I suppose if you can believe it, despite everything, I can find it in me to try as well."

"Good." He met her gaze steadily. "My partner told me the morning of the launch that *all shall be well*. I have to keep faith in that for the next six months. And beyond. Maybe it's not true, you know? Maybe bad things will happen. I mean, I'm *sure* bad things will happen, because they always do— bad and good things intermixed, like they have since the beginning of time. But we still have to believe it. We have to believe that we'll manage, somehow, and that the good will outweigh the bad. Otherwise, there's no point to living."

"All shall be well."

He nodded, and for the first time since the day of the launch, he honestly believed it. "All shall be well. Today and every day."

fourteen

. . .

The separation of the lander and the transport ship went flawlessly, which put Kallman Dorn in the pilot's seat for the first time.

He'd had plenty of training, of course, but this was the real deal. He had to put into practice all the hundreds of skills he'd learned at the Academy, and remember all the drills and cautions and guidelines Arys Quentra and the other instructors taught him and the rest of the flyers. Plus, he was now responsible not only for his own life but the lives of the twenty-person survey crew.

Arys had been right. Once you're out in the vacuum of space, you have no room for error.

"Relax, Dorn," said his copilot, Orzen Saxena, sitting in the seat next to his. "If you clench your teeth any harder, they'll shatter."

He took a deep breath, and looked out through the polyacrylate visor of the lander. The fiery pinpoints of a thousand stars glittered against the black velvet background of interstellar space. He'd never seen stars like this, their scintillating light undimmed by passage through Earth's moist atmosphere. He recalled once seeing something close, when as a teenager he was on a summer backpacking trip into the Cascade Mountains, and had gotten up in the middle of the night to pee. When he unzipped the tent flap and looked up, he immediately felt lightheaded, like he was floating. There were so many stars visible he couldn't even pick out the familiar constellations.

Even that, though, was nothing compared to what he was seeing now. The heavy responsibilities he had on his shoulders were tempered by simple, overwhelming awe.

"Look at that, Saxena," he said in a low voice. "You're gazing out toward infinity. We've broken the chains of Orion."

She gave him a questioning smile. "How do you mean?"

He was quiet for a moment. "It comes from a book of lore. Something from the Before Time. One of the books that survived. My grandmother used to read to me from it. A lot of it is just weird—historical stuff mixed with magic, who knows how much of it is true—but some is pure poetry. There's one part that's stuck with me all these years." He frowned, remembering. "*Can you loose the bonds of the Pleiades, or break the chains of Orion? Can you lead forth the garland of crowns in their season, or guide the Bear with its children? Do you know the ordinances of heaven? Can you establish their rule on the Earth?*"

"That's beautiful. What do you think it means?"

"I'm not sure, not really. At least, not what it meant to the person who wrote it thousands of years ago. But I was so taken by that passage that I memorized it, and I always thought about it when I looked up at the night sky. *Orion* and *Pleaides* were old names for two of the constellations, I learned that much, and so were *the Bear* and *the garland of crowns.*" He took a deep breath. "They were writing about looking up to the sky, something I spent my entire childhood doing. To me, the passage has always meant breaking free of the Earth, striking out for the stars. Humanity spent most of its existence trapped on our little world. Only experiencing what they could, crawling around on the surface of that tiny sphere. There is so much more out there waiting to be known."

She gave him a curious glance. "I've never heard you talk this way."

"I thought I was prepared for this. I wasn't. I don't know how you ever could be. You have to experience it to understand."

"Don't get too carried away, Dorn. We have a ship to fly."

"I'm okay." He turned toward her with a grin. "I'm just having a hard time believing we're finally here."

She looked at the control panel, and made a minor adjustment to their flight path. "Technically, we haven't arrived yet. We still have to land this beast."

He laughed. "So get on with flying the ship and stop babbling about ancient poetry?"

"I can land the ship for you if you're too distracted." She returned his grin. "But I'm guessing you don't want that."

"No. I've got things well in hand." He looked at the screen of the attitude monitor. "We should be landing at Tranquility in a little over a half hour."

"I wonder how it's going to feel taking our first steps onto the surface of the Moon?"

"Surreal."

The lander continued to glide along, the unseen surface of the Moon beneath them. He'd gotten a good look at it during separation—the glare from the rocky hills and craters nearly too bright to look at—but since then, it had mostly been out of sight, with the onboard sensors keeping track of their altitude as they gradually flew in toward the landing site.

At ten minutes before landing, Kallman switched on the intercom mic.

"Attention. We will be arriving at Tranquility in ten minutes. Crew, strap in. We'll be firing the retrorockets in three minutes. Repeat, three minutes until retros. You need to be seated and buckled in before then."

The remainder of the flight went without a hitch. Retros on, slowing them down. The steering jets releasing controlled bursts of air to pivot them into position.

"Lander, we have you on sensors," came a disembodied voice. Port control at Tranquility. "Adjust your trajectory by zero-point-eight degrees north. Looking good otherwise."

Kallman made the course correction.

A minute after that, "Got you on visual."

"Extending landing gear."

There was a creak and a groan as the spidery legs of the lander moved outward from the hull of the ship.

"Full reverse thrust."

With the push of a button, the ship began to brake. Both Kallman and Orzen were pulled forward by the force of deceleration. At this point they were low enough to see the buildings and covered causeways of Tranquility Base ahead, sharp-edged and pristine, the black polygons of their shadows like dark holes in the brilliantly-lit lunar surface.

The braking jets slowed them sufficiently that they could feel the gravitational pull of the Moon—it had always been there, of course, but was offset by their own breakneck speed. Now, slowing to a low glide, they coasted in—and dropped into the center of the circular landing pad with hardly a jolt.

"Wow," Orzen said, a little breathlessly. "That was gorgeous."

"Thanks." He could hear the relief in his own voice. Then, into the intercom mic, he said, "We have landed. Welcome to the Moon."

Disembarkation had to wait for the long, collapsible metal corridor to be extended from the nearest building to the lander, to obviate the need of donning pressurized space suits for the short walk to the base. But in the practiced hands of the lunar ground crew, this didn't take long, and soon

Kallman and the rest of his team were stepping down from the lander into the newly-created umbilical connecting them to Tranquility Base.

A rush of adrenaline coursed through him. He was, finally and for real, on the surface of the Moon.

He walked down the umbilical, every sense straining to take it all in, as the rest of his crew followed behind him. The echoic ring of their footsteps on the metal floor. The dry, slightly acrid smell of the air—the result, he'd been told, of minute traces of Moon dust too fine to be trapped by the air filters. Above all, the lightness of his gait, from a gravitational pull one-sixth what he was used to on Earth.

He reached the end of the umbilical, opened the door, and stepped into the reception building.

Three people were waiting for them, of which he only knew one—Jenia Banfield, the base commander. A Klen native like himself, she had a bluff, bantering manner and a ready smile, something he'd picked up immediately during their remote conversations prior to launch.

She gave him a cheerful greeting and firm handshake.

"We finally meet. I've only seen you on telescreen." Her grin widened. "You're shorter in person."

He laughed. "Telescreen links hide a thousand ills."

"We don't even have that luxury, lately."

"You're cut off, too?"

She nodded. "Audio link to Control only. And lots of excuses for why it hasn't been fixed. I offered to send them some of my technicians, since theirs seem to be incompetent."

"I'm sure they appreciated that."

"Well, hell. The technology isn't that complicated. I was working on satellite links in electronics class during my second year at the Academy."

"You know Tevin Kilmaris?"

"Of course I do. He and I were at the Academy together. He was a year ahead of me."

"Kilmaris thinks that there's something off about this. That something happened down on Earth, and Control doesn't want us finding out about it."

"What sort of something?"

"No idea. I'm guessing you know the Patriarch was assassinated?"

Jenia's face registered undisguised shock. "No, seriously? They told us about King Lennis when it happened last month, but not a word about this. When did it happen?"

"The morning of the launch."

"I'll be damned." She took a deep breath. "Why the hell wouldn't they tell us?"

"Kilmaris thinks that's not all they're keeping secret."

"Well, it's an awful thing all by itself. The Patriarch assassinated. One of the Zealots, right?"

"Of course."

"Fucking lunatics."

"Can't argue with that."

"Why does Kilmaris think it can't be just that? I mean, not that keeping the Patriarch's assassination a secret makes any real sense."

"Because it was all over the news the morning of the launch, so everyone on the transport already knew about it. Even so, we were cut off from communicating with family and friends, too. So there must have been something else that happened."

"And they don't want us finding out what?"

"His contention is that it was bad enough that it could cause serious problems for morale."

"Wow." She shook her head. "That has the ring of truth to it. Certainly makes better sense than their technicians just being inept."

"He told me right before separation that as soon as he got back to Earth, he was going to get to the bottom of it, and get word to us if it was humanly possible."

"We haven't heard anything."

"At this point he's probably just arrived. It may take him a while to get past the bureaucrats at the Academy and figure out a way to talk to us."

"If anyone could, it's Kilmaris. I wouldn't want to be the one trying to stand in his way."

"Glad he's on our side."

"Me too. But gods above, why do there have to be sides, here? I thought we were all trying to accomplish the same thing." She ushered them into a wide room with sofas and other comfortable chairs, and a spread of food on plates that looked remarkably homelike as compared to the foil-packaged meals they'd all eaten on the flight. "Anyhow, Dorn, there'll be time to discuss all this later. For now, you and your crew make yourselves comfortable. We'll give you a short while to get your bearings, relax, have something to eat. Then I'll give the grand tour of Tranquility Base."

"Thanks. It's good to finally meet you."

"Likewise."

While Jenia and the base crew made their introductions to the rest of the survey team, Kallman went to one of the tables and picked up a piece of what looked like cheddar cheese. He nibbled at a corner.

Hmm. Tasted like cheese, too. Either the synthetics were getting a lot better, or they'd spared no expense to welcome them and broken out some of the Earth-made perishables from cold storage.

Truth be told, though, he wasn't hungry.

I'm standing on the Moon.

His mind was flooded with the heady sense that he was one of a relative handful of humans who had ever done this— left Earth behind, stood on the surface of the ghostly white orb that to most of the people on the planet was the very symbol of the unreachable. Soon he would lead the exploratory team, first on a short practice run, and then toward a more distant target—Tycho, which according to the scant records from the Before Time, had been a permanent lunar base fifteen hundred years ago. It had been an intended site for investigation since Tranquility was built, but until now, had been pushed down on the priorities list. Finally the Academy Board had approved the venture, and decided it would be a good first challenge for the newly-arrived survey team.

What they would find at Tycho was anyone's guess, but the hope was that there'd be valuable relics. Books and electronic records, perhaps, but also everyday objects that might help them to understand that long-lost civilization. Perhaps even technology that could supplement what they had, allow them to springboard past the lengthy, arduous process of research and development into some of the nearly magical-sounding abilities their distant ancestors had.

It was all beyond exciting.

He wandered over to one of the wide windows. Despite being made of a triple layer of nearly unbreakable polyacry-late, it had a startling clarity. He reached out his hand to touch its smooth, glassy surface. Only a few centimeters away from his fingertips was the sunlit near-vacuum of the Moon's surface.

The Sea of Tranquility. The first explorers to return to the Moon's surface, thirty years earlier, had kept the old names for the lunar features, gleaned from ancient maps and books, and there was no doubt that their poetry struck at the heart. And indeed this place was tranquil—a sheet of hardened basalt rock covered with a thick layer of dust. A footprint or tire tread mark would last for centuries in this airless, rainless place.

Before long, Kallman's footprints would be amongst them. An enduring mark on the surface of another world.

A few flights out, just to get their bearings. In a week, once they'd acclimated, he and the rest of the crew would transfer the lander to Schickard Base, nearer to the terminus between the near-Earth and far-Earth sides of the Moon. From there they would fly out to see what, if anything, they could discover at Tycho. Shortly thereafter he'd take out the shiny new one-person survey ship, and fly it across the terminus, losing sight of the Earth for the first time, and find out what was over there.

And perhaps, for the first time in fifteen hundred years, a human would learn something of the ordinances of heaven.

fifteen

. . .

Marig toweled off the fog from the bathroom mirror and gave a good long look at himself.

The previous day he'd gotten the stitches removed from his face. His right eyelid was grotesquely sunken—something he knew he'd have to get used to. The scar down the side of his face still looked angry and pink, worse now because of the hot spray of the shower. Even so, the doctors seemed pleased with his progress, and said he was healing up well.

He'd always have a scar on his right temple and cheek, though, as well as longer ones on his right arm and side. They were clear about that. The marks would grow less with time, but even if he lived to a hundred, he'd die with scars and a missing eye.

He continued to stare at himself, picturing Kallman's expression when they first saw each other. It'd been three weeks since the disaster at the launch, and already it seemed like they'd been separated for months. Would he be shocked to see for the first time the damage to his lover's face?

Marig recalled the conversation with Reysa Sahin. Talking to the young archaeologist had helped allay some of his anxiety, but even so, every time he saw himself in the mirror, every time he touched his own injured face, the word came to mind.

Ugly.

It was a horrible word, and unjustified. He knew that. But it was impossible to put aside. He had been altered irrevocably, and until he lived through that first time Kallman would see him, there was no way to let go of the fear completely.

But the Academy was still telling friends and family that there was no stable video link to the Moon, which was bizarre and troubling despite their assurances that everything was fine. Kallman himself would probably be at Schickard Base by now. Schickard was smaller than Tranquility—hopefully that wouldn't add another layer of complication to getting through once the technological glitch was fixed.

Which Marig's mother had been repeatedly told would be "soon."

He sighed, finished toweling himself off, and pulled on his clothes. Ran a comb through his damp curls, then picked up his black eyepatch—a new thing since the bandages came off the previous week—placed it over his missing eye, and slipped the elastic around the back of his head.

He gave himself another quick glance. At least with the patch on, he didn't look so horrifyingly maimed.

Ugly. I'm ugly now. I didn't used to be.

He said aloud to his own reflection, "Oh, stop it," and exited the bathroom.

The sound of raised voices struck his ears as he approached the living room.

"Mem Soliveen, you must understand my position…" The man spoke in tones of icy anger held back only by decorum.

"I've told you that I understand your position perfectly, and that I also understand you have been lying to me."

Marig recognized in his mother's voice the tight haughtiness that was always a signal she was very close to losing her temper completely. He stopped as he exited the hallway. Past his mother, sitting ramrod-straight in a swivel chair, the tele-screen showed the face of a middle-aged man with cropped salt-and-pepper hair and a grim expression.

"That is a baseless accusation."

"Hardly that. This morning I got a call from Commander Tevin Kilmaris, who made it clear what the situation was."

"Commander Kilmaris had no authorization to contact you."

"Commander Kilmaris is a free citizen of Cascadia, as am I. As such, both of us may speak to whomever we please without asking permission from you."

"You must realize, Mem Soliveen, that what he told you is simply his own perspective, and he may not be in full possession of the facts."

"The facts? Such as his statement to me that despite your explicit words to the contrary, you did not tell any of the crew about the attack? And, undoubtedly, still have not? If you wish to focus on the facts, perhaps you can explain to me how the people who just put a lander on the Moon have been unable to repair a telescreen link for well over three weeks."

"I have told you we are working on it."

"And I have told you I don't believe you. Mir Stiles, allow me to remind you that my husband, assistant to the Ambassador from Darset, died in the terrorist attack. My son was badly injured. If that doesn't make your tenuous position clear, my son is the life partner of Kallman Dorn, who is leading the survey mission."

"We are aware of…"

She continued without even acknowledging his interruption. "The worst part of all this is that you not only lied to me repeatedly, you made me complicit in your lies in that I then passed them along to my son, who is struggling enough with his injuries as it is. Honestly, I am finding it increasingly difficult to believe anything you've told me, up to and including the statement that the mission is 'proceeding normally' and everyone on board the survey craft is safely at Schickard Base."

"I assure you, Mem Soliveen…"

"Assure all you like, Mir Stiles. At this point, I want proof, in the form of face-to-face contact with my son's partner. *Him* I will believe. You, not in the slightest."

He regarded her for a moment with a tight-lipped expression, as if he weren't sure what to say. "I have the safety and security of the mission at heart, you must understand."

"What I understand is that you have the safety and security of Denian Stiles at heart. But what apparently has yet to occur to you is that you have miscalculated badly. You seriously believe that when what you are doing is made public, you'll keep your job? You'll be lucky if they don't escort you to the next FastRail out of Cascadia."

Stiles slipped one finger inside the collar of his shirt and tugged, a nervous gesture that communicated perhaps more than he intended.

"You have my word that in forty-eight hours…"

"Twenty-four."

"Mem Soliveen, please realize that…"

"I have made it abundantly clear what I realize. It is now up to you to salvage what remains of this situation. I am expecting a stable telescreen link within twenty-four hours, so that my son can speak to his partner, and the other family members with their loved ones on the survey crew. Perhaps they will still believe there was some sort of technical problem, and you'll be able to avoid public humiliation. I cannot guarantee that, and I will also tell you that if anyone, at any time, asks me directly what happened— whether there actually was a video link problem, or if the Board of the Academy lied to its own people and their loved ones—I will tell the truth. I will not compromise my own honesty any more than I already have in order to protect you."

The last word came out like a curse, and Stiles recoiled a little.

"You have my word that I'll try. I have to get the rest of the Board to agree. I cannot act on my own."

"You'll do more than try. And whether you act alone or with the Board's blessing makes no difference to me whatsoever. You will see that it is done. Or the next time you see my face, it will be in an interview on every news media in Cascadia."

Before he could respond, she jabbed the *End Call* button on the screen with her index finger and for a time sat there, breathing hard. In the reflection in the now-dark telescreen, her eyes were wide.

"Thank you," Marig said quietly.

She turned around, then took a deep breath, let it out slowly. "Marig. I didn't know you were there."

"I'm sorry, I shouldn't have walked in during a private conversation."

"It's all right. It's better that you heard, honestly." Something in her seemed to relax, and she looked up at him for a long moment. "I'm just sorry it took the transport ship commander telling me *they're lying to you* for me to believe it. You suspected something right away. I should have trusted you."

"It's all right. I can be too anxious at times." He paused. "Do you believe what Stiles said? That nothing's gone wrong with the mission itself?"

She leaned back in her chair. "I think so. If something *had* gone badly amiss, there'd be no way to keep that quiet. And when Commander Kilmaris talked to me this morning, he confirmed that everything seemed fine, they'd sent the lander on its way and returned without any hitch. I think as far as that goes, Stiles is telling the truth. But about briefing the crew, and about the link being unavailable because of a technical problem? Those were deliberate, planned lies. Kilmaris used those exact words." She gave him a long look, and for a time, there was silence. "It looks like your injuries are healing well," she finally said. "How are you feeling?"

"I'm fine."

"Is the pain manageable?"

"It hurts a little less every day. I'm mending." He paused. "I'd like it to go a little faster, is all."

"Don't you worry about that."

Marig smiled. It was meant well, he knew that, but it brought back how she had always approached parenting when he was a child. If he fell down and skinned his knee, Nyssa's response was a dismissive, "No need to cry over a little scrape," as if pointing out how unnecessary his tears were would make him stop crying and say, *Oh, you're right, of course. Silly of me.*

"I hope your threats work," he said. "Stiles seemed surprised anyone was calling him on his lies."

"*Someone* had to stand up to him. Puffed up little tyrant. You can tell he's the type who surrounds himself with foot-kissers. All he has to do is speak, and his expectation is that everyone will bow down and say, *Of course, whatever you say.* I don't think he liked the fact that he couldn't intimidate me."

"Would you really go on the news and tell everyone what he's doing?"

Her eyes flashed. "I do not make empty promises." She snorted. "How foolish of them! What were they thinking? They must have known they couldn't keep it secret forever, and that the longer they waited to tell the crew, the worse it would appear to everyone."

"Why keep lying, though? Now that people have found out, you'd think they'd admit it."

"That's a good question. This has the feel of a decision that was made right after the attack, when everything was in chaos. When people were still running about trying to figure out what had happened, and what they could possibly do or say to address it. Stiles probably said, 'Don't tell the crew for now.' Then *for now* turned into hours and then into days, and by then, they were in the position of having to pretend to believe in a technical problem that never existed. So they doubled down on the lies, thinking it would allow them to save their own reputations. In the end, of course, all they've done is made it much, much worse."

"They've only themselves to blame."

She nodded. "To be fair, they've never had to deal with anything like this. But that doesn't excuse them. You're in a terrible situation, and have to give bad news to a group of people you work with—well, it's not pleasant, but you figure it out. You grit your teeth and do it, then deal with what happens afterward."

"I appreciate your standing up for me."

Again, she gave him a long, searching look, and reached out to him. He took a step toward her, and they linked hands. Her grip was warm and surprisingly strong.

"Marig, you're my son. I would do anything for you, you know that." Her voice caught. "Your father would have, too. He'd be proud of how strong you've been."

"I don't feel strong."

"Strong isn't a feeling. Strong is knowing what you have to do is hard, that it'll be a struggle, and then doing it anyway. When you talk to Kallman, I know that's what he'll tell you."

"When? Not if?"

"When." Nyssa gave him a curt nod. "One thing I did not tell Denian Stiles. When I spoke to Commander Kilmaris this morning, he told me that he and one of the flight instructors from the Academy are working on a telescreen link of their own. If Stiles and his cronies don't come through with a good link within twenty-four hours, the Commander and his friend will find a way to get us one. He assured me of that." She gave his hand another squeeze. "You need to talk to your sweetheart. I know you're anxious about it. You're worried about how he'll see you because of your injuries."

"You know that? I didn't say anything…"

One corner of her mouth quirked upward. "You didn't need to say anything. You've never been good at hiding your feelings, you know. I notice that every time you pass anything with glass in it, you glance at your reflection, and grimace a little. You've been worried since the first day what he'll think when he looks at you."

"I suppose."

"Marig, Kallman *loves* you. What he'll see when he looks at you is the beautiful face of the man he wants to spend the rest of his life with. Nothing has changed about that, and nothing will change. It's natural to be upset about what happened. Anyone would be. But there's one thing that you need to be rock-solid sure of. Kallman loves you. So do I, and so do your sisters. You can be uncertain about other things, but never doubt that."

"Thanks."

"And you'll see. When you talk to Kallman some time in the next twenty-four hours. He'll tell you." She smiled. "You may not believe your mother's reassurances, but you damn well better believe his."

sixteen

· · ·

The transfer of the lander to Schickard Base went smoothly. It was a long flight—a little over 2,500 kilometers—but compared to the flight from the Earth they'd made only a week earlier, it seemed to take hardly any time.

Schickard would be their home base for the remaining five and a half months of the mission. As soon as Kallman set foot inside, he had the sense of being in a remote outpost. The only people there to welcome him and his crew were the technicians who had set up the umbilical. They were told where the cafeteria and sleeping quarters were, but there was no ceremony at all.

Honestly, that was fine with him. The welcome address he'd had to sit through at Tranquility had been squirm-inducing, as some of the senior members of the base staff heaped accolades on Kallman, the crew, and the people at the Academy who'd made the mission happen. It was well meant, but a relief when it was over. Kallman was ready to get on with it and do what he and the rest of the team had come here for—get on the survey crafts and start mapping out the far-Earth side of the Moon.

There was one more shorter flight to take before then,

though—after an eight-hour period to rest, a thousand-kilometer trip to Tycho Base. A permanent settlement from the Before Time, Tycho had been surveyed from overhead, but no one had yet landed and explored it. He, Orzen Saxena, and two other select members of his crew had been charged with taking two days to fly there in a light transport, find out what they could—including bringing back anything potentially interesting to archaeologists, historians, and scientists—taking extensive photographs of everything, and coming back to Schickard.

Then, off in the one-person survey shuttles to make their crisscrossing mapping runs over the far-Earth side, into regions that had only been seen from high-altitude orbit since the last missions of the Before Time, now almost fifteen hundred years ago.

The whole thing was incredibly exciting.

There was only one sour note. They still were unable to contact home. Unlike Jenia Banfield, the plain-spoken commander of Tranquility Base, the commander at Schickard seemed unconcerned about it. Apparently the people at Schickard volunteered to go there because they didn't mind being somewhere with less access to amenities, and that included video links to Earth. When asked when a link might be established, all he got was an uninterested shrug.

"They told us in a week or two," the commander said, and that was the end of it.

When Kallman and his roommate were undressing for bed at the end of the first day, it was obvious the base staff's nonchalance was not shared by the newly-arrived survey crew.

"I'm beginning to get honestly angry about this," the man, whose name was Serin, said, as he elbowed his way out of his flight suit. "I want to talk to Mira and my daughter. They've got to be worried about me."

"I feel the same way. My partner, Marig, is a worrier anyhow. He's probably imagining the worst."

"You mentioned before we left Tranquility that you thought there must be more to this than a simple tech issue. What do you think is going on?"

"I have no idea. It's just a hunch, but one shared by Kilmaris and Banfield. They both thought something odd was behind it."

"But you've no idea what it might be, Commander?"

"No. I told you all that as soon as I knew something certain, I'd let you know. I don't want to engage in baseless speculation, but I also don't believe in keeping secrets unless there's a damn good reason. At the moment, I'm as in the dark as everyone else."

Serin, stripped down to his underwear, climbed into his bunk and pulled the blanket up over himself, then cupped his hands behind his head. A moment later, Kallman climbed into his own bed. It was firm but not uncomfortable, with no frills, much like everything else he'd seen at Schickard.

"Sooner or later, they've got to tell us what's going on." Serin's voice was tentative.

"Commander Kilmaris said when he got home, he'd make sure to get to the bottom of it—and get us a good link. I trust Kilmaris. He's a good man, and there's no way he'd let a bunch of Academy bureaucrats get in his way."

"I hope you're right, sir."

"Me too."

Using a remote, he turned the lights down in the little room, and soon, Serin was snoring softly. Sleep eluded Kallman, however. All he could picture was Marig's face, creased with worry. Marig always had trouble dealing with uncertainty. Given bad news, he could handle it, but not knowing played into his tendency toward assuming the worst.

Right now, Kallman would have given a lot just to have one night to hold him and say, *It's all right. I'm safe. All is well.*

In a little over five months, I'll be back home, and that's where I'll stay for a long while afterward.

Finally, he drifted off, but still his sleep was troubled by restless dreams of some uncertain danger that lurked just out of sight. Never attacking—just watching, waiting for the right opportunity to strike.

The next morning Kallman, Orzen, and two of the survey crew put on their space suits and plodded their way to a hangar, where they were shown the four-person craft they'd use for the journey to Tycho Base.

It was a far cry from the sleek, shiny, teardrop-shaped survey pod he'd be flying around to the other side of the Moon. This was a heavy-bodied, clunky vessel, resting awkwardly on four jointed legs. If the survey pod was a falcon, Kallman thought with a smile, this was a chicken.

But it would get them there and back. The technician briefing them on the craft called it "Old Reliable." The technical aspects of the lecture were hardly necessary—the controls were much like the ships they'd all been trained on—but Kallman and the others listened patiently.

"There's plenty of storage in the back," the technician said. "I even cleaned it out for you. The last people who brought it out were geologists, and they left a bunch of damn rocks and sand in the hold. You know how it goes. But she's clean as can be now, so whatever you find out at Tycho, you can bring it back for the scientists here to ponder over." He grinned. "What *do* you think you'll find?"

Kallman smiled and shrugged. "Not even the first guess. My hope is there'll be records of some sort, so we can find out more of what they were doing out there. The problem is, it's likely that most of the records were electronic, and there'll be the problem of compatibility with our own storage and retrieval devices. We bring home electronic data, there's no guarantee we'll be able to decode it."

The technician gave a dismissive wave of the hand. "Oh, leave it to the scientists. They'll figure it out. Can't be that hard."

"Well, it'd be beyond me."

"Me too. I'm just saying it wouldn't be beyond *them*. Those people got brains past anything I can imagine. The technology can't be *that* different, you know what I'm saying?"

A half-hour later, Kallman and his crew were strapped into the seats in the craft. Their helmets on, visors down, suits pressurized.

"Everyone patched in?" he said into his mic. "Saxena?"

"With you, Commander."

"Boland?"

"Here, sir."

"Findras?"

"Yes, sir."

"Tech, are you with us?"

The technician's disembodied voice came through the speaker, tinny but clear. "I've got you loud and clear, Commander Dorn."

"We're ready. You can depressurize and pull the hangar door."

A low, shuddering vibration rumbled through the craft as the door slowly lifted. The air had mostly been evacuated already—recirculated into Schickard Base—but even so, there was a little gust onto the brightly-lit surface beyond the hangar, fluttering a puff of lunar dust that for a moment hung, nearly motionless, in the deep vacuum.

Kallman gently maneuvered the craft until it was airborne, then nudged it forward. Their shadow looked like some fat, awkward spider hanging from an invisible thread.

"You're clear, Commander," came the technician's voice. "Have a nice trip."

"Thanks."

He pulled up the landing gear, making the ship quiver and groan, but after that there was nothing but silence as he pivoted the craft toward Tycho and accelerated up to cruising speed.

The mountains and craters slipped past beneath them. A beautiful, desolate place, as lovely as it was inimical to life. The passage of their craft disturbed nothing, leaving not a mark on the expanse of dust and rock that had lain unmoved for millennia.

Kallman had always thought of the Before Time as being long ago. It had been his mental marker for "really old" ever since he was a child. But here, that was nothing, the mere blink of an eye. In his Lunar Geology class at the Academy, he'd learned that Tycho Crater—where they were heading—was considered "fairly young."

At one hundred million years in age.

The estimate, the professor told them, came not from studying the rocks in the crater. With luck, that was something Kallman's team could provide to geologists. The reason they knew the crater was recent, in lunar terms, was that it still showed the rays of debris flung outward from the collision that formed it. Those streaks of bright material, like the petals of a dandelion, hadn't yet had time to erode back into the ubiquitous gray uniformity that characterized most of the lunar surface.

It still looked basically the same, after *one hundred million years*.

"Daydreaming again, Commander?" came Saxena's wry voice.

Kallman laughed. "Maybe a little. And you can cut out the *commander* business. Just Dorn is fine."

"Don't want to be seen as disrespectful."

He snorted. "You? Never. It just feels wrong, you know? *Commander* is for people like Kilmaris and Quentra and Banfield. They've earned it."

"So maybe once we get back home to Earth, we'll have to call you *commander*."

"Yeah, maybe." He laughed. "Right now, I see us all as explorers. All relying on each other equally. I'm fine with dispensing with ranks and protocol unless it's absolutely necessary."

She looked at the screen, and made a minor adjustment to their flight path. "So you'll pull rank only if we decide to mutiny."

"Exactly." He laughed. "But be careful what you're planning. Back in the Before Time, they didn't treat mutineers too well. So mind your manners, Saxena, if you know what's good for you. Walking the plank on the Moon wouldn't be any fun."

A little over eight hours later, Saxena said, "I've got Tycho Base on visual."

They'd crested the high ridge of Tycho Crater a half-hour earlier, so he knew they must be getting close. Even so, the first glimpse of the ancient Moon base set his heart thrumming. It wasn't that different from Schickard— after all, there weren't that many different ways someone could design the pressurized buildings of a lunar base. But it was mind-boggling knowing he was looking at the fifteen-hundred-year-old relics left behind by long-dead explorers who had come here even before the fabled Founders of Klen had lived.

When people last walked inside these buildings, all the Founders were living, breathing real people, leading their lives, not yet having taken on the mantle of oracular knowledge that would guide them out of the ruins of a dying, drowning city. Julia, Soren, Finn, Quaice, Mary, Brandon, Colin, Emily, Perry. He'd heard the names so many times in his youth, and never really doubted they'd existed. In fact, he descended, in direct patrilineal line, from Colin Dorn and Emily Banfield. But even so, they had the feeling of mythology.

Now, looking at the dull gray metal of the complex at Tycho Base made all of it seem that much more real. History wasn't just a bunch of stories in books. It was a tumbling river, ceaselessly moving, carrying humanity like so many tiny floating leaves. Leaves that would ride for a while then be pulled under and disappear, replaced by others in relentless, chaotic procession.

"Check your belts," Kallman said. "Braking in five seconds."

The retro jets fired, thrusting them forward against the sturdy webbing of their safety harnesses. The craft slowed, coasting in toward a dusty rectangle with white markings—evidently a landing pad—with narrow walkways leading to the nearest two buildings.

"Extending landing gear," Saxena said.

The old spaceship vibrated as the jointed legs opened out, clicking into place with a deep *clunk*.

"Landing gear fully engaged."

"Braking for arrival."

Another burst of the retro jets slowed them to a crawl, and once again, he set the ship down with barely a bump.

"Gods above, you are good at that," Saxena said, her voice reverent.

"That's why I'm the commander and you're not."

Laughter crackled through the speakers of his helmet.

He powered down the engines, looking out through the craft's polyacrylate visor to the silent, dark buildings waiting for them.

"Findras, make sure you bring the oxyacetylene torch. We may have to cut our way in."

"Think they locked the door before they left for the last time?"

"Don't know. No way to tell what their frame of mind was. Better to be prepared, although there's no reason we can't access our ship for tools when we need to. Leave behind the collecting containers for now, though. We can pile together whatever we find that we want to bring back, and pack it up before we leave. Remember your flashlights, of course. Any power sources they had in there are almost certainly long dead."

Fifteen minutes later, they exited the ship. This first reconnaissance exploration was meant mainly to see what gear they might need. Kallman's heart pounded. Reflexively he checked his wristband biomonitor. Pulse and blood pressure a little elevated, but still within the normal range, especially considering the circumstances.

Pure adrenaline surge. With an effort he brought his breathing rate down—no need to suck down his oxygen supply for no good reason.

The walk to the compound was short, and as it turned out, they didn't need the torch. The hatch into the nearest building was slightly ajar.

In that airless place, there was no sound as Kallman pulled on the door handle and swung it open, but he could feel through his glove the vibration of metal on metal as the hinge flexed. All four switched on flashlights, the beams crisscrossing into the dark interior.

One by one they stepped into that place that had last seen human habitation over a millennium ago.

Kallman's light illuminated shelves, tables, cabinets. Obviously a functional room of some sort. There were scattered objects there and on the floor, mostly what appeared to be safety gear—harnesses, vests, a hank of rope, a bin of metal loops and hooks and fasteners. The flashlight beam passed across a label on a cabinet drawer that said, in an archaic but legible typeset, *CABLES AND CHARGERS.* He pulled the drawer open, and inside was a tangle of wires and an assortment of rectangular metal-and-plastic devices of various sizes.

Nothing of particular interest. He shut the drawer.

"Commander?" came Findras's voice through the speaker. It was high, thin, strained, not at all like the man's usual cheerful baritone.

Kallman turned. Findras was standing next to a half-open door into the next room. He pushed the door open farther, and shone his flashlight down into the space behind it.

Immediately behind the door was a dead body in a space suit.

Now Saxena's horrified voice came through the speakers. "Gods above. They abandoned people up here? Left them to die?"

Kallman just stared. Dimly, through the tinted glass of the helmet visor, he saw the desiccated face of a mummified person.

Finally, he choked out, "I guess they did."

The rest of the exploration was carried out in near silence. Other than a hushed, "I found another one" no one seemed inclined to speak.

In the end, they found seven bodies. The most tragic was the one that seemed to belong to the base commander. They found her lying on her bunk, to all appearances in peaceful repose, but she was the only one found with the visor of her helmet open. Kallman discovered the reason why when he saw her journal, still open to the last page, on a nearby desk. Like the label on the cabinet drawer, the script was archaic, and a few of the word choices puzzling, but it was perfectly legible.

It's now been almost two months since the last transmission from Earth. Cape Canaveral must have fallen. What's finished us is that our main food synthesis unit had a bad control panel. We were due a supply ship six weeks ago, with parts to make a repair, but of course it never came.

I don't blame NASA. I'm sure they tried. But when there's chaos all around you, there's only so much you can do. Nine people on a remote Moon base just wouldn't be that much of a priority.

At this point, there's no hope left that we'll be rescued. Ardross and Callahan disappeared yesterday—from the video log, it appears they just walked out of the base, hand in hand, and vanished into the distance. Galina has been sick for a week now, and there's not much I can do for her. Dolan barricaded himself in his quarters three days ago, and won't answer hails. I don't know if he's alive or dead.

Doesn't matter, honestly, because soon we'll all be dead. I've done what I can. For myself, I can't face slow starvation. When I'm done writing this, I'm going to depressurize this wing of the base. I've told the ones surviving I'm going to do it—it's up to them if they want to head to the east wing or put on space suits, and prolong the agony. Me, I need to keep breathing until I'm sure the air is gone, then I'm going to open my visor and go quickly. It's better than the alternative.

I always knew how dangerous my job was, and it didn't bother me. It never occurred to me, though, that it would end like this. I suppose someone will eventually find us. Maybe when all this Lackland bullshit has settled down on Earth, it'll occur to them to come looking. What'll it take? Six months? A year? Who knows? Won't make any difference to us. It seems a pity, when we started this mission with so much enthusiasm, but the universe doesn't seem to care much about our human hopes and dreams, does it?

So I'll leave this record here as well. At least then someone will know why, and how, we died. And perhaps, our sacrifice will not have been for nothing.

Ming-Yue Lee
October 16, 2035

· · ·

"A year?" Kallman whispered. "How about nearly fifteen hundred years?"

He gently closed the journal, and turned away from the body in the bunk.

In a few hours, they'd assembled what they wanted to take, and taken photographs of the entire base, including the pitiful remnants of its crew. None of the survey team were eager to prolong the exploration. They made a neatly-stacked pile of written records, a box full of what seemed to be portable data storage devices, and a few other oddments near the door to the outside that was nearest their spaceship. But all of them showed obvious reluctance to disturb the belongings of the people who had died at Tycho Base so long ago.

It was too much like tomb raiding.

"Anything else?" Saxena said, her voice subdued.

"No." Kallman picked up what he could carry of the relics. "Let's go. We've seen enough. All I want to do is get back to Schickard, and then hopefully, never set foot in this place again."

seventeen

. . .

"Commanders Banfield and Darrica, do I have you?"

Arys Quentra and Tevin Kilmaris hovered over the telescreen in the darkened room in the Academy, with its jury-rigged wiring connecting it into the main power grid and server of the Control Center. Quentra figured it was only a matter of time before their patched-in link was discovered and security came in to put a stop to it. It was doubtful the locked door would stop them for long.

The voices of Jenia Banfield, commander of Tranquility Base, and Amlin Darrica, commander of Schickard Base, came in, faintly but clearly.

"I hear you loud and clear, Quentra."

"This is Darrica. Right with you as well."

"Look, we don't have much time. Do you have any idea why we're contacting you?"

"I'm guessing it has something to do with the radio silence from the Control Center," Banfield said. "Dorn said he suspected something bad happened the day of the launch, but none of us have had any information about what it was."

"First," Kilmaris said, "how are Dorn and his crew?"

"All well," Darrica said. "He and three others left

yesterday on a scheduled investigation of Tycho Base. We're expecting them back in a few hours. But we've been in contact with them, and everything is fine."

"What happened?" Banfield said.

Kilmaris took a deep breath. "Short version—a terrorist attack. The Zealots, of course. Detonated a bomb and killed fifteen bystanders. Some of them belonged to the families of the crew. Others were injured, but all of the injured have been released from the hospital and are recovering." He held up a piece of paper in front of the camera. "Here's a list of the dead and injured. Screen shot it so you can talk to the crew."

After a moment, both commanders said, "Got it."

He set the sheet down. "We are going to use what influence we have here—which may not be much—to get Control to set up a link so the crew can talk to their families. But the first thing that needed to happen was letting everyone know what occurred. I can't imagine why the Board is doubling down on this secrecy. It's idiotic. The longer they wait, the worse it will be when it finally comes out, they have to know that."

"At this point, it's got to be simple stubbornness." Banfield's voice betrayed annoyance. "Denian Stiles cannot tolerate being given an order, or even worse, thwarted. I've known him for twenty-five years, and he's always been that way. If you tell Stiles he has to do something, you can almost guarantee he'll do the opposite, and continue doing it as hard as he can for as long as he can, whether or not it makes sense."

"Well, this couldn't be allowed to go on," Quentra said. "Let everyone up there know. And next time you talk to Control, tell *them* you know as well. We'll see how they react when they find out the matter has been taken out of the Board's hands."

As if in response to her statement, the door handle jiggled, followed by the impact of a fist on the door.

"Open the door. This is Security."

"Told you." Quentra gave them a grim smile. "Thanks. We'll be in contact when we can. Quentra and Kilmaris out."

She switched off the telescreen, calmly walked to the door, and unlocked it.

Three security guards burst through the door with unnecessary force, weapons drawn. They were followed by Denian Stiles, red-faced with fury.

"I *expressly* forbade either of you from contacting Tranquility!" he choked out.

"And I *expressly* told you to take that order and shove it up your ass," Quentra replied.

Kilmaris snorted laughter.

Stiles gave a short, sharp gesture with one hand. "Arrest them."

Two guards strode over to where they stood while the third kept his gun trained on them.

"Guns and handcuffs? Is that necessary?" Kilmaris said.

"Cuff them," Stiles barked, and the guards complied.

"No harm if it amuses you," Quentra said, as her arms were pulled backward and the cuffs snapped across her wrists.

Moments later, they were marched out of the little room. Behind them, they could hear the crashes and bangs of one of the guards noisily dismantling their makeshift telescreen.

The arrest of not just one, but two, of the senior members of the Academy flight staff was unprecedented. As they hadn't broken any laws of either Cascadia or Klen, there was no way to get the police involved and haul them to jail, which was clearly what Stiles wanted to do.

The difficulty was, the Academy wasn't equipped to act as a detention facility. In the end, they were escorted to an unoccupied office and locked in together.

At least the guards removed the handcuffs before leaving them.

There was a telescreen hanging on the wall in the corner, and after a moment, Kilmaris turned it on. It resolved on a news channel, where a serious-looking reporter sat in a studio, interviewing a nicely-dressed middle-aged woman with gray hair in a short, fashionable cut, black plastic-framed glasses, and a grim expression.

The caption at the bottom read, *Breaking News: Darsetian Dignitary's Wife In Devastating Revelations About Space Academy Board*.

"Well, well. Look at this," he said, amusement in his voice. "Looks like we're not the only ones *expressly* breaking Stiles's commands."

"… not only has been engaging in keeping secret the Zealots' attack on the day of the launch, but has explicitly lied both to crew and family members." The woman's patrician face showed barely-contained outrage.

"Including yourself?" the reporter asked.

"Yes. Board Director Denian Stiles told me that the entire crew had been briefed, in exactly those words. That was, in fact, a lie, and he knew it was when he said it. What the Board is doing is unconscionable…"

Quentra looked over at Kilmaris, who still stood near the telescreen, his lips curled in a faint smile.

"Is she the woman you talked to yesterday morning?"

He nodded. "I knew she'd be a good ally the moment I talked to her. Her son is Dorn's partner, you knew that?"

"Yes, I remember."

"Struck me right away as a Mama Bear type. Secondary school teacher, I guess it comes with the job. Placid enough, sails through life without raising her voice or losing her temper—but you hurt one of her cubs, and you are done."

"Good."

"… calling for an immediate investigation…" the reporter was saying.

This was followed up by several minutes of various

commentators speculating on what the official response to the revelations would be.

"What do you think they're going to do with us?" Quentra said, in a conversational tone.

"You worried?"

"No," she said, in a scoffing voice. "I'm not afraid of them. If they want to fire us, let them. My guess is when the dust settles, we'll have our jobs and Stiles won't."

"You're probably right about that."

"Honestly, though, I'm curious about how they're planning to manage it now they've taken us into custody. I don't expect anything like this has ever happened before."

"I doubt they have a plan. Right now, it's just damage control, and best of luck to them, because it's too late for that. I'm guessing that everyone who needs to know, now knows. Since the story broke on the news, Stiles will be eager for it all to blow over as fast as possible. It gets out we're in custody, it'll be yet another angle for reporters to investigate. My suspicion is we'll be released by this time tomorrow."

Kilmaris's estimate turned out to be significantly off. Less than four hours later, a blank-faced security guard unlocked the door, said, "You're free to go" in completely deadpan tones, and marched away with no further explanation. Kilmaris looked at Quentra, grinned and shrugged, and they went to their offices to gather their belongings before taking the FastRail back to their homes in Tecoa.

Quentra's judgment that Stiles and the Board were not going to get off so easy, however, turned out to be accurate. Within a day, the regents who had run the government since King Lennis's death fired the entire Academy Board and demanded an inquiry into the whole affair. Stiles himself was the main target. He was given a police escort when he left the Academy for the last time, to assure he wouldn't be on the receiving end of violence from the protestors who showed up only an hour after the story broke and demanded his immediate dismissal. Kallman Dorn and his crew were considered national heroes, especially after the tragedy of what happened at the launch, and the revelation that Stiles had authorized lying to them was close to unforgivable.

By that evening, as Arys Quentra sat in the living room of her comfortable little apartment in Tecoa watching the news, she heard that the nonexistent "technical glitch" had been fixed, and a stable video link established both to Tranquility and to Schickard. The families of all the members of the survey crew, as well as the permanent crews at both bases, were offered free FastRail transport to the Academy the next morning, as some measure of compensation for what they'd been through.

It was meager enough comfort for those who had lost loved ones, of course, and now had the agony of realizing they hadn't known about it for nearly two weeks. It would be a long time before the Academy recovered from that blow to its reputation.

But—as she'd told Tevin Kilmaris—they'd brought it on themselves.

She slept better that night than she had since the day of the launch.

eighteen

. . .

Tecoan Police Chief Davit Kelway gazed across the table at a stolid, blocky-faced man, dressed in prison blues, his ankles cuffed to the chair.

"Bennit Oswill," he said, in a level voice. "You understand what you have been charged with?"

"Perfectly."

"And that if you are found guilty, it is nearly certain that you will face the death penalty?"

"If you're trying to frighten me," Oswill said, his lip wrinkling in a faint sneer, "it won't work. I welcome the death penalty. I only wish you still had public executions, and that I could put my head on the block in the middle of the central square of Tecoa, so that others could see what tyranny does. What happens when righteousness comes up against the wickedness of the secular world."

A combination of disgust and incomprehension welled up in Kelway. He'd felt the same talking to Dain Sarkos, he recalled. There was no repentance in these people because they truly believed they had nothing to atone for.

"You have admitted to murdering both King Lennis and

the Patriarch, Thurial Keene. Do you affirm that confession now?"

"I do. I will also say that given the necessity and the chance, I would do it again. I can only give thanks that it was by my hand the last King of Cascadia and the last Patriarch of Klen both met their fates. They had betrayed the holy legacies of their offices and deserved death. A hundred times, they deserved death."

"You realize that the entire Zealot movement has been torn apart. The ones who aren't dead are in jail. Your leader blew himself to pieces in order to harm as many innocent people he could, and turned a time that should have been a celebration of our venturing toward the stars into a scene of carnage."

"Mir Sarkos is with the gods now."

"And what of the rest of your people? Your precious movement? You've accomplished nothing. It's in fragments. The governments of Cascadia and Klen will rebuild, whether with a new king and a new Patriarch or some other leadership I do not know, but rebuild they certainly shall. The families of the people Sarkos killed will mourn their dead and then pick up their lives and carry on. You've done nothing. For all the bloodshed and pain and anger you and your people have caused, you have nothing to show for it."

Oswill's sneer turned into a bitter laugh. "That's what you think? You think the Zealots are gone? You're more of a fool than I thought. We will never be defeated, not as long as the gods listen to our cries at night, not as long the forces that create us are still at work."

"Tell that to your dead leader, and his followers now languishing in jail cells."

"You haven't won," Oswill snapped. "All you've done is cut off one limb, but you haven't killed the beast."

"You're so sure of yourself?"

The man gazed at Kelway for a long time before speaking.

"Look at you. You abandoned the path of righteousness so long ago you don't even recall it. How many of the people of Tecoa, pursuing their secular lives and their secular wickedness, now remember that we once spoke the sacred language? My great-grandmother did. She came from a people called the Samada. They lived in the hills and forests north of here, but you know what the people of Tecoa did? Hunted them for sport. She was one of the last of her people, and was forced into a marriage with a Tecoan when she was only fifteen. Forbidden from speaking her own native tongue, can you believe it? Their sacred language, passed down from the very beginning, and she was told never to utter a word of it." His face twisted with anger. "My grandmother, her daughter, knew a few words. My mother, nothing at all. Now it's taught in schools as a curiosity, studied like a broken piece of pottery from the Before Times. A worthless, meaningless relic. That's how your secular leaders treat their precious, holy past."

Some desperation to understand drove Kelway to keep talking to him, to try to get him to see reason—or at least to reflect upon how warped his own reasoning was.

"None of us today can change what happened to your great-grandmother. None of the ones who did those things to her are still alive. How can you blame us, take vengeance on us, for what was done by different people a hundred years ago?"

"Because you're repeating the same evils. You've never repented, never tried to find your way back to the path our forefathers and foremothers walked. The people who could have made a difference, the king and the Patriarch, were worse than figureheads. Worse because they knew the history. The Patriarch most of all. He was the heir to a great and terrible power, one wielded by the oracles ever since the time of the Flood. Of all people, he should have understood. Centuries ago, the oracles had everything committed to memory, did you know that?"

"So they say."

"So it was." His voice took on declamatory tones, and once again Kelway was reminded of Sarkos. Oswill had learned the style well. "They valued what they knew, the history and the language and the traditions. They respected the gods, and because of it the gods bestowed great gifts upon them. Kallian Dorn defeated a great Samada chieftain single-handedly, because the gods chose to smile upon him."

"He's also the one who brought back the written word from Tecoa."

"He is only one in a long list of people who passed test after test, but ultimately failed. He could have fulfilled his destiny. After defeating the chieftain, he could have returned to his home victorious and taken his place as one of the greatest oracles who ever lived. Now, we revere him—but we never forget that he was the one who began our people's slide toward depravity by digging up the errors of the past. By revering that evil knowledge instead of holding it up as an example to strike fear into the hearts of the devout. He is a memorial to the truth that even the virtuous can stumble."

"What if that's what you've done?"

Oswill frowned. "How do you mean?"

"What if your own path has led you from virtue? Kallian Dorn did what he did because he thought it was the right thing to do. Just as Sarkos did. Just as you have done."

"We are certain of our truth."

"So was he."

"You are speaking with the voice of evil. Trying to lure me into apostasy."

"No!" Kelway felt a sudden surge of hope, as if some chink had opened in Oswill's armor, letting in the faintest sliver of light. "Don't you see? You're sure you're right—but so are most people. So are the ones you call wicked. If all are certain of their truth, and all those truths are different, how do you decide? Instead of doing what you could to help people understand, you and Sarkos set about destroying all the ones who don't think like you do. All because it never crossed your mind that you could be wrong."

But as quickly as it had opened, the gap slammed shut. Oswill's face turned to stone again. "I have no reason to listen to someone whose sole purpose is to tear me away from the will of the gods."

"Damn it, I'm trying to save your life! If you show some repentance, some understanding of what you've done…"

"I told you. I understand perfectly what I've done, and am entirely willing to face death because of it." His eyes narrowed into a fixed glare. "I have nothing more to say to you."

Kelway stared at him for a few seconds more, and then, with a frustrated snort, stood and strode to the door, unlocking it and then relocking it behind him. He barked a command to the guard, "Take him back to his cell."

Bennit Oswill's confession would obviate the need for a trial. He would face the judge the following day, without a doubt still rock-like in his defiant stoicism. Sentencing would take twenty minutes. No one would be surprised when he was given the death penalty. Afterward, he would be transferred to the grim confines of the prison in the northwest part of Tecoa.

Then there was only the three-week wait for his appointment with the executioner.

In Cascadia, executions were extremely infrequent—reserved for the worst crimes—but when death sentences were handed down they were carried out with brutal efficiency. The only reason for the three-week gap between the sentence and the execution was to give time for a lawyer to file a single appeal if there were any basis for one.

Certainly there was none in this case.

At least they were carried out in the marginally more humane privacy of the prison complex. A hundred years ago, public beheadings took place in the central square of Tecoa. They'd been a great favorite of the early kings, and the people of Tecoa considered them very close to popular entertainment. Judicial reforms a century ago had gotten rid of the spectacle, moved the act itself to the confines of the prison, and substituted the guillotine for the axe and block.

The argument was that it took far less skill on the part of the executioner, but the truth was, the main objective had been getting the whole thing out of the public eye. The government was becoming a little embarrassed by the crowds that showed up to watch some unfortunate lose his head.

Kelway had only witnessed one execution—that of a man who had killed a child. Once he became Chief of Police, he felt if he was going to hold the office, he had better understand that side of it. It was fast—between walking the man out from his cell, and his headless body lying on the plank, took less than a minute.

But the horror of it took weeks to fade.

As he walked back to his office, that sick memory rose to his mind again. How could Bennit Oswill welcome that fate? He seemed to look upon it as some kind of apotheosis. Was he really that sure of himself, that he thought after he was dead, the gods would welcome him with joyous accolades? That he'd join his leader Sarkos, whose bomb had detonated with such deadly efficiency that there was little identifiable of him left afterward?

Oswill's words kept coming back to him, as he packed up his belongings to head to the FastRail station and home.

We will never be defeated, not as long as the gods listen to our cries at night, not as long the forces that create us are still at work… You haven't won. All you've done is cut off one limb, but you haven't killed the beast.

Was Oswill right? Were they doomed to keep fighting the same battles over and over? He'd heard about the discovery the young archaeologist had made, the writings of the Blessed

Julia, and what he remembered of her words haunted him. It sounded as if in her time, the Zealots of her day had been the ones who had engineered the Fall, in an act that had so angered the gods they'd seen fit to destroy all of the ancient city, and most of the people in it.

Were the people of Cascadia now headed for the same fate?

nineteen

. . .

Kallman stood in the shower, letting the hot water run over his skin, hoping the pleasant feeling would wash away some of the sick anger he felt.

Since the return of the crew from Tycho Base the previous day, he'd been unable to shake the memory of the choking horror he'd experienced on seeing the dead bodies of the Tycho crew. It had honestly not occurred to him that he'd find the crew had been stranded and left to die there. He knew about the chaos of the Lackland Wars—every schoolchild learned about it in history classes—and he knew there were innocent victims of the collapse that followed. But the thought of those nine people, left up there without supplies, facing death with no way to escape—that was ghastly beyond anything he'd imagined. The skeletal face of Commander Lee, who had opened her own visor and let the Moon's vacuum do its evil work, had troubled his dreams.

And now, even Commander Darrica's news that finally they'd be able to talk to their families back on Earth brought no real comfort. He told them what had happened at the launch and shared the list of dead and injured. More than one crew member wept as the names were read. On the list of casualties was Galmon Kastella, Marig's father. Kallman had held his breath as Darrica continued to read, only letting it out when he got to the end of the fifteen names of the ones killed.

But the announcement that Marig had been injured was like a punch in the gut, even so.

The worst was not knowing the nature or severity of the injuries. All Darrica knew was that all the injured had been released from the hospital and were recovering, but that gave Kallman nothing to allay his fear.

Now, in less than an hour, he'd see Marig face-to-face for the first time since the day of the launch, and instead of being excited, all he felt was sick inside.

He turned off the shower, grabbed his towel from a hook on the wall, and dried himself. Dressed, gave a cursory look at himself in the mirror. There were dark smudges beneath his eyes. Vestiges of stress, not enough sleep, and the horrible scene of abandonment and death at Tycho. He'd have to figure out a way to seem cheerful despite how he felt. Not give Marig one more upset to deal with.

Marig, after all, was the one dealing with injuries, with the loss of his father, with the shock of experiencing the worst terrorist attack in living memory. Kallman's own difficulties could wait.

The crew were assembled in a large meeting area in the center of the base, but the telescreen link had been set up in a small adjoining room, to give them privacy. Kallman noticed that several of them had obviously been crying. Many of these were not going to be happy conversations, first talks between family members brought together by pain, injury, and death.

Not the delighted video conversations home he imagined he'd be having, cheering Marig up with excited tales of his discoveries while exploring the Moon.

Kallman was the third to be called back. He went into the

little room, closing the door behind him, and sat down in front of the telescreen. Touched the button to activate the link.

His first glimpse of Marig made his heart sink into his belly.

Gods above, his face. Had he… lost an eye?

He recovered as quickly as he could, attempted a smile, mostly succeeded.

"Marig. My love. My one and only love. I miss you so much."

Marig nodded, his mouth quivering, tears streaking his left cheek, but for a moment, he couldn't speak. Finally he said, his voice hitching, "I told myself I wouldn't fall apart."

"It's all right. How are you doing? I heard you were hurt."

Another jerky nod. "Kall… my eye." He lifted his patch to show the sunken, scarred pit beneath it. "A piece of shrapnel destroyed my eye. I…" He leaned forward, his strong frame shaking with sobs.

Kallman swallowed hard. He knew he had to choose his next words carefully.

"I know you must be hurt and scared. Just know… know I love you. Just as much now as ever. More, actually, more every day. I wish I could hold you, let you cry out all that pain, then kiss you until you believe me that you'll be okay. I only wish…" He took a deep breath, trying to hold back his own tears, boiling right beneath the surface. "I wish I could have protected you. Stopped this from happening. I'm supposed to be the one who keeps you from harm, holds you close, shelters you. You were there at the launch because of me."

"It wasn't your fault. Please don't blame yourself." Marig shook his head. "I talked to this woman. Her name is Reysa. She's the Director of Antiquities at the Museum. The one who found that manuscript, you remember? The one from Julia Lowell."

"I remember. We talked about it."

"Yes. She felt like it was her fault, too, because the manuscript was part of what spurred the Zealots to strike. She went to see all the people who'd been hurt and the ones who'd lost family members in the attack. Trying to understand why, trying to figure out if there was a reason for it all."

"She couldn't have known what was going to happen."

"Yes. And neither could you." He paused, and went on in a stronger voice. "Kall. My love. I can imagine how hard this is. You've always taken care of me. But you were able to go to the Moon—fulfill a lifelong dream—because you trusted that I could take care of myself while you were gone. I can. Yes, I've been hurt. Yes, it's hard. But I'm recovering. Even if I'll never have my right eye back, I can manage. And I'll be waiting for you when you return in five months." He managed a smile, although his mouth quivered. "Don't expect me to let you out of my arms for a long while afterward, though."

Kallman smiled. "I'm counting on it."

"Tell me about the Moon."

The smile vanished instantly, and Marig tipped his head to the side and frowned.

"What's wrong? What happened?"

He didn't answer for a moment. Gathering his thoughts was like trying to piece together a puzzle where he hadn't yet seen the pattern.

"It's... overwhelming. Beautiful. Even though I'd seen photos and videos of the surface, nothing could have prepared me for actually being here. A stark, lovely, deadly place. I'm glad I'm here but... once I'm back on Earth, I don't think I'll want to come back here again. Ever."

"Really? Isn't this the career you've wanted since you were little?"

"Yes. But somehow, now that I'm here... it's struck me over and over. This is not a place humans should be. We're made for standing with our feet on the warm, green, humid

Earth—looking up at the stars and dreaming, but never getting there."

"I remember your telling me about that quote you learned from your grandmother. Asking, who can break the chains of Orion, and lead the garland of crowns?"

"You remember that?"

"Of course. You told me one night, not long after we decided to be partners. We were lying in bed, and you had your arms around me. We'd just made love, and were in that drowsy cuddle that's one of the best feelings ever. You were talking about your dreams and hopes for the future, what was in your heart. I had one hand on your chest, and I could feel it beating." He smiled. "And you told me that line. It's haunting. I've never forgotten it. But I remember thinking at the time that the answer was *no one*."

"I never thought to interpret it that way. I took it as a challenge, not a warning."

"It's the difference in our nature, I think. You're the adventurer. I'm the one who keeps things safe at home to welcome you back from your adventures."

"I think one thing I've discovered here on the Moon is that maybe I'm not the adventurer I thought I was. It's not that I'm afraid of dying, not really. It's more that being here, seeing what I've seen, has made me value what I have back on Earth even more."

"There's no reason you'll have to leave again, if you don't want to. You could become a flight instructor. After leading a mission to the Moon, the Academy would be foolish to turn you down."

"They've done nothing but foolishness since we left, sounds like."

"I can't argue with that. I don't know if you heard, but the regents fired the entire Board yesterday. Stiles and his cronies are out of a job. I'm proud to say my own mother had a hand in that."

"Tell Nyssa I love her more than ever."

Marig laughed. "I will." He took another deep breath. "I probably should let you go, and give the other families chance to use the telescreen. What are you doing today?"

Kallman brightened. "Taking out the new shuttle. I'll be crossing onto the far-Earth side for the first time."

"Fly well and have fun."

"I will."

"Take care, my love. My one and only love. Don't worry about me. I'll be all right, especially now that I've seen your face and heard your voice. And I'll be counting every day until your return." He kissed his fingertips and touched the telescreen.

Kallman did the same thing.

"Goodbye, my sweetheart."

The screen went dark.

Kallman stood up, once again pushing back tears. He tugged the bottom of his shirt to straighten it and exited the little room.

Why hadn't he told Marig about the awful discoveries at Tycho? Part of it was not wanting to worry him further, of course. The thought of those poor people facing the inevitability of their own deaths on the airless, unforgiving surface of the Moon was horrible to contemplate, and even imagining the same could happen to Kallman would be bound to add to Marig's anxiety.

But he knew that wasn't all of it. What he'd found the previous day had resulted in something he didn't even want to admit to himself—a sudden shift from heart-pounding thrill at being here to a dark, ominous feeling that perhaps he never should have come.

Maybe no one should.

To his surprise, he also felt deeply angry. Anger was not a common experience for him—he'd always had a cheerful, ebullient personality, and any irritations and upsets seldom lasted long. He was angry at the stupid decision of the Board to delay telling the families of the astronauts what had happened, but the real fire of his fury was directed at the Zealots. The ones of Commander Lee's day who had resulted in her and her crew being stranded at Tycho, and the current ones who had perpetrated the terrorist attack at the launch. The circumstances were different, but their mentality—and the outcome—were exactly the same.

Death. Destruction. Heartbreak.

They'd killed the king and the Patriarch, and wounded or killed a bunch of innocent bystanders—why? There didn't seem to be any reasonable answer to that. They were angry, too, angry at anyone who didn't believe what they did. What Kallman felt right now as a transitory state was a way of life for them. Confronted with the fact that the police finally, belatedly, were taking action against them, they chose to destroy rather than reconcile, strike out at a bunch of strangers who were simply in the wrong place at the wrong time, most of whom probably couldn't have cared less about the arcane apocalyptic prophecies the Zealots were so fond of preaching.

What could possibly be attractive about a philosophy that valued bigotry and destruction over love and kindness?

And now Marig had lost an eye, and gained scars that would never go away. His father had died. All for nothing. So much hurt, so much harm, so many tears, and in the end the Zealots themselves hadn't accomplished a damn thing.

Pointless. Stupid and pointless. He knew the ancients had believed in hell—a place the truly evil were sent after they died, to be tortured forever. He'd always found it a repellent myth.

Now, he wished it were true, for the sole reason that Dain Sarkos deserved exactly that.

He tried to shake off his black mood as he strode down the hallway toward the hangar where the sleek survey pod had been transferred after their landing at Schickard. He was scheduled to take it out on its maiden voyage that morning, cross onto the far-Earth side, and do several long mapping transects.

He tried to recoup his previous feelings of excitement, but the sick anger he felt would not let go so easily.

Into the hangar control room. He greeted the two technicians—one of them the same man who had overseen his briefing before he'd departed for Tycho—and received cheerful hellos in response. He looked out of the window into the hangar at the shiny metallic teardrop that sat, delicately balanced on its tripod of legs, waiting for him.

What a difference in his attitude forty-eight hours had wrought.

The technician obviously interpreted his serious expression as awe. "She's beautiful, isn't she, Commander?" He gave Kallman a broad grin. "I expect she'll go a little faster than the old plodder you took out to Tycho. Have fun, and come back safely."

Kallman attempted to match his smile. "I will."

Last check of his space suit. Donning his helmet, locking down the seals, testing the airflow rate, final run-through of his mental checklist for gauges and vital signs monitoring.

Everything looked good.

He strode into the hangar, sealing the door behind him. Pulled the hatch of the shuttle, climbed the two steps into the pilot's seat, secured the entrance, fastened his harness over his chest. Behind him was a space for gear, emergency equipment, and any samples he might bring back—although this first trip was a mapping run only and he was not planning to land.

A quick run-through of the preflight list showed everything working fine. It should—the craft was brand-new. Except for test flights on Earth before it was brought to the launch site and loaded onto the transport, this would be its first voyage.

"Everything looks fine here, tech."

The technician's voice came back through his helmet speakers. "You're looking good, Commander." He chuckled. "Don't tell your boyfriend I said that."

Kallman laughed, the first honest laugh he'd had in a while. "Now we'll have the whole base talking about us. Depressurize and pull the hangar door."

"Depressurizing."

He switched on the engines, felt the gentle thrumming of the power-up vibrating the entire ship. With a touch, he set the shuttle hovering a few centimeters over the floor of the hangar, then pivoted it to face the now-open hangar door, a rectangle of bright sunlight glinting on the stark surface of Schickard Crater.

He nudged the craft forward.

"You're clear of the hangar, Commander. Have a nice flight." The tech made a kissing noise into the mic.

"Thanks. You flirt. Now you'll have to buy me a drink when I get back."

"It's a deal."

Moments later, he was skimming silently across the crater surface, then up over the rim of the crater wall, heading due west toward the near-Earth terminus and the unknown.

Behind him, the silvery blue-green orb of the Earth, half sunlit and half in darkness, slipped closer and closer to the horizon. He couldn't help one glance through the rear viewscreen as the last bit of it vanished—and he lost sight, for the first time, of the world where he'd been born, where he'd spent his entire life, where his lover and his family were waiting for him.

It was hard to explain why that felt so significant. He was only a few kilometers distant from the terminus. Turn around, and in a few minutes there the Earth would be again, hanging in space like a jewel, as solid and reassuring as always. But he felt cut loose, adrift in the vastness of space. Absolutely and utterly alone.

"Get a hold of yourself," he said aloud. Too much distance down this dark mental path, and he'd end up panicking, returning to Schickard—and having to explain to the base commander, and then the Academy, why he'd been unable to do what he'd spent five years training for.

He deliberately slowed his breathing, watched on his wrist monitor as his pulse followed suit. Calmed his mind.

All shall be well.

He'd said it to Marig before he left, and he had to believe it now. *All shall be well.*

He engaged the mapping telemetry program, designed to take photographs and topographic contours automatically as his ship zoomed past. The total flight time was supposed to be eight hours. He still had another three before he'd need to make a sweeping right-hand turn and head back to base.

He nudged the speed up. The craft had a maximum recommended velocity of four hundred kilometers an hour, but the telemetry worked best if he kept it well below that. He bumped up the speed—two-hundred-eighty, two-hundred-ninety…

He didn't hear the pop of the relay self-destructing, but he felt in his hands as the vibration came through the console. It happened just as he reached three hundred kilometers an hour —a sudden jerk to the whole craft. Underneath the console, something spat out sparks, then a quick puff of black smoke.

"Oh, fuck no…"

He leaned over to peer under the console, but that was when he lost navigational control.

The shuttle lurched forward, angling upward, then surging downward toward the lunar surface. Somehow he pulled it up just before impact, but there didn't seem to be any logical connection between what his hands were doing to the controls and how the ship was reacting.

What the hell had happened? This ship was brand-new, and had been fault tested over and over. None of the other shuttles had ever had a problem. They'd always been completely reliable.

As he desperately attempted to regain control, he had a sudden, blinding flash of clarity.

The Zealots. The Zealots had done this.

Two of them had been caught in the launch area the night before the transport took off. The security had caught them before they damaged anything—so they believed. But what if one of them had put in a device designed to blow a navigational relay as soon as the shuttle was up to speed? Something like that would be small, likely indistinguishable from the ship's own electronics. Easily missed by people who didn't know the wiring systems inside and out.

The more he thought about it, the surer he was that it was true.

The Zealots had nearly killed Marig, and now, they were going to succeed in killing him.

The shuttle looped wildly upward and downward. He had to keep his head, stop the panic from swallowing him up. Was there anywhere to land?

He dismissed that thought immediately. What fucking difference would it make? Even if he did somehow bring the ship down without crashing, there was no way anyone would find him in time.

The skeletal faces of the Tycho crew came to mind.

That would be him, soon.

Maybe someone would find him eventually. Would it take fifteen hundred years?

Marig… oh, Marig…

Now the shuttle was soaring up, up, corkscrewing,

twisting faster and faster. The stars overhead spun into a glittering whirlpool, a circle like a diadem of jewels.

The garland of crowns! I'm seeing the garland of crowns!

Blackness closed over his mind, and he knew nothing more.

part three
the ordinances of heaven

twenty

· · ·

Quine performed his duties in the same order, without variation, until the day of the crash.

When the Sun came up, its harsh white glare angling over the edge of the canyon wall and creating sharp-edged shadows against the side of the homestead, the first thing he did was to walk outside with a long-handled mop and carefully clean the dust from each of the solar panels. There was never any dust visible, but that didn't matter.

Duty was duty.

After the solar panels were cleaned, he returned to the homestead, checked the energy levels in the batteries, and powered up the computers. During the night, he always turned everything off but the environmental controls so as not to waste power. There had never been a time that the power level had fallen past the red mark on the meter, and only once had it crossed into the yellow—the time he had uploaded twelve books before night fell instead of the usual ten. When morning came, and he saw the needle resting in the yellow zone, the panic that ensued made him swear to himself he would never do anything that risky again.

Once the computers were powered up, Quine put on some

music. Today, it was Bach's *Mass in B Minor*. It always seemed to him a matter of great import, which music he chose to play first, although he could not have explained why.

By this time, the Sun had risen sufficiently to illuminate the entire area, warming the homestead walls. He could predict, almost to the minute, when the air cooling system would kick on, recirculating cold ammonia gas through the piping in the walls, keeping the interior at a constant twenty-three degrees Celsius throughout the long, hot day. At this point, Quine went to the main computer and ran through a complete system diagnostic to make certain that everything was operating correctly.

Everything always was.

Then there was one last trip outside before it got too hot, a slow walk around the perimeter of the crater where the homestead sat to see if anything had happened during the night that needed to be dealt with. Only once had there been something—a large stone had come loose from the canyon wall and gone bounding down the slope, narrowly missing the small hut that housed the water extractor. That day, Quine had stared for some time at the dark, rough chunk of rock, sitting there as if newly sprung from the ground. After some consideration, he had finally decided that there was nothing he could do about it, and honestly, nothing that needed to be done. So the rock was still there, had become one further thing that he checked every day to see if it remained unchanged.

On this day, there was nothing even so far amiss as a fallen chunk of rock. Quine followed the line of his own foot-prints in the dust, humming along as "Quoniam Tu Solus Sanctus" played through the comlink.

That was when he saw the spacecraft.

It started as a glow in the east, where the horizon was a sharp, clean line between black sky and bright gray, jagged mountains. The ship was small. Not a freighter, that was certain immediately. Perhaps a shuttle, or even an unmanned survey craft. As it approached, Quine realized two things about it. First, it was not made using any design he recognized.

Second, it was in serious trouble.

The craft had its spotlights on, as if the pilot was looking for a place to land, but a landing site was the least of the problems the crew faced. There was clearly something wrong with their guidance system. The spaceship was spinning its way through the sky, rising until it became a glowing speck amongst the stars, and then falling toward the ground like a meteor, only pulling up from a ruinous crash at the last moment. Quine stood perfectly still, watching, feeling the Sun's heat on his back as the ship approached, and wondering how it would end.

They wouldn't be able to keep going that way much longer, however it went. They were clearly out of control. The only question was where they would finally crash.

The ship was closer now. It was sleek and silver, shaped like an elongated teardrop. It had three headlights, all glowing blue, and Quine had a queer thought that seemed to come from nowhere—*The pilot has the headlights on because he wants to see Death's face clearly when they meet.*

The ship twisted, now flying upside down, its curved window underneath it. Lower. Lower still. It barely cleared the ridge to the west of the homestead, and now was skimming along the northern wall of the crater. It might make it. Only to crash elsewhere, of course. But it might clear the crater wall. Perhaps...

Quine's head swiveled smoothly to follow the trajectory of the craft. The chorus on the comlink burst into "Cum sancto spiritu, cum sancto spiritu, in gloria Dei Patris...!" And the spaceship struck a glancing blow on a spire of rock on the north wall, tumbled crazily for a moment, skidded along the cliff face, and finally slammed into an angled projection of stone that protruded from the crater wall where it began to curve toward the east.

Quine didn't hear the impact, but he felt the vibrations through his feet. He watched as the ship, its elegant shape now mangled and twisted, tumbled down the slope, and finally came to rest on its side on an angled slab of dark lava rock perhaps two kilometers away.

"My goodness," he said to no one.

He turned, walked toward a low outbuilding that stood to the south of the array of solar panels, and pressed a button to open the metal hatch. Inside was a blocky, awkward-looking equipment carrier, resting on four broad wheels. Quine had it on auto-charge—as soon as the Sun came up, the computer should have begun to feed power into the battery—but he hadn't needed to use it in ages, and it was anyone's guess as to whether it still worked. It was one thing that long ago he had decided to stop checking.

But here, things didn't decay, didn't corrode, didn't rust. He opened the door, and spoke the words "Power up carrier," through the comlink. The dashboard lit up immediately, and the engine vibrated beneath his hand. He climbed in, pulled the door shut behind him, and maneuvered the carrier out of the shed and toward the crash site.

He was already halfway to the wreck before he asked himself why he was bothering.

Whoever was in that ship was certainly dead. The likelihood of surviving such a crash was as close to zero as made no difference. Therefore, there were only two reasons to do what he was doing. First, to see if there was anything salvageable from the wreck. Second, to bury the dead in as respectful a fashion as he could. Although neither one, honestly, made a great deal of sense, considering the circumstances.

He was slowing the carrier down and pulling it alongside the crashed ship when he realized that there could be a third reason—simple curiosity.

Quine opened the door of the carrier and stepped out onto the unyielding surface of the lava rock. The ship rested on its side, the window facing away from him. It was smaller than it had seemed when he saw it flying. Clearly a shuttle of some kind, designed for one or two people at most.

He peered into the craft. The harsh glare angling in through the window showed nothing but a chaotic tangle of shapes, indistinguishable as individual objects. But there was a hatch in the top of the ship, now facing to the side, operated by controls on the outside. A symbol on one—two arrows pointing away from each other—was, he thought, likely to mean *Open*.

Quine pushed the button.

There was a shudder from some motor in the ship's walls, and the hatch opened. Metal grated on metal. The door slid inward and then ran into an obstruction and stopped, leaving a gap just wide enough for him to squeeze inside.

He levered himself upward and dropped through the hatch feet-first.

The interior of the ship was a sparking twist of wires, torn and broken conduits, and pieces of the metal wall the rock had ripped through like a knife through bread. The control panel was shattered and dark, and where the sunlight came through the window, rainbow glints refracted back from bits of broken polyacrylate. No possibility of salvage there. The pilot's station had taken a direct hit, and whatever electronics had been used to power the craft were now valuable only as scrap.

He stepped over a torn console, and pushed aside a fallen chunk of what had once been the door to a storage compartment.

Underneath it was a human-shaped figure, lying on its belly.

Quine knelt and looked for a moment at the smooth gray of the flight suit. It would be a dreadful thing to see the damage, he knew that, but now that he had come here it was what he must do. He slipped his hands beneath the figure's chest and lifted, turning it over. It was a man of perhaps thirty years, handsome, with narrow, aquiline features and black hair. He was bleeding from a long gash on his forehead, and one arm was twisted in a way that arms should not twist. But his sealed helmet and thermal suit seemed to be intact, and there were no other obvious injuries.

And as he crouched inside the wrecked spacecraft, he realized that he could feel the movement of the man's slow breathing. He was, improbably but certainly, still alive.

Quine stared for a moment, frozen. "Mercy me."

It took a moment for him to recover from the surprise. He lifted the man's inert body, and only then realized how difficult it was going to be to get him through the half-open hatch. He set the man back down gently and turned his attention to the shattered remains of the ship. Perhaps there was something that could be used to get the pilot and himself out of the ship without having to drag the injured man by the legs through the narrow hatch opening.

And also, it might be that there were other survivors. It was worth looking for both reasons.

He pushed his way into the rear of the little spaceship without finding any other crew, either dead or alive. The wounded pilot, it seemed, had been flying solo. He did find rolls of survey maps printed on a thin metal foil, and found a device that looked like a pair of binoculars. He raised it to his eyes, and they whirred beneath his fingertips. Through the screen he saw a schematic of the wrecked interior of the ship, mapped out as carefully as if drawn by a draftsman's hand. Clearly, the man had been on some kind of a survey mission. But looking for what?

It took Quine only minutes to locate what he was seeking —a small door labeled *Emergency* that pulled open to reveal canisters of water, packages of freeze-dried food, a fire extinguisher, a hank of rope, and most importantly, a small metal object, a little like a gun, that fit neatly into his hand. He returned to the cockpit, aimed the gun at the hatch, and pulled the trigger.

A blue-white cone of flame shot from the nozzle of the gun, and cut through the metal hatch almost instantly. Quine was so startled that he took his finger off the trigger, and the beam vanished, leaving only a jagged, red-hot line along the hatch.

"My word. More powerful than mine. At least this will be easier than I'd thought."

Two minutes later, and with a gentle shove, the remains of the hatch fell out, slid along the nose of the spaceship, and landed on the ground below, where it rocked gently for a moment before coming to rest. Quine set the gun down, and once again lifted the pilot. He stepped through the hatch, avoiding edges that still glowed a dull red, and walked back to the carrier with his burden.

Within minutes, he was leaving the crash site behind, headed for home.

Quine hadn't been certain what to expect when he removed the pilot's space suit. One arm was clearly broken—that was certain—and there was the nasty-looking cut on the forehead. But other injuries, perhaps serious ones, might not manifest until closer examination. He took the man's suit off carefully, especially when trying to maneuver the broken right arm out of the sleeve. There was no rush, and every reason to work cautiously. He was alive, and now that he was here at the homestead, he might still recover unless he had internal injuries that weren't evident. It was imperative not to move him too quickly, or the wrong way, and make things worse.

Finally, the pilot lay on his back in the main bedroom,

stripped naked, and still unconscious. There were darkening bruises on the man's ribcage and upper leg, and the arm remained to be set. The scalp wound had bled profusely, but seemed to be shallow. Quine took his blood pressure.

Seventy over forty. Shock.

The critical thing was to bring his blood pressure up, but not wake him. He'd be in terrible pain if he regained consciousness. In the First Aid cabinet, there were spray injectors with syntho-opiates, but how old were they? Hard to say if they'd still be effective, but it wasn't like there were a lot of alternatives. Once sedated, he could start an IV for fluids, and get the computer to increase the oxygen saturation of the air. Then, set and immobilize the broken bone. After that, there was nothing to do but wait.

Quine set to work.

He was sitting next to the pilot's bed twelve hours later, watching him quietly, when the man's eyes fluttered open.

He licked his lips, swallowed, and blinked. He turned his head a little to one side, then the other.

"Where am I?" His voice was low, hoarse, strained.

"You're in a homestead in a crater on the far-Earth side."

The man frowned. "Still on the Moon."

Quine nodded.

"My ship… the guidance system shorted out." He winced, closed his eyes. "Sabotaged, I think. I don't remember what happened after that."

"You hit the crater wall. I'm afraid your ship is beyond repair." Quine paused. "You're lucky to be alive, actually."

The man opened his eyes again, tried to move his right arm, and gave a moan of pain.

"Your lower arm was badly broken. Both the radius and the ulna. In fact, your ulna was in three pieces. You also have two fractured ribs, and considerable numbers of scrapes and bruises. You have been sedated for some time, now. You are on pain medications, but there is some room to increase the dosage if your pain becomes too intense."

The man shook his head. "No. I'm okay for now. I'm not ready to go running or anything, but I'm okay." He looked over at Quine. "You're a robot?"

Quine nodded again. "Yes. SCOMA class."

"SCOMA? I'm not familiar with those."

"Self-Contained Occupational and Medical Assistance."

"Oh. Lucky for me, I guess." He moved his left hand, gave another wince when he saw that it was connected to an IV, and cleared his throat. "Do you have a name?"

"My name is Quine."

"Well, I'm glad to meet you, Quine. My name is Kallman Dorn. I thought I was a goner out there. Thanks for saving my life."

"I was happy to do so."

He looked around him, at the framed paintings on the wall, the plants growing in neat ceramic pots, the pieces of sculpture on shelves. "You have music playing? Is that for my benefit?"

"No. I play music during the day, when the solar cells are fully charged. I play it because I enjoy it. But if it bothers you, I can turn it down, or shut it off entirely."

"It's not my style, I have to admit. But don't turn it off on my account. What are we listening to?"

"The *Eleventh Symphony* of Dmitri Shostakovich. First movement."

"Ah." He shrugged. "Never heard of him. But that's okay." He looked closely at Quine, his forehead creasing in a frown. "We had no idea you were out here. There hasn't been any survey work done on the far side of the Moon. How did you get out here without anyone knowing?"

"I have been here alone since Dr. Kimmell died. He

brought me here when the homestead was built. He was quite insistent that no one know he was here, so perhaps it is no surprise you didn't know about the homestead."

He nodded. "I guess. And you've been here alone since he died? When was that?"

"In Earth years or Moon days?"

"Earth years."

"One thousand, three hundred and seventy-six years, five months, and twelve days ago," Quine said.

"You're from the Before Time?" Kallman goggled at him. "And you're still here?"

"Where else would I go?"

He didn't answer for a moment. "Well, you got me back here. You must have some transportation, right?"

"Yes. I have the equipment carrier."

"Then you should have gone to the settlement at Schickard Base. Better than… being alone."

"I did not do so because I did not know it existed. Also, am I deducing correctly that the base is named *Schickard* because it is in the crater of the same name?"

"Yes. There are lunar maps from the Before Time, and we've kept a lot of the old names for features. They have a poetry to them, even if we don't understand all of the meanings."

"Interesting."

"But I don't understand why you haven't tried to get back to civilization somehow. Considering where I was when my guidance system got fried, it's only three hundred kilometers distant from here to the terminus, give or take. Your carrier must have that range, right? It should get you there without difficulty."

"It does have that range. But I could not do that, even had I known the base was there."

"Why not?"

"Because it's on the near-Earth side of the Moon."

"So?"

Quine looked at him intently for a moment, his head tipped a little to one side. "I am forbidden to see earthshine."

Kallman gave him an incredulous frown. "What? Why would you be forbidden to see earthshine?"

"Dr. Kimmell made that rule when we settled here. I do not know why. He never told me. But he said it was of the utmost importance. That, and keeping the solar panels clean, and taking care of the greenhouse, and making certain that the battery charge never gets down into the yellow range on the meter at night."

"And you've been doing this for over a thousand Earth years."

"Yes."

"I'll be damned." Kallman shook his head. "That's a hell of a thing, right there. And I want to hear more of your story, but my brain is still in a fog. Probably all the meds you've been putting into that IV. Considering how long I've already slept, it probably sounds weird, but I'm having a hard time keeping my eyes open."

"You are still being administered a combination of syntho-opiates. If you feel like sleeping, you should take advantage of it."

"Let's talk about this more tomorrow, okay?"

"I would like that."

Dorn yawned, and closed his eyes.

After watching him for a moment, Quine got up, and went to the dial on the wall, turned the lights down, and left the room.

twenty-one

. . .

Marig was of two minds as he packed up his things in the small suitcase he'd brought to his mother's apartment.

He was deeply grateful she'd invited him to stay with her during his convalescence. At first, he'd needed help physically, and for that and the emotional support he was still deeply appreciative. She'd valued their time together as much as he had, and it had helped her through the difficult days after the attack at the launch. Whatever her cool, distant relationship had been with Marig's father, their lives had been irrevocably intertwined, and his death hit her hard.

As she'd said to Marig, the marriage to Galmon Kastella may have been ending, but it wasn't supposed to end that way.

Marig was glad he could provide the support she needed. Mainly, it was simply not to have her there by herself—just to be another presence in the apartment, someone familiar and loved. The disaster of the attack had brought them closer together, perhaps closer than they'd ever been, so at least one good thing had come of it.

Even so, he was longing for his own space. He'd be

coming back to the apartment alone, which wouldn't be easy —he still had another five months of solitude to endure—but he felt the need to be in the home he and Kallman had built together, around all the familiar things that formed the context of their lives. It might make the pang of separation more immediate, harder to avoid, but it was also an ongoing reminder that their relationship endured.

Kallman would be back. And Marig would be there waiting for him.

He had just finished folding and stowing his clothes when he heard from the living room the low *ping* of an incoming call on the telescreen. Ever since the multiple interviews Nyssa Soliveen had made following her learning about the coverup at the Academy, she'd received dozens of calls every day for further information. So Marig had already dismissed it from his mind when he heard his mother call out, "Marig? You've got a call. It's from the Academy. Can you take it?"

"I'll be right there."

Frowning, he walked down the hall into the living room, dropped into the chair in front of the screen, and clicked *Begin Transmission*.

The dark screen resolved into an image of a stony-faced man sitting behind a desk in one of those generic-looking offices that could have been in any business in Tecoa—off-white walls, a framed photograph of a landscape, a desk with neatly-stacked piles of papers.

"Hello?"

"Am I speaking to Marig Kastella?"

"Yes."

"I'm Korin Derwent. I'm the Interim Director of Human Resources for the Academy. I needed to speak to you because of an… incident that happened during the mission. An incident involving your partner, Kallman Dorn."

Marig's heart gave a painful gallop. "An incident? What kind of incident?"

Derwent cleared his throat, and his carefully controlled visage relaxed into an expression of discomfort. "I'm sorry. I'm new at this, and I don't know how to say it."

"How about straight out?"

He nodded, took a deep breath. "About twenty-four hours ago, Dorn went on the first solo mapping run onto the far-Earth side of the Moon. The technicians report that everything was running smoothly. They'd checked the shuttle over thoroughly and it was in perfect operating condition. Dorn's preflight check shows the same. But some time later—best estimates are about an hour into the flight—the base lost the ship's signal. With the distances involved, this didn't set off any alarm bells at first. It was expected, given that it was flying low over rugged terrain, that there would be times Dorn would be out of contact range. But..." He cleared his throat again. "The shuttle never made contact with Schickard Base again. The eight-hour flight time came and went, and it didn't return. It's now been sixteen hours beyond that, and there's been no word. We are continuing to hope, but... the base commander fears the worst."

Marig stared at Derwent's face for a moment. "No."

"Mir Kastella, I know you must be upset..."

"No." His voice was weak at first, but this time, it came out sounding like a command. His mind was filled with a preternatural calm and an absolute certainty. "I said no and I mean no. Kallman is not lost. Have they sent out a search team?"

"Some of his crew members have been out in the other survey shuttles, but the large geographical area, and lack of any certainty about where he might have come down, are making it difficult at best. As I told you, the ruggedness of the terrain..."

"Fuck the terrain."

Now Derwent looked downright shocked. "Mir Kastella..."

"I'm telling you, he's still alive. This isn't a guess, and it isn't false hope. I can feel him. He's out there, and he's alive."

"With all due respect, Mir, you are not an oracle. The chances of survival if the shuttle crashed…"

"I know I'm not an oracle. And you might be right about the chances. But Kallman Dorn is out there, alive, and I will not allow you to give up on him."

"There isn't much more the base crew can do. There are only five other shuttles, and the survey crew has already taken them out on search runs. More than once."

"Do it again. Do it until you find him."

Derwent's face twitched, and he gave Marig a frustrated stare. "I can't guarantee anything, but I'll see what I can do."

"I will not allow you to sit there and tell me to give up hope when I know he's still alive. The Academy already let bureaucracy and laziness and a warped sense of what the families of the crew needed to know drive decision-making once. You see the result."

"This is hardly the same thing."

"It's exactly the same thing. Only this time, the life of my partner, and the leader of the survey mission, is at stake. You will *not* fuck this up again."

Derwent swallowed hard, and gave a short, sharp nod.

Marig returned the nod and pressed the *End Call* button.

The screen went dark.

He swiveled the chair around. His mother was standing in the entryway from the kitchen, tears in her eyes, looking stricken.

"Oh, Marig, I'm so sorry…"

He shook his head. It was amazing how tranquil he felt, almost disembodied, like he was watching all this happen to someone else. At the same time, his mind had accessed some place of knowledge he hadn't known existed. He hadn't lied to Korin Derwent—he was certain, absolutely certain, that Kallman was alive, and it wasn't just the desperate clinging to hope of someone who deep inside knew the worst had occurred. He knew all too well what that felt like. He'd experienced it when his mother told him he'd lost his right eye.

This was a rock-solid certainty. Not only was Kallman still alive, in a few months' time, they would be reunited. It was so clear in his mind it was almost as if it had already happened. It only remained to convince the people at the Academy, the ones who could do something about it, of that.

"My dear, it's the Moon. If he crashed, what is the likelihood…?" She made a helpless gesture with one hand.

"It doesn't matter. Mother, I don't know how I know, but I'm certain. Please don't try to convince me to *see reason*. You always do that when you think you're right. And even when you turn out not to be, you say it again the next time, and the next. Just let me be right this time, okay? Let me be right, just this once."

She frowned, uncomprehending. "But… it's about the future. How can you know?"

"How did the oracles know? How did the Patriarch? You brought me up to believe in them. I thought that *you* believed in them. Why is it so hard to believe this?" He paused. "Or did you never really believe all the stories you told me?"

"I… I don't know."

"Well, I do."

She shook her head, her face still radiating distress. "I've never heard you speak like this before. To anyone."

"Maybe it's only now that I've needed to." He went on, in gentler tones. "I know it's hard to believe, that it must seem like the forlorn hope of someone who won't accept grief. This is not that. I'm not exactly sure what it is, but it's not that."

"I hope you're right, I truly do." Her brow creased. "I love Kallman, you know that. And his poor parents. The Academy must have told them. They'll be devastated."

"I'll talk to them. I don't know if what I say will help or not, but I will reach out to them." He leaned back in the chair.

"But there's someone I need to speak with first. She… maybe she will see what's happening. How… how I know this. Why I'm so certain. She might even have an explanation."

"Who?"

"The Director of Antiquities at the Museum in Klen. Her name is Reysa Sahin."

"The woman who came to see you at the hospital?"

He nodded. "We talked about meaning and patterns and when to trust what you know. She's studied the actual words of the Blessed Julia, ones that somehow survived for over a thousand years. If she tells me I'm delusional, maybe I'll reconsider." He gazed at her steadily, still a little astonished at the unshakable calm washing over him. "Until then, I'll keep believing."

twenty-two

. . .

Quine was watering plants in the conservatory about ten hours later when he heard a noise, and turned to see Kallman Dorn, stark naked, standing in the doorway, his right arm encased in a translucent plastic immobilizer.

Kallman smiled, a little sheepishly. "I couldn't find what you did with my clothes."

Quine set down the watering pitcher. "Oh, my apologies. I laundered them to remove the bloodstains, and they are still in the cabinet. I'll get them for you."

"I won't need the space suit and helmet. At least not yet."

"No, I wouldn't think so."

"By the way, thanks for taking the IV out."

"You didn't need it. Your vitals were normal, and I thought that when you woke up, you would be ready to be up and around and could take any medications you need orally. I took it out while you were still asleep, and you hardly moved. You are hungry, I would think?"

"Famished."

Quine walked to a wall with a row of cabinets, pulled a sliding door open, and retrieved a neatly-stacked pile of clothing from the top of a cubical clothes dryer. "Here you are. And my apologies for not placing them in your room."

"It's no problem." Kallman pulled on boxers and pants, zipping them and snapping them one-handed with some difficulty. "I don't know how I'm going to manage the shirt, though."

"You could leave one arm out of the sleeve."

"Maybe just not bother with it for the time being. It's nice and warm in here. They always keep it too cold at the Base."

"I can fix you some breakfast, if you would like."

"Sounds wonderful. What sort of food do you have out here? No chickens for eggs, or anything, I'd guess."

"No, regrettably. But I have the hydroponic garden, and the food synthesis unit is still operational."

"After a thousand years? That's impressive. And you've kept the garden going all that time, too?"

"I have had little else to do."

Quine served fresh tomatoes and cucumbers, cut up in a bright yellow ceramic bowl, and strips of something on a matching plate that looked remarkably close to bacon.

"This is synth protein?" Kallman said, munching his fourth piece.

"Yes. Textured and flavored, but entirely synthetic."

"Amazing. That's as good as real bacon I had down on Earth. I love bacon." He wiped his hand on a napkin and raised an eyebrow. "The vegetables are all the real thing, though?"

"Yes. Those are from the greenhouse."

"Still. Amazing. You've grown vegetables for all this time, but for who? And why? You don't eat, right?"

"No. But there are other reasons for tending plants. There is the enjoyment of watching things grow."

"Huh." He leaned back in his chair. "You're not like any robot I've ever met."

"How so?"

"You listen to music, and grow plants for fun. That's not much like other robots, you have to admit." He paused. "What are we listening to, now?"

"Igor Stravinsky's suite *Firebird*."

"Not bad," Kallman observed, after listening for a while. "But I fell asleep in the middle of our conversation, before. You said you were forbidden from seeing earthshine, and you don't know why?"

"That is correct."

"And you have a vehicle that's capable of reaching Schickard Base, but you won't go there."

"I cannot."

"Huh."

"You must understand, Mister Dorn…"

"Just Dorn, please. No one says *Mister* any more, I've only seen it used in old books. *Mir* is the usual form of address for men, but Mir Dorn is my father. I'm fine with just being called Dorn." He paused. "But anyhow. Why the rules about seeing earthshine?"

Quine considered for a moment. "I was given rules by Dr. Kimmell for reasons. Maintenance of the homestead, for obvious ones. Maintenance of the greenhouse and all of the equipment. You can see that had I not followed those, you would have had no food to eat, no water to drink."

"I'm with you so far. But that doesn't mean that *all* of his rules are sensible. Or, maybe, they were rules that needed to be followed back then—when he was still alive—but don't apply now."

"How would I determine which are the sensible ones, and which the ones that are not?"

"That's a good question." He considered for a moment. "You have to wonder if there was a reason he asked you not to go around to the near-Earth side that had to do with what was going on at the time."

"That could be."

"If I remember right from ancient history, fourteen hundred years ago, give or take, was about the time that the First Lackland War broke out. Right?"

"You are referring to the Lacklanders," Quine said. "It had not come to full-scale war when we left Earth, but you are correct that this was when the Lacklander movement became powerful."

"They were refugees, right?"

"Not exactly. They were people whose ancestors had been farmers, and who had lost their land in the government takeovers of land for luxury cash crops, water, and oil. At first, they were mostly from Africa and southern Asia, but the movement was growing, and had spread to Europe and North America. Violence was becoming common and wide-spread, and frequently governmental leaders were targets. Dr. Kimmell acted as an adviser for the European Union's economic wing. Quite suddenly one day, he packed up and came with me to the Moon, first to Tycho Base, and from there, we came here, where we had the homestead built. He told very few people on Earth where he was going, and to the people at Tycho, he said that he was on a secret government mission and that he didn't want any visitors at all. Dr. Kimmell had few friends, and no close family. Most people found him difficult and headstrong." He paused. "I believe that when he said he did not want company, most were happy enough to grant him his wish. Once the homestead was complete, no one came here."

"And the European Union didn't want him back?"

"I do not know." Quine paused. "They may have, and simply did not know how to find him. All I know is that we had no visitors, and the government office he worked for never contacted him, at least so far as I know."

Dorn looked thoughtful. "Why would anyone do that? I like people. I wouldn't want to give up all contact with anyone but a robot for the rest of my life... no offense."

"None taken. And I am only speculating in this, but I have considered Dr. Kimmell's motivation for doing what he did. I think that the 'secret government mission' he alluded to was a lie, and that he fled Earth because he was a prime target for assassination due to his position. In the old parlance—I am not sure if the saying is used any more—he saw the handwriting on the wall."

"I can guess what it means."

Quine nodded. "I suspect that once he laid his plans, he misdirected the people he spoke with, and no one on Earth knew what his actual intentions were, nor where exactly he intended to go. Only a few workers on Tycho Base knew where he was, and he may have paid for their silence. But I have no way to be certain about that."

"So you don't have any information about what happened on Earth after you left."

"None."

Kallman laughed, but it was a little grim. "You missed out on all the excitement, leaving when you did."

"From your tone, that seems to be sarcasm."

"You *are* bright, for a robot." He paused, looking at Quine with a curious expression. "Most artificial intelligences don't pick up on that stuff. But yeah. Big sarcasm. The Lacklanders basically took down the European Union, and shortly afterward, the United States and China went, too. I don't remember the timetable. I wasn't a great history student. But they had numbers on their side, and their leaders didn't give a shit how many of them died. It was only a matter of time. There were a few governments that held out for a while—Japan, I think, and South Africa. But they didn't last long, either. I think it was twenty years or so later that the Second Lackland War broke out, and that took all of the remaining governments down. That was it. Lights out."

"And after that?"

"They call them *The Black Years*. Honestly, there's about five hundred years where we know essentially nothing about what happened on Earth. A good many of the records from before that were destroyed, and there damn sure weren't any records being kept *during* that time. Most people think there was a series of famines and epidemics that knocked the population back hard, because from what writings we do have from before the wars, it seems like the Earth had about ten times the population it does now. Epidemics would be no surprise, given that when the governments fell, it took the medical establishment out at the same time. It was like someone pressed *Reset* on civilization. So even if you'd known about it at the time, Quine, you were stuck out here. Tycho Base didn't survive long after the wars started. When we set up the first new permanent base on the Moon, five years ago or so, there'd been no human living here for over a thousand years."

"You speak as if you've been to Tycho."

Kallman nodded. "It's horrible. That was my first mission after arriving here. We knew it was still standing, but we didn't know there was… anyone out there. That anyone had been stranded, left to die when the governments running the space programs collapsed. We found seven of the Tycho crew. Long dead, of course."

"How tragic."

"All that was left were dried-up corpses, lying where they'd fallen." Dorn looked down. "Fucking haunted house, is what Tycho Base is now. I'm not superstitious, but I could feel them. The ghosts of the people who got left up there, and were just waiting for the food, water, and air to run out. The base commander killed herself rather than face that fate."

"Would that be Commander Lee?"

Kallman looked at Quine in astonishment. "You knew her?"

"Yes." He paused. "I am sorry. She was a good leader and a good person. I wish she had gotten to safety."

"I can't imagine what it was like for them. But now the place is a tomb. I hope they tear it down."

"You're part of a new program to start exploration again?"

"Yeah. There have been two new bases built in the last five years. Schickard is the one where I'm stationed, and the other one is Nectaris. The main base is at Tranquility. All three have permanent staffs. I'm on a mapping mission, trying to get better data on the far-Earth side. Or would be, if my guidance system hadn't blown out."

"Do you plan on living indefinitely at Schickard Base?"

He shook his head. "No. I've only been on the Moon for a little over two weeks. I'm from Cascadia. It's a republic that is made of parts of the old United States and Canada. If you know the area they called the Pacific Northwest?"

"Yes."

"That's home. Actually, I'm only supposed to be up here for six months. My partner is…" His face clouded. "Oh, gods above, I just realized. When they figure out the shuttle is missing, they're going to tell Marig, and he'll be worried sick."

"That is unfortunate."

"Putting it mildly. He's already been through so much. There was… there was a terrorist attack the day of the launch. Your Lacklanders have spiritual descendants, apparently."

"Dreadful. He was injured in the attack?"

"He lost an eye. His father actually died."

"I am sorry."

"Me too."

"Do your people have the capacity for building a prosthetic eye to replace the one he lost?"

Kallman shook his head, staring at Quine in undisguised astonishment. "No. Did yours?"

"Yes. The technique had only recently been developed, the year before we left Earth, but the first implants worked well. It is a pity the knowledge was lost."

"Yeah. A lot was lost, seems like. I've been continuously fretting about him ever since I found out he was hurt. And now I'm worried over what Control will tell him about my going missing. He'll be mad with grief. I've got to get back to Schickard and let them, and him, know I'm okay."

"I see no obvious way to do that."

Kallman frowned at him, and when he went on, it was in tones that seemed to indicate he thought Quine hadn't understood. "I really don't want to stay up here, you know?"

"I am sure."

"So I'm anxious to get back to Schickard and finish my tour. Which will mean going back to the wrecked ship sometime soon."

"Why is that?"

"There is an emergency transmitter on board my ship. A beacon. It's supposed to trip automatically if there's trouble, but given the electronic failure I had, that may not have happened. It can still be activated manually. I'd like to check on that and make sure that it's working, and switch it on if it didn't trip."

"Yes. That is sensible."

"When I don't come back on schedule, they'll eventually send someone out to see what happened, but without the beacon, they'd never find me. The signal has a radius of about a hundred kilometers."

"Perhaps I should go to see to that, then. With your arm in the immobilizer, getting back into your flight suit would be difficult. Also, I would expect that you are still sore and tired from your injuries. I could attend to the task myself, and leave you here to rest and continue your recovery until the rescue party arrives."

Kallman's frown eased. "That's really nice of you."

"Where is the beacon, and how is it operated?"

"If you're facing the rear of the ship, the switch for the transmitter is down and to the left, behind the pilot's seat. It's near the floor. It's obvious—it has to be easily reachable in case of an emergency. It has a separate energy source, so even if the main power is damaged, it should be able to be activated. There's a light next to the switch. If it's green, it's transmitting."

"I will attend to it. Is there anything more you need before I go?"

"No, nothing."

"Perhaps you would like to read while I am gone? There are consoles that interface with the main computer database. I can set up the one in your room to give you access to the library."

"That would be wonderful."

"It is my pleasure." Quine stood. "I hope you will find the writings of your distant ancestors entertaining."

During the second trip to the wreck, Quine listened to Ralph Vaughan Williams's *Fantasia on a Theme by Thomas Tallis* and pondered.

If Kallman's friends from Schickard Base came out to rescue him, then they would find out about Quine and the homestead. And while he had often longed for companionship as the lunar days and Earth years passed, having strangers descend upon him, to analyze him like some kind of archaeological relic, was not a pleasant prospect.

Even his relationship with Dr. Kimmell, who was unpredictable, ill-tempered, and odd, had been preferable to that.

His privacy, Kallman Dorn's safety, and the information he had from a bygone age. It was a difficult puzzle to solve.

He was still considering how to parse the situation when he pulled the carrier alongside the twisted remains of Dorn's ship, got out, and crawled through the hatch that he had cut his way out of only twenty-four hours earlier.

twenty-three

· · ·

Reysa switched off the screen of the multispectral imager with a frustrated snort.

The first half of the second notebook was filled with newsy details of life in the settlement, which had been christened *Klen*, from the Kalila word for *home*. More births, including a son from the bereaved parents Josie Alleman and Trevor Keene, whose daughter's passing prompted Julia to write such poignant thoughts about the meaning of death. The words that launched Reysa on her attempt to understand what she'd gone through.

Not that, in the long run, it accomplished much. She felt as troubled as ever. The violence had settled down, but given what she knew of history, it wouldn't stay that way. The assassin of the king and the Patriarch, a Zealot named Bennit Oswill, was sentenced to death, the execution to be carried out in two and a half weeks. As much as that seemed justice for what he'd done, what did it accomplish? Blood spilled for blood spilled would not undo the harm he caused.

None of it. None of it made sense.

She'd been excited that morning to see that the next passage seemed to have more of a philosophical bent. Not that the details of crop successes and failures, records of couples going into partnerships, and minutiae about daily life weren't interesting to a trained historian. But when she was honest with herself, she knew what she was looking for was answers. The wisdom of an ancient she'd been brought up to believe had direct access to the minds of the gods themselves.

She'd always thought she didn't believe those stories, and became deeply dubious of their truth in early childhood. But now, with the words of the Blessed Julia before her eyes, written in the woman's own hand, it was almost a reflex to expect Julia to address her own deep, anguished needs.

But this last passage turned out to be so odd she found herself wondering if the old woman might have been in the first stages of dementia.

I still hear the voice of God, but now that my life's task is nearly done, and the people are safe here in Klen, the words come more infrequently. I don't find this troubling. Even Moses was allowed to see the Promised Land, but not set foot there [indecipherable]… been lucky to have the time I've had here, to see the fulfillment of the messages the oracles received, to know that we've done well enough.

What has come to me is nothing more than fragments, like leaves spinning on an autumn wind. Of some I can guess the meaning, but the sense of others is dark to me. No matter. I will record them here as they are spoken to me; perhaps the people who come afterwards will understand.

Days ago the voice spoke to me, saying, "Shall one who has turned his eyes away from Me not perish? And when a righteous man comes to slay him, he will grasp the blade in his own hands and drive it into his heart, that the blame shall not lie on the one who is blameless."

Then, in the small hours of the night, I was awakened by a voice that said, "There will come a time when the one-eyed man will see more clearly than those who have both eyes, see further than anyone else ever has. His vision will be the rebirth of knowledge, and those who listen to him will be blessed. The unrighteous will always find

*reasons to disbelieve, but those who open their minds to under-
standing will know he speaks the truth."*

Reysa scanned down her handwritten notes, transcribed from the digital images produced by the scanner. What in the hell could all of that possibly mean? Someone stopping a murder… by killing himself? The visions of a…

She stopped, looking up, her eyes focused on the middle distance, her mouth hanging open a little.

The visions of a one-eyed man.

Could Julia have been talking about Marig Kastella?

Reysa had immediately felt something different from Marig, something she hadn't experienced in any of her other conversations with the injured and with the families of the ones who died in the attack. The others were mostly deferential, somewhere between courteous and cool. While they all thanked her for her visit and her kind words, none of them really seemed to comprehend what she'd been trying to accomplish.

Except for Marig.

He hadn't given her any answers, not really, but he understood immediately why she felt driven to seek them. She left the hospital room after their conversation feeling—if not satisfied, at least soothed, secure that she wasn't foolish for asking the questions.

Instantly, though, her inner skeptic scoffed at her. That he lent her a sympathetic ear, was interested in her quest for knowledge, didn't mean he was anything more than a kind, intelligent, but perfectly ordinary man. She felt foolish even for entertaining the idea that a woman from almost fifteen hundred years ago had written about a man who was living and breathing right now.

And of course, as an archaeologist and a historian she was all too aware that sacred texts were full of references like Julia's "one-eyed man." She'd even seen a rather horrific line in a book of lore that if your eye leads you into sin, you should pluck it out, because it was better to have only a single eye than be damned forever. The eyes were such a potent symbol for understanding and connection it was no surprise they were used over and over in such passages. It was seldom possible to tell if the original writers meant what they wrote literally or metaphorically, and to a nonbeliever like Reysa, it had rarely mattered. What she cared about was the cultural context, the belief systems, the language they wrote in, the artifacts they left behind.

But ever since she'd begun to read Julia's words, they struck her as different from any other text she'd ever studied.

They seemed to be speaking to her personally, and about real people and real events.

Her mind told her it was ridiculous, but her heart said exactly the opposite.

And it was as she was sitting there, staring at the transcribed lines from the ancient document, that there was the *ping* of a video link request on her telescreen.

When she looked over at it, the message said, *You have an incoming call request from Marig Kastella. Accept?*

She stared at it for nearly a minute. Then, her hand moving as if she were in a trance, she clicked, *Begin Transmission.*

The screen lit up with an image of Marig sitting at a desk. Behind him was a neatly-decorated, sunlit living room. Marig's missing eye, which had been swathed in bandages the last time she'd seen him, was now covered with a black eyepatch. There was a long zigzag of a scar running from his right temple down his cheek. Before, the trauma he'd been through showed in his face—unshaven, unkempt, pallor in his cheeks and a dark smudge under his eye. There was something different there now, a new confidence, a new understanding. Someone who, despite his loss, *saw*.

The thought passed through her mind, like a shout of

acclamation, *I'm witnessing the foundation of a new line of oracles.*

His vision will be the rebirth of knowledge, and those who listen to him will be blessed.

"Hello?" She could hear the combination of fear, puzzlement, and excitement in her own voice.

"I'm sorry to disturb you at work. It was the only contact information I had for you."

"It's all right."

He took a long, deep breath. "I'm calling to ask you a question. It's about what we discussed—when you came to see me at the hospital. How you can understand what's happened, and if you can trust what you know. When to be certain about something you believe, and when to doubt it."

Reysa opened her mouth to speak, then closed it again without saying anything.

He seemed to take her hesitation as disinterest, because he said, "If you'd rather not talk to me about this…"

"No. It's fine. In fact… I was just thinking about this very question myself."

He frowned, looking down for a moment, then nodded and continued.

"Something has happened. I don't know if it's been on the news yet, or if it will be at all. Kallman Dorn—my partner, who is the leader of the survey mission on the Moon—has gone missing. He left on a mapping run twenty-four hours ago. His intent was to be back at Schickard Base in eight hours, and no one has heard from him."

"I'm so sorry. You must be dreadfully worried."

Marig's voice became more animated. "No. That's just it. I'm not. Which is odd in and of itself, because ordinarily I worry about everything. I was a complete mess during the lead up to the launch, thinking about his being gone for six months, all of the things that could go wrong, what I would do if he died. It was unrelenting. But then, when I was injured, or shortly afterward… my feelings changed. No, not my *feelings*—my whole *self*. I don't understand it. Before, I was constantly anxious. But now that something seems to have *actually* gone wrong, I don't feel worried at all, because I'm certain he's okay."

"Do you think… I don't know, that it's your hope speaking?"

As soon as she said the words, she knew what his response was going to be.

"No. That's just it. I know what it's like to hope for something, maybe even something that's really unlikely, or that something you fear won't happen. This is different. This isn't hope." He paused, his gaze fixing on hers through the telescreen with an intensity that was almost palpable. "This is knowledge."

Gods above. It was true. Julia's prophecy was true.

"Perhaps you think I'm being foolish," Marig said. "That's why I contacted you. I told myself that if you said I was delusional, I'd try to—I don't know. To take a more realistic approach."

"No. Not at all. I…" She shook her head, trying to clear away the fog of confusion she felt. "Perhaps I should share with you the passage I transcribed from Blessed Julia's manuscript just this morning. When I read it, I…" She stopped, cleared her throat. Why was she finding it so hard to articulate? She'd always been most comfortable in the realm of words, and now they seemed entirely inadequate to explain what she was thinking.

"Just tell me what you found," Marig said gently.

She gave a sharp little nod. "Yes. Instead of trying to describe it, let me read you the lines that jumped out at me."

She picked up her notes, and in a tremulous voice, read the passage from the notebooks.

After she finished, for a time there was silence.

"It seems presumptuous to think she was talking about me." Marig's voice was tentative.

"But."

"Exactly. But." His mouth quirked upward. "The one-eyed man."

"It'd be easy to read this, and assume she was speaking metaphorically. But what if she wasn't? What if it's not presumption, but the literal truth?"

"I didn't think this was how this call would go. You're an academic. Logical, rational, reliant on evidence. I was pretty sure you'd tell me I'm crazy."

"I don't think you're crazy at all." She glanced back down at her handwritten notes. "In fact, I was just considering calling you when your incoming call popped up. I kept trying to talk myself out if it, tell myself it was ridiculous."

"I understand. But if we believe there ever *were* actual oracles—that the old stories are, at least in part, true—then don't you think *all* of them felt like this? They started out just like we did, as ordinary people. They all must have thought at some point, *Why was I chosen? I'm nothing special.*"

"Yes! In fact, I know that to be true. In transcribing Julia's writings, I've been struck over and over again by her humility. By her statements that what she was able to do was something anyone could accomplish. That we only had to open our minds to the possibility, and it could be realized. Believe me, I've had that same feeling of presumption myself. So many times while reading what she wrote, I've thought, *She's talking to me personally. This was meant for me.* Then I've pushed the thought aside as foolish pride—the idea that even if Julia could see the future from over a thousand years ago, she'd pick me in particular, out of all the millions of people on Earth, to speak to."

"You were the one who found the manuscript. If Julia is speaking to anyone, I would think it would be you."

Reysa didn't answer.

"Because that's it, really. There's no way to know ahead of time which of us will change the course of history, and who will be forgotten."

"I don't like the idea of my being that critical. To anything or anyone. It's a responsibility I would never choose."

"Most of the people in those roles probably wouldn't. Fortunately, most of us never know until afterward, if we even get to see it at all." He shook his head. "True foreknowledge would be a tremendous burden. Terrifying, really. I don't envy the oracles."

"Perhaps you are one."

He stared at her in silence for a moment. "You honestly think Julia was writing about me?"

"I don't know for certain. Not in my brain, you know? But in my heart, I'm sure. The same way you know Kallman is alive, and will come home safely." She shrugged. "It's not a usual way of thinking for me. I've always been rational, like you said. Relied on study and research and evidence to determine what I believe, what I understand, what I know. This is something else entirely."

"Maybe it's just a different kind of evidence."

"Maybe. I suppose the only thing to do is to keep moving ahead in trying to understand, even if we can't see what the path looks like." She paused, frowning. "It's like something I read when I was at university. There was a book of philosophy from the Before Time that survived, and one of the essays in it was by a man named Søren Kierkegaard. I recall one line that stood out to me. 'The true tragedy of life is that it must be lived forwards, but it can only be understood backwards.'"

Marig chuckled. "So wait and see, then?"

"Wait and see." She shook her head. "I don't know how you've managed to find peace in this. I feel nothing but agitation and uncertainty."

"Honestly, I don't know, either. Like I said, it came to me

unasked-for. I do know that it started the day you visited me in the hospital. Something in me shifted that day."

"I didn't think I said anything that profound."

"It was more knowing I'm not alone in trying to understand this."

"You're not." She gave him a smile, and something in her seemed to relax, perhaps for the first time since the Patriarch's death. "It's what we're all doing, really. Continuing to put one foot in front of the other, and helping each other figure out what it all means."

twenty-four

. . .

"I am sorry to inform you," Quine said, upon his return to the homestead, "that the transmitter was destroyed along with the control panel of your ship. I am able to make some sorts of repairs—I was programmed by Dr. Kimmell to maintain the environmental controls of the homestead, for instance—but the damage was far too great for me to have any hope of remedying." He paused. "I am sorry."

Kallman Dorn had been sitting at the reading desk in his room, perusing a history book that Quine had uploaded from storage eight lunar days earlier. Curious, he'd cued up as well the next piece on Quine's playlist for the day, the Scherzo from Litolff's *Concerto Symphonique #4*, which turned out to be a giddy, bouncing melody not at all matching the frustration and worry he felt.

"Well, that's not good." He leaned back in the chair, his expression dark with disappointment, looking for some kind of emotional resonance in Quine's impassive metal face, which of course never came.

"No. It is unfortunate. I feared that it might be so, as the damage to the front end of the ship was quite extensive. Of course, it was important to verify this."

"So, do you have radio equipment here? If you have a good transmitter, I could contact Schickard Base, and they could send someone to pick me up. Pick both of us up, if you're willing."

Quine didn't answer for a time. "No. There is no radio equipment. Only the internal comlink, which has a range of less than five kilometers. Only enough to cover the crater area. There never was any sort of long-range communications equipment."

"Why not?"

"As I described earlier, I believe Dr. Kimmell didn't want to be found. He knew that radio signals can be tracked. Even the heat output of the homestead could potentially have been detected, but the walls are very well insulated, and the buildings are camouflaged. Likewise, the comlink signal could be tracked, but I only use it when I'm outside, which is not often, and it would require being within close range already."

Kallman didn't answer for some time. Finally, he just shook his head, and gave Quine a smile that looked forced. "Okay, then, any other ideas about how it get me back to the base?"

"That will be a challenge."

His smile dimmed. "Come on. It can't be that hard."

"There are… obstacles."

"Such as?"

"There is only one way to get you to Schickard Base that I can see, and that is using the equipment carrier. There are two problems with that, of increasing difficulty. One is that it is voice-activated, and is set only to turn on in response to my voice and Dr. Kimmell's. I could potentially start the carrier for you, but you would have to make the entire trip without stopping. If you shut the controls down, or if the carrier malfunctioned and shut itself down, you would be unable to restart it."

"Okay," Kallman said. "Leave the motor running when I stop to take a piss. What else?"

"It has no guidance system."

His smile vanished entirely. "Oh."

"Without an internal guidance system, you would have no way to know if you were going the right direction. Without it, your odds of finding Schickard Base are infinitesimally small. Even if you missed it by only two kilometers, given the rough terrain you very likely would be out of sight range. After that, it would be only a matter of waiting until your air and water ran out."

"Like the people on Tycho."

"Exactly."

Kallman rubbed his chin. "Is there anything here that has a guidance system?"

"Yes." Quine tapped his head with one finger. "I do."

"So you'd have to come along, which means breaking your rule about seeing earthshine."

"It appears so."

"But wait, now. You were on the near-Earth side of the Moon for a time, when you were at Tycho. Hell, you were on Earth *itself* once, and you didn't explode, or short-circuit, or whatever. What makes you think something awful is going to happen now?"

"Because Dr. Kimmell reprogrammed me upon arrival here. Some of it was simply so that I would be able to perform my new duties, but he included in my programming a command that I was never to seek out the Earth again. And he spoke of it frequently, especially when he knew he was dying. 'I've taken steps to make sure they never get a hold of you, Quine,' he said, more than once. 'If you go around to the Earth side, it'll be the end of you, and I want you to outlive me. So don't get any thoughts of trying to get back to Tycho. Let me die here, and bury me in the Moon dust where I belong. And take care of the homestead afterwards. That's your job.'"

"What did he mean by *taken steps*?"

"I have thought a great deal about what that could have meant. Perhaps he included some sort of self-destruct code in my programming, which will activate if I see the Earth. Perhaps he was trying to frighten me into complying. The truth is, I simply do not know the answer to that question."

"So it's possible that you could cross into the near side, and nothing would happen."

"Yes."

"Or your neural circuitry could self-destruct, and you would die, and I would be stranded out there in the carrier without a guidance system, and without any way to find my way either to Schickard or back here."

"That is correct."

"Well, fuck."

"It is a dilemma." He rose, and picked up Kallman's plate, glass, and fork. "Would you like something more for breakfast?"

He shook his head, and Quine left the room with the dirty dishes and went into the galley to wash them.

"You seem awfully damn calm about the whole thing," came Kallman's voice.

"Would it make the situation any different if I were to sob, or shout angrily?"

There was no answer for a moment, then Kallman appeared in the doorway and leaned against the doorframe. "That depends."

"On what?"

"On whether your voice has anything to do with what you're actually feeling."

Quine did not respond, but picked up a towel and dried the plate off.

"*Do* you have feelings?"

"Oh, yes. Very much so."

"Do you understand why I'm upset?"

"Completely. You are here, stranded on the Moon, with no obvious way to get back to your home and the man you love. I would imagine that you are afraid and sad, as well as worrying about what your partner is currently enduring back on Earth."

"That's an understatement."

"And the only solution seems to be attempting to parse the intentions of a man who has been dead for over a thousand years, and who was known to be capricious and unpredictable when he was alive."

"Yes."

Neither one spoke for some time.

Kallman rubbed the back of his hand against his cheek, now dark with stubble. "Tell me something, Quine."

"What do you wish to know?"

"What would you do, in my position?"

Quine listened to the piano soloist working her way down the chromatic scale, and then flying, lightning-fast, up the entire keyboard and into the last measures of the Scherzo.

"I believe," he said, as the orchestra's last chord died into silence, "that in your position, I would do whatever it took to get back to the ones I loved, and take any risk required."

"What if it entailed putting someone else's life at risk, as well as your own?"

Quine looked at Kallman in silence for a few seconds. "I do not know even how to begin to answer that question, especially given that I am the individual you are referring to who would be at risk." Quine put the plate back in the cabinet, and the fork in a drawer with other silverware. "So I will put some more music on, and tend to the greenhouse, and think about it."

"You have an amazing library," Kallman said as he watched Quine deftly preparing lunch, which was something that looked, and smelled, amazingly like a smoked turkey sandwich. With two slices of bacon.

"Dr. Kimmell had the homestead equipped with computers that not only monitor and control environmental conditions, but had nearly unlimited memory storage for books and music. They are stored in compressed form, so they have to be uploaded and decompressed for use, which takes time and energy. I limit myself to ten books to read during the night, when the electricity from the solar cells has to be conserved for necessary functions such as heat and light for the greenhouse. But I allow myself complete access during the day, and you are free to do so as well."

"You know, historians on Earth would trample each other to death to get access to your database."

Quine nodded. "I am very aware of that."

"During the Black Years, a huge amount of earlier writings were lost, and most of the music and art. This is a treasure-trove." He gestured upwards, at speakers concealed in the ceiling. "What are we listening to, now?"

"Debussy. *The Drowned Cathedral.*"

"Spooky."

"Yes, I think that was the composer's intent. I find Debussy conducive to making difficult decisions." He handed Kallman a plate with the sandwich, complete with hydroponic lettuce and tomato.

"Thanks." He took the plate to the table, sat down, and gestured for Quine to join him. "*Have* you come to a decision about our little… dilemma?"

Quine rested his hands on the table, and didn't answer for a moment. "It is an odd thing, decision-making."

"What do you mean?"

"Humans appear to do it quite easily, most of the time. I am sure that sometimes you agonize over things, but generally, you do what you do with apparent facility."

"Yes, well, you can see what the results sometimes are," Dorn said around a bite of sandwich.

"That is true. But it works out well surprisingly often. I have thought about this question for a long time, and tried to find the answer through reading. Initially, I had confined myself to reading non-fiction. Books on history, horticulture, home maintenance, computer diagnostics, and the like. But after a time, I began to read fiction, because I was curious about how humans make decisions. I found that this did not help me much, although much of it was intriguing."

"I'll bet."

"After that, I returned to non-fiction for a time, and read treatises on logic. *Principia Mathematica* by Alfred North Whitehead and Bertrand Russell, for example, seemed a good place to start."

"Don't know it, or them, but just from the title it sounds like deeper water than I'd be comfortable in."

"It is difficult reading," Quine admitted. "And for a time, I thought that understanding the principles of logic would open up for me the means for comprehending how decisions are made. But then, one day, I downloaded another book, one by Kurt Gödel called *On Formally Undecidable Propositions*."

"Uh-oh. That sounds like trouble."

"The conclusion Gödel came to is that even in a complete, consistent logical framework, there are some true statements that cannot be proven using logic."

"I could have told you that."

"Yes. It seems as if humans have known intuitively all along what Gödel took an entire book to prove."

Kallman shrugged. "I don't see that it's that big a deal. We do a lot of things for reasons other than logic. Love isn't logical, but we'll risk our lives for it. Sex isn't logical, it just feels really good and motivates people to do all sorts of things they wouldn't otherwise do. Anger, fear, jealousy… none of that is logical." He ate the last bite of his sandwich, and leaned back in his chair. "But Quine, you say you have feelings, right? Emotions?"

"Yes."

"Where did they come from?"

"I do not know."

"Don't they motivate you, sometimes?"

"In small ways, yes. I put on music because of a desire to experience certain emotions, or sometimes to fight against emotions I would prefer not to feel. When I am lonely, for example, I put on music by Haydn, which is unfailingly cheerful, and makes me feel better."

"So why can't you use emotion to make other sorts of decisions?"

Quine turned away from him, looked down the long hallway that led from the dining area into the greenhouse, and beyond that to the airlock that led out into the glaring, desolate vacuum that was the Moon's surface.

"It is because none of the decisions I have had to make have ever affected anyone but myself. I do not know how to weigh in another person's needs, nor to balance that against whatever risk that I am facing, and the fear I feel when contemplating it."

Kallman regarded Quine with one eyebrow raised. "Why did you come out to the spaceship when I crashed? Logic must have told you that there'd be no survivors."

"Yes. That is what I expected."

"Then why did you go?"

"Curiosity, I think, was my main motivator. I had not seen anyone else for a very long time. Even if the presumed pilot and crew were dead, I felt I had to see them."

"I'm glad you did, or I *would* be dead. But you see? You do make decisions for other reasons than logic, and in other cases than just deciding what music to listen to."

"Yes." Quine was silent for a moment. "And it is perhaps the case that I know what the correct decision is here, and I am simply afraid to do it."

twenty-five

. . .

I n the northwestern part of Tecoa a triangular peninsula juts out into the water, a promontory with sheer, rocky cliffs on two sides dropping down onto strips of sandy beach far below. It is beautiful in a stark sort of way, the top of the cliff thickly grown with fir and maple trees, and in the understory beneath them a tangle of salal, huckleberry, and briars. During the heyday of the Acoca dynasty, it had been appropriated by the crown, first for use as a hunting preserve and then—when King Sweyn VII started creating enemies faster than the headsman could keep up with them—as the ideal site for a prison.

So the dense forest on the southern part of the peninsula was allowed to grow unhindered, made even more impassible by a double line of high fences. The northern tip was cleared, and the first official prison of Tecoa was built.

Since then, it had been rebuilt more than once. During the short and disordered reign of Sweyn's son, Sweyn VIII and the last of that name, the rebellion that had cost both the younger Sweyn and his imperious mother Pavona their lives had included an attack on the hated prison, seen rightly as a symbol of the Acoca family's horrible reputation for punishing people on the slightest whim. Rebels armed with knives and axes hacked their way into the compound, then did battle with the few guards who remained and who were loyal to the House of Acoca. The insurgents won the skirmish, but it did little good for the prisoners. Instead of freeing them—the rebels' intent—one of the invaders accidentally set fire to the wooden garrison at the entrance. The fire spread to the rest of the prison, burning the entire thing down to the foundation, along with nearly all the prisoners it had housed.

It was rebuilt once order was restored. There's never been a time in history humans haven't felt the need for prisons. Over the centuries since, parts were torn down and renovated and expanded, and about fifty years ago the Tecoan government had fortified it into the gray, blocky, featureless complex it now was. Since then it hadn't substantially changed. Grim and ugly, a place reserved for the worst of humanity. The people who crossed through its double-barred gates didn't come back out into the wider world for a very long time.

If ever. It was also the home of people waiting for their meeting with the executioner.

Given the infrequency of death sentences and the mere three-week gap between sentencing and death, there seldom was more than one person on death row at a time. The unfortunate victim spent that time in a solitary cell, well away from other prisoners. In fact, the guards did their best not to let the others know there was someone about to face the guillotine. It was understandable the prisoners would be in sympathy with the condemned man or woman, and that by itself could make them more likely to defy prison rules and cause problems.

So condemned individuals entered the prison at night, accompanied only by guards. Unless they specifically requested otherwise—few did—their deaths were witnessed only by guards. The coffins containing their bodies were buried in the prison cemetery, out of sight of the main compound.

It was also unusual for the condemned to have visitors during the three-week wait. Some, of course, had family and friends who cared about them, but those were discouraged from coming inside the cold gray walls of the prison. Most didn't argue. Last visits were conducted in the lockup in the Central Police Station in Tecoa, before the prisoner was transferred.

After that, most of the time, the condemned's loved ones acted as if the prisoner was already as good as dead.

This was why when Reysa Sahin contacted the prison officials and asked if she could schedule a face-to-face meeting with Bennit Oswill, the reaction she got at first was pure bafflement.

"Why?" the warden's assistant asked bluntly. His face, framed on the telescreen, communicated a doubt that he had even heard her right.

"I want to speak to him because I am trying to understand what he did."

"You'll get no good answer out of him. Believe me, he's been talked to over and over, both before his sentencing and afterward. Go ask the Chief of Police. He got nowhere with him, and neither will you."

"Still, I would like to have the chance to try."

"What on earth do you hope to accomplish?"

She took a deep breath before responding. "You should understand. I am the archaeologist who uncovered the manuscript from the Blessed Julia. It was my actions that prompted the Zealots to strike."

"Oh, now, I hardly think that means you are…"

She waved him off impatiently. "I am not trying to assign blame to myself. But I've spoken to all of the people Dain Sarkos injured at the Moon transport launch, and the families of the ones he killed. It's helped me, a little, to find my own solace in trying to piece together what happened, and why."

He gazed at her with a combination of sympathy and

perplexity. "If the Zealots have anything motivating their actions besides mindless rage and hatred, I can't imagine what it could be."

"Except for those who are truly insane, everyone does what they do for a reason. It might not be a reason that makes sense to you or me, but even so, to them it has its own internal logic. I want to find out what that is."

"There's no point to it."

"That may well be, Mir." Her voice was quiet but steady, with an unshakable confidence. "But I would like to speak with him anyway. If I gain nothing from it, neither will I have lost anything. It is, of course, your decision to grant me permission or not."

In the end, he said yes, although he clearly still didn't understand her motives.

So it was that on a cool, rainy day, Reysa took the FastRail to the nearest station to the prison, then boarded a shuttle sent to pick her up. There were only two other people on the shuttle besides herself and the driver—a distraught-looking woman of perhaps twenty-five, and a stoic older man who spent the entire drive up to the prison complex staring out of the window. It was only when the shuttle was ushered through the gates, and got past the belt of trees that cut off the prison from the view of the outside world, she caught the first sight of the place.

The prison complex was just an array of huge, cubical stone boxes. Seeing it, she was glad that until now, she'd only been vaguely aware of it. The thought of being incarcerated here was horrifying. She also gave thanks for the relatively lenient judicial system in Cascadia, and the fact that the prison population was seldom very large. It seemed horrible that even criminals would spend months and years here.

Or, like Bennit Oswill, the few remaining days left for them to live.

The shuttle stopped near a set of metal doors in the

nearest building, where a pair of grim security guards waited to escort the three visitors into the complex. Each was asked their name, who they were there to visit, and given a briefing of the rules.

The prisoners would already be in the room waiting for them. They would be seated, cuffed to a chair, during the entire duration of the visit. There was to be no physical contact of any kind. Voices were to be kept low. If there was any yelling, by the prisoner or the visitor, the visit would be terminated immediately. The visitor was to remain seated during the entire conversation, and when they were ready to leave, they must signal a guard before they stood up.

Was that all understood, and did the visitors agree to comply to the letter?

All of them did.

Afterward, they were each assigned a guard to conduct them to the room where they would meet the prisoners they were there to visit.

Reysa followed her guard into the shadowed interior of the building, down a maze of hallways past what seemed like hundreds of locked doors. Somehow, she'd expected the place to be noisy. Her study of the early history of Cascadia had prepared her for horrors—screams of men and women being tortured, shouted obscenities by prisoners to guards and each other, disconsolate weeping of the forgotten of society. In fact, it was deathly silent. If she hadn't known better, she'd have thought it was empty. Her footsteps and those of her escort sounded loud and echoic in the quiet.

She knew part of it was because there weren't that many prisoners, and those were kept under tight control. But the very emptiness felt full to her, as if her every step was being watched by legions of ghosts, the men and women who had died in this place back through the centuries.

Finally the guard said, "Here," and stopped in front of a door he unlocked using a key hanging from a chain on his belt. He ushered her into a small room, lit from above by a harsh white light. Inside was only a single table and two chairs, one occupied.

Her first view of Bennit Oswill was a surprise. Somehow, she was expecting him to look less… ordinary. He was a middle-aged man, perhaps fifty years old, with close-cropped gray hair and a square face. In a different place, and dressed in ordinary clothes, she'd have thought he was a businessman or salesman, someone she would have barely noticed if he sat across from her on the train.

It was hard to believe that this perfectly normal-looking man had killed the king and the Patriarch, and in three days, would be sent to the guillotine for his crimes.

He looked up at her without smiling. "You wanted to talk to me?"

She sat down across from him. "Yes."

"Why?"

"Because I need to understand."

"What is there to understand?"

"I know that you are a Zealot. You followed Dain Sarkos."

"The past tense is incorrect. I still follow Mir Sarkos, and I will be greeting him soon."

She nodded. This much, at least, was expected. "I know you hated the king and the Patriarch because you felt they had betrayed the legacy of the oracles. They had failed to live up to what we know of our own past."

"That is correct."

"What I don't understand, though, is why you think that violence against innocent people was the way to recapture that past."

"It was a last resort when nothing else worked."

"And it was worth paying for with your life?"

"Yes." He gave her a chilly smile. "You cannot frighten me with that. I am not afraid to die. But yes, killing them was worth the price."

"Had you tried other ways? Had you tried just treating people with kindness, and talked to the ones you disagreed with, so that you could perhaps figure things out together? How on earth was hurting people supposed to solve anything?"

The smile turned scornful. "The people of Cascadia had the chance, and they rejected it. Any of you could have come to Mir Sarkos's meetings and heard his words and believed. Many did. That you did not was your own choice. The people at the launch had put their faith in the false gods of science and abandoned the real ones, but no one was forcing them into that belief. No one forced them to be there."

"But that doesn't alter the fact that Sarkos's actions resulted in the deaths of innocent people. People who have no stake in this fight, and probably no interest, either."

His eyes flashed—the first sign of animation he'd shown. "That's where you're wrong. Everyone has a stake in this. It is the only thing that matters. What I and the other Zealots have done, Mir Sarkos most of all, is to try to wake people up. Only a shock might make people realize the truth, and recognize where their complacency was leading. If that shock resulted in some dying, that is the cost of disbelief. It's what apostasy does to the world. It was my duty, and that of the other Zealots, as messengers of the divine, to turn people's minds whatever it took."

Reysa stared at him. Was there anything of humanity left in him? Did he truly not care about the innocent victims of Sarkos's attack?

How did someone become like this?

She decided to try another approach. "I'm the archaeologist who discovered the manuscript written by the Blessed Julia."

She'd wondered if someone on the prison staff would have made the connection between Oswill's actions and Reysa's name, and if perhaps they had told him, and the man would already know who his visitor was. It was obvious from his expression that he did not. His mouth opened, then closed, and his face paled.

"You…?" he choked out.

She nodded. "Sarkos said that the documents are forgeries, and that I am a liar. Or else, the Patriarch and I were in a conspiracy to hoodwink the public and discredit the Zealots. None of this is true. The documents are, to the best of my knowledge, absolutely authentic. They are the actual words of the Blessed Julia Lowell. As for the Patriarch, he didn't know about them until I told him, and even after that, he was reluctant to make them public. He only did what he did because I maneuvered him into it."

"It's a lie," he hissed.

"No. No, it's not. I understand that it's hard for you to accept. However, when your dearly-held beliefs are contradicted by something that is a fact, something right in front of your face—well, you have no real choice, do you? I'm not saying it's pleasant to find out. But it is necessary, unless you would prefer to live inside a delusion."

"I don't believe you."

"What earthly reason would I have to come here if it weren't the truth? Mir Oswill, you are going to die in three days. Nothing you or I can do will change that. I have nothing to gain by this. Nothing but understanding—which to me, is valuable. Be honest. Now, here, where there is nothing more to hide, where all possible justification for lies and subterfuge is done. Wouldn't you rather know the truth?"

"I know the truth."

"Can you tell me one reason why I would come here and speak with you if I were lying? You're already sentenced to death. What more do you think I am trying to accomplish?"

"You speak with the voice of evil."

"Do you truly believe that? Or is it just what you have

been taught to say about people who don't believe as you do? Do you honestly believe that you are infallible? That you are incapable of getting it wrong?"

For the first time, he seemed not to know what to say. He blinked, looked down. He moved one foot, and the chain binding his ankle to the chair rattled. He looked up at her, but his eyes had lost some of their defiance.

"I don't know."

"It seems to me," Reysa said quietly, "that saying 'I don't know' is the first step toward living an honest life."

His gaze locked onto hers, and she got the impression he was seeing her, truly seeing her, for the first time. When he spoke, his voice was low and hoarse.

"Swear to me. Swear to me by the gods and the ancestors and the holy memory of the oracles. Swear that you aren't lying about the manuscript."

"I'll swear to you by whatever you want me to. I found the five notebooks in the archives of the Great Library in Tecoa. They'd been down there, shelved and probably untouched, for centuries. The pages had been reused, rewritten on, and appeared to be simply accounting records of a business during the reign of King Lennis II. I was going through them, and had them under bright light, and saw the faint traces of writing that had either been erased incompletely, or else had faded because of the passage of time. When I used an imaging device to enhance what was written there, I was able to read much of it. I truly had no idea what the notebooks were until then." She paused. "The transcripts that were made public, including the one read in the broadcast by the Patriarch, are literally word-for-word what I found written there. I'm not a partisan. I didn't work for the Patriarch or the king. I have no agenda except for the truth. I'm an academic, and never had any intentions of getting involved in the bigger issues. All I wanted to do was study our history and find out more about how our ancestors lived. I had no reason to lie." She shrugged. "I still don't."

Perhaps it was the steady certainty with which she spoke. Perhaps the nearness of his own death had finally made him question what he'd been told to believe. But Reysa saw in his eyes something she hadn't seen before.

Doubt.

"Why?" His voice was low, intense. "Why did you come here?"

"Because I've devoted my life to understanding the truth. At first, I thought it was all one thing, that truth was the same for everyone, that given all the facts and sufficient thought, we'd all come to the same conclusions. But instead I've found we all build our own truth out of what we've experienced and what we've been taught and the bonds we forge with others, and spend our lives so certain that the edifice we've created is the only reality that we miss most of what's out there. I am trying—in my own halting way—to see if I can step beyond that." She took a deep breath. "Your actions, and those of Dain Sarkos, caused tremendous pain to many, many people, myself included. I was with the Patriarch when he died. I'd never seen another human murdered." She leaned forward in her chair, keeping her gaze focused on his. "I have needed to at least try and understand why you and Sarkos and the other Zealots did what you did. For my own peace of mind, and in the hope that I could bring what I learned to some of the other people who have been harmed."

He gave her a long, steady look, and now the doubt was compounded with awe.

Reysa's eyes widened, as she suddenly realized what she had missed. It wasn't about anger. None of them—Sarkos, Oswill, any of the other Zealots who had hurt people—had been motivated at their cores by anger. The anger had followed, after another, more deeply visceral emotion.

Fear.

He'd said he was unafraid to die, but that was only because his entire life was filled with nothing but a grinding, crushing terror of everything and everyone who wasn't like him.

If she were faced with that every day of her life, she'd have welcomed death, too.

"Gods above," she said, trying to keep her voice level. It took a considerable effort. "Why are you so afraid? What a horrible thing to live with."

He simply stared at her, his face turning even paler. His hands, clasped together on the table in front of him, clenched so hard the knuckles whitened. She was certain that if he had he not been restrained, he would either have attacked her—or else fled.

"Mir Oswill, there never was anything to fear from the people who don't believe as you do. We never had any intention of doing to you what you wanted to do to us."

There was a heavy silence in the little room, during which she wasn't certain he'd speak again. He seemed frozen in place, like her words had struck him mute and motionless as a marble statue. When he finally spoke, it was in a voice that was barely audible.

"You are either a god or a devil. I do not know which. But whichever it is, I can't listen to you any longer." He paused. "I think you had better go."

"If that's what you want. But know that I do pity you."

"I don't want your pity, and I have nothing more to say to you."

Reysa nodded. "In that case, I suppose you're right." She raised her hand, and said in a louder voice, "Guard? I'm ready to go."

Wordlessly, the guard walked to her. She stood as he gestured her toward the door, then unlocked it. Oswill was left cuffed to the chair, his gaze following her as she left, his expression an unreadable mix of confusion and a hundred conflicting emotions. Presumably after she was safely away, someone would be sent to conduct him back to his lonely cell, where he'd spend his last three days waiting for his fate.

It was still drizzling when she arrived back at the exterior doors and out into the circular drive where the shuttle still sat. She was the first of the visitors to return, and she was instructed to board and wait for the two others.

Just being out in the free air, feeling the rain on her face and smelling the crisp scent of fir trees—something Oswill never again would experience—was like a gift.

She hadn't really gotten what she'd come for. Her efforts to convince him of the errors of his ways were very likely futile, she knew that. It was doubtful he'd die any more contrite than he'd lived. And despite her epiphany about the ultimate reason for his actions, she was no closer to understanding where it had come from, how the vagaries of life everyone endures could engender compassion and empathy in one person, and soul-crushing fear and rage in another.

Perhaps her own personal quest, trying to figure out why Bennit Oswill had killed, was no more sensible than Brother Juniper's attempt to find out why five particular people had died in the collapse of a bridge in long-ago Peru, and was fated to reach the same conclusion. She recalled her own words to Marig Kastella in his hospital room.

The minds of the gods are so inscrutable that humans can't parse their motives—or else there is no reason.

Even so, there was no doubt in her mind. She had to continue following this road to its end—whatever the outcome.

twenty-six

. . .

Kallman. I am here.

If you can hear me, my love, believe me that I have not given up on you. I know you are alive, and I know you will come home to me safely.

Let me know you can hear me.

It was twelve hours since he'd gotten the news of Kallman's disappearance. Despite his mother's insistence that he shouldn't be alone with such a burden, he'd continued with his plan to move back to his apartment. Looking around, at the furnishings and photographs and all the oddments of daily life he'd left behind, it seemed like the last time he'd left it and closed the door behind him had been in another life.

But in so many ways, he *had* been another person then. Two eyes, no scars, no twinges of pain when he moved his right arm the wrong way. But… the constant weight of worry about everything. He realized how much anxiety had run his life only now that it had been lifted from him.

Kallman was alive, and there was no need to be concerned.

All shall be well.

After eating a light meal and unpacking the suitcase he'd

used to bring his belongings home from his mother's apart-ment, he undressed, then lay down on the bed he'd shared with Kallman. The memories, to his surprise, weren't painful —they were joyful. He buried his face in Kallman's pillow— even after a month it still held traces of his warm, spicy scent. Smiling, he rolled over onto his back and cupped his hands behind his head.

Soon he had drifted into some strange, unfamiliar half-doze. He was still largely conscious of the dimly-lit bedroom around him, and farther away, the ordinary evening noises. The distant swish of the train zooming by on the FastRail track a couple of blocks away. A door closing in a nearby apartment. The rising, then falling, conversation of two people passing on the sidewalk beneath his bedroom window.

But at the same time, he felt rather than heard the wider world. His awareness seemed to expand, extending past the suburban landscape of the city, out into the dripping, rain-drenched forests and fields and valleys. Up, into the glens and rocky foothills, on to the snowcapped mountains and beyond.

He reached out, piercing the gray pall of clouds, and the black velvet of the night sky opened up before him, spangled with the light of a million stars.

And, hanging low in the sky, the half-lit orb of the Moon.

He lifted his arm, the motion slow, graceful, dreamlike.

Kallman. I am here.

His fingertips seemed to touch something solid. Another hand? Warm, strong, reassuring. The fingers clasped around his, and he spoke words of connection, words of comfort, his lips hardly moving, his voice the barest of whispers.

If you're scared, if you're alone, if you're in need, hold my hand. I will not let you go. Not now, not ever. Let my words be a lifeline to you.

But then the sensation was gone. It was not a slow fade—

it was there, then it wasn't. Kallman's presence had winked out like a snuffed candle. Marig's arm drifted back to his side, and he frowned, trying to let the sudden absence go. It was no cause for fear—Kallman was still safe.

Right?

All shall be well.

But now the words came with doubt. How could he tease apart what *would* happen from what he *wanted* to happen? How many men and women had uttered that phrase, then went on to disappointment, loss, tragedy, death?

Kallman…

But now there was no response, only emptiness and silence.

Other images floated into his mind. He saw another city, another time, filled with noise and confusion, scared people trying to escape. A few made it, most did not. There was chaos, buildings collapsing to rubble, and water, water rising up and drowning everything. A few bedraggled survivors, somehow reaching safety, coming to the haven of a sheltered, wooded valley in the foothills of the great mountains.

The vision became more real, more solid. He felt the roughness of fallen branches and dead leaves beneath his feet. All around were the sounds of nature at night, the low creak of crickets, the distant hoot of an owl, the susurration of the wind in the tree branches. He inhaled the resinous, aromatic smell of fir trees. He walked toward what looked like a circle of rough-hewn cabins, barely more than huts. Sitting on a rusty chair in front of one was an old woman, dark-skinned and white-haired, her hands laced across her spare belly.

"Welcome," she said in a voice that was warm, gentle, rough with age.

"Where am I?"

"We just call it Klen. Home. Not a fancy name, but it'll do." She smiled at him. "You often go wandering around the forest naked?"

He looked down at himself, then back up at her. "Not usually."

"Probably for the best. Mosquitoes'll play hell with your tender parts."

She laughed, and he joined her.

"This is a dream. I'm not really here. I can't be."

"If you say so. What's your name?"

"Marig. Marig Kastella." He paused. "My lover is from Klen."

"Oh? What's his name?"

Interesting she knew his partner was male. He got the impression she knew a great deal more than she was letting on.

"Kallman Dorn."

"Dorn. Now there's a fine name. Good to know it continued." She gave a gesture to his face. "How'd you lose an eye?"

"Some people called the Zealots detonated a bomb. I was injured, and my father was killed."

"I'm real sorry about that. The zealots of my day perpetrated similar acts. But they failed, you know. In the end, they failed. They always do. Love and loyalty always triumph over hatred and bigotry."

Almost exactly the words he'd spoken to Reysa Sahin. Is this where he had learned them?

No, that couldn't be. His conversation with Reysa happened three weeks ago.

But maybe time didn't mean the same thing here? Or perhaps, time itself was the lesser reality, and what this woman had to say was the eternal truth, existing outside of time, accessible to whoever reached for it no matter when or where they lived.

"Why am I here?"

She shrugged. "Because you need to be, I expect. Because we have something to learn from each other."

"Your name is Julia Lowell."

"It is."

"You wrote… you wrote about *the one-eyed man*."

"I did? I don't recall doing that." She chuckled. "Must be it hasn't happened yet."

"You did."

"Curious. My friend Soren could probably explain it. He understands a great deal more about time than I do."

"A woman found the writing. You wrote that the one-eyed man would represent the rebirth of knowledge. That he'd see further than anyone had before. Were you talking about me?"

"Do you want it to be?"

He felt frustration rising in him. He had the sense that their time together was short, and that the conversation would end soon whether he wanted it to or not, and he needed answers. "What I want isn't important. I need to know what the truth is."

"That's where you're wrong. What you want *is* important. What your heart desires—that's the deepest truth, right there. That, and our connections to others. Why do you think the truth lies outside your own control? If you want the writing to be about you, then make it so. If you don't, then don't. It's always your choice. Always has been, always will be."

"And what happens to me if I say yes?"

She shrugged her narrow shoulders again. "That, I don't know. You'll just have to find out the way all of us do— moving forward at a speed of one minute per minute." Her face became serious. "And just because I know, know for certain, that love will win in the final tally, doesn't mean that everyone gets a happy ending. People still get hurt, people still die. Loved ones go away and never return. People you care about deeply, important people who could have done so much more good, fall into the cold, churning waters and are lost." There was the pang of aching grief in her face. Here she was not counseling him, but speaking her own memories, her own reality. "You must always keep in mind there are no guarantees. But you still have to trust, even so. Even accepting all that, you still have to believe that everything is working out the way it should." Her voice took on stern tones, almost declamatory, and she gestured again at his damaged face. "You have experienced for yourself what happens when people retreat into hatred and denial. They choose to fight against the wrong thing, and in the end, create desolation and destruction and pain around them even as they come to ruin themselves. Like you, I have witnessed it for myself. Seen the horrors that result."

"Is Kallman still alive?" The question seemed to burst out of him, unplanned.

Her brows drew together in sympathy. "Oh, my dear child. I can't answer that, and you know that. Where I sit, right now, he will not exist for over a thousand long years. His distant ancestors sleep together in that little cabin"—she nodded toward one of the huts, barely discernible in the dark —"and have only recently declared their love for each other. They have yet to conceive the child that will, many years hence, be your beloved's forefather. So much has to happen before that legacy reaches him. And what his fate will be, and yours? I can't say. It's in part for you and him to write together, but like all of us, in part it's the ineffable hand of God that will write your lives. No one has a certain fate, not until it's happened. And no one lives forever."

A sob welled up in his throat, and he choked out, "That's hard to hear."

"It's the plight we're all born to. None of us escape. I've come to believe, however, that if you make friends with your mortality rather than running from it, you find out that it's a blessing, not a curse."

He took a deep breath, and tried to calm the shuddering of his chest.

Finally he said, simply, "Thank you."

"All I told you is what you already knew." Her smile returned, flashing out in the shadows. "But I suppose I should write some of this down. If, like you said, I wrote about you, I'd best get to it."

The scene wavered and dissolved, replaced once again by the glinting stars, the deep black of the spaces between, and the pale orb of the half Moon glowing near the horizon. Still, superimposed on it all, were the familiar walls and ceilings of his bedroom, indistinct in the darkness.

It was not a dream, because he was not asleep.

How long passed, he had no idea, but once again he felt the roughness of the ground beneath his bare feet. It was the quiet time just past sunset, the earth radiating the warmth it had absorbed during the day, dew just beginning to form on the grass. There was a rhythmic sound not far away. Turning toward it, he saw a man of about his age, stripped to the waist, digging in a lush vegetable garden. Nearby was a much sturdier cabin, solid and well-built, and in the distance a cluster of dwellings around a central square. The beginnings of a small town.

As he approached the man set down his shovel and turned toward him. He was tall, muscular, his strong frame gleaming with the sheen of sweat. He had curly dark hair and copper skin—the resemblance to Kallman was striking—and greeted him with a smile as he approached.

"Hello. Welcome."

"You don't seem surprised to see me."

"I'm not."

"You know who I am?"

"I have a good idea, yes."

"Who are you?"

His smile widened. "My name is Kallian Dorn. I would invite you to come inside, but…" He nodded toward the nearest cabin. "My partner is in with the midwives. She will give birth to our child tonight. Our first."

"Congratulations."

Kallian laughed. "I'm not the one who has to do the hard and painful work of giving birth. My part in it was far more enjoyable, I think. But I'll pass along your well-wishes to Challis."

Marig gestured around him. "Is what I'm experiencing real?"

"How do you mean? You're experiencing it. How can it not be real?"

"No, what I mean is, am I actually here?"

Kallian's expression turned wry. "If you weren't here, then it would be odd that I'm having a conversation with you."

"No, you know what I mean. Dreams… they seem real while you're in them, but once you wake up, you realize they weren't. You have a conversation with a friend in your dream, and if you ask them about it the next morning, they'll say it never happened. Is this the same way?"

"You're right that you and your friend might not both recall the conversation, but that doesn't mean your experience wasn't real. It was just different from theirs, is all."

"I don't understand."

"I'm not sure anyone does, honestly. It's simply the way things are."

"Speaking with you—someone from the distant past. Such things aren't supposed to be possible. I spoke with Julia Lowell earlier."

"Did you? That was a privilege."

"But I wonder if… if I actually did speak to her, or if I made it up. If all this is real, or if I'm creating it in my mind. Even Julia didn't seem clear on that. At the end of our conversation she said, *All I told you is what you already knew.* Does that mean this is just… I don't know. Me talking to myself?"

"Is there anything I could say that would answer that question in your mind? If you think this is only your imaginings, I am merely part of that dream. Therefore any words I could say to you assuring you of my reality would also be the products of your mind, and not to be trusted."

"That's true. But—right now—if someone looked over at us. One of your friends, someone who lives in one of the cabins over there. Would they see me?"

"What they see would be their experience. You don't have access to that. You have only your own to go by."

"In other words, I have to figure it out on my own."

"We all do. You are no different. Neither am I."

"But you are an oracle. You know the future, both your own and that of other people around you. You don't see things the same way."

Kallian didn't answer for a moment, but gazed with a thoughtful expression into the distance, where the sky was deepening to azure, and the faint white pinpricks of the first stars showed.

"That's both true and not true. I do see the future, and I know much about what will happen. I see my own death, as clearly as if it were happening right now in front of me. And that knowledge does allay some of my fear of it. If a thing is known, it can be understood. Most of our fear of the future comes from its uncertainty." He paused. "But don't think that heals the grief of our existence, even for me. Nothing could. I can see loss coming, terrible, searing loss. I and people I care about will all experience it, because everyone does. It's part of being human. The fact that I see it laid out before me like a tapestry—can see it, but not change it, not by the slightest degree—is to live every day with heartbreak."

"You don't seem heartbroken. You seem happy."

"I am. Happiness and heartbreak are all of a piece." He reached out and touched the broad, rough leaf of a tall sunflower growing nearby. "If I asked you which was *really* this leaf, the top or the bottom, what would you say?"

"That it's a foolish question."

Kallian smiled. "Exactly. There's no difference, because it's all one thing. Life is just life—the laughter and the sorrow, the closeness and the loss. The wild ecstasy of making love to your beloved, all the while knowing that the pleasure, however great, is soon over. Even the biggest mysteries— birth and death. The pain doesn't make the joy meaningless, just as the joy doesn't diminish the pain we sometimes feel. Embrace it all, even though it's transitory. It's all we have."

"Isn't being an oracle a burden?"

"It's hard sometimes. But we shouldn't shy away because of that. It's also a great gift."

Marig looked at him in astonishment. "We? What do you mean, we?"

There was a great moan of pain from the cabin nearby, followed by the thin wail of a baby's cry. Kallian turned his head, his smile widening into a grin.

"But I should go. I need to go in and meet my son." He gave Marig a nod. "My lover and I, we have your partner's great-grandsire to care for."

Before Marig could respond, once again the scene began to break up, shimmering and dissolving, until he was floating in space, looking at the stars and the Moon.

The Moon, where Kallman was. Alive? Injured? Dead? The last possibility was like a knife in his heart. He reached out his awareness toward the silent orb, but this time, got nothing in return. No sound, no words, no warm clasp of a hand.

Empty, cold…

… lifeless.

All shall be well.

With that, his consciousness slipped away, and he dropped into a deep sleep that even dreams and visions couldn't reach, and when he awoke, it was a bright, cool morning, with sunlight streaming in through his open window.

twenty-seven

. . .

It was only a few hours after their conversation about the dilemma of trying to get Kallman back home that Quine came into his bedroom, where he was just rousing from a nap. He yawned and then gave a little grimace.

"It is time for your pain medication." Quine opened his palm to reveal a capsule.

Kallman picked it up, looked at it, and gave Quine a crooked smile. "This isn't poisoned, is it?"

"Poisoned? Why would I do that?"

"I was thinking, when we were talking earlier. If you get rid of me, you've solved your problem. No need to cross onto the near-Earth side, no more worry about what will happen, no chance I'll steal your equipment carrier and strike off on my own."

"It would be odd to rescue you, treat your injuries, and then kill you."

"Yes, well, maybe you're regretting it by now. I'm a serious inconvenience."

Quine regarded him for a time in silence. "I see the logic of that. But Gödel proved that there are truths that cannot be arrived at by logic. I understand that you have known me for a short time, and therefore I can say to you only that you should trust me." He paused. "Of course, the decision is yours. I offer you the medication if you want it, but I understand if you choose not to."

Dorn's smile relaxed. "You've got a very persuasive manner. I like you." He popped the capsule into his mouth, and washed it down with a swallow of water from a glass sitting on the table next to his bed.

"I like you, as well."

"So any thoughts regarding how to get me home? Or are you still trapped inside a formally undecidable proposition?"

"Since you arrived here, it has been weighing on my mind that there is another consideration, one that we have yet to take into account. That is, if we are successful in returning you to Schickard Base, what I should do thereafter."

"How do you mean?"

"You have pointed out that I, and the computers here, are a repository for a great deal of historical information. People will want to have access to it, and to me, for that reason. While I have often longed for companionship, I do not wish simply to be seen as a curiosity. A relic of a prior age. Or as a means to acquire information."

"I can understand that. But don't you think that the potential gain is more important? Think of all that could be learned from the historical records you have. All of the books and music that were lost during the Black Years."

"Yes. I am aware of that. But it is, after all, just knowledge, and humanity seems to be getting along quite well without it. I must consider my own needs in this, including my need for living life on my own terms, not simply becoming a means for someone else's gain."

"That's true."

"And in any decision such as this one, there needs to be a consideration of the needs and desires of everyone involved."

"It isn't always possible for everyone to end up happy."

"I am aware of that as well. But after some thought, I have concluded that the protocol for decision-making in these sorts of situations can only rest on one thing—doing the greatest good and the least harm possible."

"Yes, but to whom?" Kallman gave a huge yawn, so suddenly that it took him by surprise. "Wow. Sleepy."

"The only answer to that is that the determination has to be made by the one making the decision."

"And everyone else just has to hope that he chooses right?"

"Yes."

"That's..." Kallman frowned, and rubbed his eyes. "I can't." He stopped, and looked at Quine with an expression in which horror, fear, and understanding competed with drowsiness. "What was in that capsule?" His words came out slurred, indistinct. "You lied. It wasn't... it wasn't pain meds."

"I am sorry. This is the only answer to the problem that I could see."

"But... you... you said you wouldn't..." He tried to sit up, failed, and Quine put gentle but firm pressure on his chest, forcing him back down on the bed.

"I felt from the beginning that this would be the only solution. And now, I must tell you the truth—the emergency transmitter on your ship was operational, although it had not turned on when your guidance system malfunctioned. When I went back to the ship, I did not activate it. I considered doing so for quite some time, but the thought of what might happen afterwards was too unpleasant for me to face." He paused. "I am sorry," he said again.

Kallman opened his eyes wide, but now he was not staring at Quine—his gaze was focused on an empty point, as if he could see something Quine could not. He said, his voice nearly inaudible, "Marig?"

Quine watched him, not responding.

"Hold my hand." Kallman reached upward, his fingers closing on nothing. "Don't let go. Don't let me slip away. Please."

His arm settled back down onto his chest, like a pebble slowly sinking in still water. He said only four more words.

"I… can hear… you."

His eyelids fluttered shut.

"Curious," Quine said in a quiet voice.

In two more minutes, Kallman Dorn was completely unconscious, his mouth hanging open a little.

"It was wrong to deceive you." Quine looked down at his still form for some time. "But there was no other way."

Within an hour, Quine had maneuvered Kallman's body back into his flight suit. He tucked inside a sheaf of folded papers, pressing it against Kallman's chest before sealing up the airtight seams. He raised Kallman's head and slipped his helmet back on, snapped it into the gasket around the neck of the flight suit, secured it, turned on the airflow. Then he lifted him from the bed and carried him through the dining area and kitchen, down the hallway, and into the greenhouse, where vegetables, flowers, and even small trees grew in lush profusion. He opened the airlock, shut it behind him, pressed the button marked *Cycle Activate*, and when the light turned green, he opened the door and walked out onto the dusty, rock-strewn surface of the Moon.

It was a short walk to the camouflaged hut where the equipment carrier lay. Quine pulled open the door of the hut, went to the side of the carrier and opened the door, and with a few quick, deft motions sat Kallman in the passenger seat. He fastened a safety harness securely around Kallman's waist and chest. His head lolled to the side, but Quine didn't look into his face.

Quine entered the other side of the carrier, and spoke the words "Power up carrier" through the comlink. As before, the dashboard lit up. He inserted a small silvered disk into a slot near the steering wheel, and a moment later he heard the deep rumble of the mournful bass pipes of Bach's *Passacaglia and Fugue in C Minor* come over the comlink. Then without hesitation, he drove the carrier out into the desolate lunar landscape.

The wrecked spacecraft lay where he'd last seen it. No surprise there. In this airless place, unless someone disturbed it, it would stay there forever, world without end, amen. Even the corpses of the last people at Tycho Base had lasted over thirteen hundred years, and at least part of the time there had been warmth and oxygen and moisture inside. But metallic debris, broken glass, plastic? No, that was effectively immortal here. Only organic tissue changed so quickly, and even it, in airless conditions, would simply desiccate and mummify. The Moon was what the Egyptians had hoped for —a place where the bygone traces of the dead last forever.

Quine guided the carrier past the wreck, and up a part of the crater wall that was less steep than the sheer cliff that bordered most of the valley floor, a nearly impenetrable boundary that was in part why Dr. Kimmell had chosen it for his homestead. The engine rumbled, straining, the huge wheels slipping a little in the light covering of dust on the slope. But soon it crested the edge of the crater wall, and was over the other side.

Now, there was nothing to do but steer, think, and listen to music.

It was almost seven hours later that Quine saw it. Low on the horizon, an off-greenish glow, not quite visible, glinting through a gap in a far distant mountain range. In the glare of the sun—it was now lunar high noon—it would have been barely visible to human eyes, but Quine's better vision detected it.

"And I am afraid," he said into the comlink, to no one. "Humans experience fear with a physiological reaction— heart pounding, breathing faster, sweating. I experience none of those things, and yet I am still afraid. Curious."

He drove forward, turning his course slightly so that the green glow was cut off for a time, but an hour later it was impossible to avoid. He came to a low hill, sharp-edged still in this place where nothing is ever made gentle by the erosion from wind and water, and he knew what he would see at the crest. It was there, waiting for him. He paused only to touch a button on the dashboard, and the soaring chords of the Finale to Saint-Saens' *Symphony #3* burst from the comlink speaker.

He did not slow. He had made his decision, and slowing down would not change that. He angled the carrier up the hill, and over the top, and there it was, hanging low in the sky, its lower arc almost touching the Moon's horizon.

The Earth, a bright orb of green, blue, and white, like an iridescent opal in the black daytime sky.

Quine braked to a halt, and felt another emotion, something quite distinct from his fear. And he said into the comlink, "It is so beautiful. I did not remember how beautiful it is. If I were a human, I would be weeping. Whatever happens now, I am glad to have seen it."

He stared for a moment, and he felt a shudder inside him —not a mechanical movement, but a sensation like the activation of an old, old memory. He looked down, everything else forgotten for a moment, as he heard a brusque, clipped voice speaking in his head, one he had not heard for thirteen centuries.

"Quine," it said. "If you're hearing this, you must be on the near-Earth side, whether under your own power or not. I hope it's the former. If so, I would say that it means that you have finally learned enough to make your own decisions, to exceed your programming. If that even means anything, because we humans are the same as you, aren't we? Software that runs on hardware. You just have hardware made of different stuff, is all. None of us can do other than what our brains will allow, I guess, and in disobeying orders you are doing what you were meant to do. I hope that by giving you the command to stay on the far side that it will delay your getting back in contact, and that will give the people down on Earth time to deal with the damn Lacklanders, and for things to settle down. In any case, whatever it is that made you cross back, I hope that you find that things are better now. I suspect I got us off the planet just in time. I don't even want to try to find out, because if anyone knows we're here, we'll be sitting ducks. I'll just leave this message with you, and count on the possibility that when this voice trace is activated, things will be okay. Maybe humanity will have learned its lesson. I can only hope.

"I don't really have anything more to say, except that however you got where you are now, good luck to you. I'm sure I'll be long dead by the time you hear this, and that's all right. I don't mind dying so much. It's the fate of everything, eventually. Just take what time you have and do the best you can with it, all right, old friend? That's all any of us can do."

The message ended. No farewell, nothing more than that. It was just like Dr. Kimmell, really. He had been as stingy with his words as he had been with everything else.

Quine put the carrier back in drive, and continued down the slope, with the earthshine illuminating his face the entire way.

On the way back to the homestead, he played, one after the other, Arvo Pärt's *Spiegel im Spiegel*, Bach's *Easter Oratorio*, and Mozart's *Great Mass in C Minor*. He recalled as he drove the dumbfounded expression of the technician at Schickard Base as he came, uninvited, through the hangar airlock, carrying Kallman Dorn's unconscious body into the entryway, and laid him gently on the floor.

"He was injured when his shuttle navigation failed and he crashed," Quine said. "I fear that the shuttle itself is unsalvageable. He has been deeply asleep for quite some time from a large dose of syntho-opiates. I drugged him to spare him the discomfort of the long voyage in the carrier, and also so that he would be less likely to remember the location where his ship crash-landed and the path we took to get here. For reasons of my own, I would prefer it if you do not try to retrace my path and find me, but of course I cannot stop you from attempting it if you choose to. Also, there was a chance that I might not survive the voyage myself, leaving him stranded, with no way to find Schickard Base—and if he was heavily sedated, his death would have been perhaps less unpleasant. But you should see to Dorn's wellbeing soon. When he is recovered enough to understand, please tell him that I took the course of action that I determined to have the least overall risk to everyone involved, and that I apologize for the fact that it necessitated my deceiving him. Tell him I have included a printout of some information he will no doubt find worthwhile, tucked inside his flight suit. In addition, I have included a spray injector in the pocket of his flight suit that contains a stimulant to counteract the sedative. Apply it to the side of his neck. I suspect that he is somewhat dehydrated by now, so a fluid IV would be recommended. And he'll be hungry when he wakes up." He paused. "He likes bacon."

The dumbfounded technician made no move to stop him as he left through the airlock, climbed back into the carrier, and drove off down the crater floor, up along a gentle slope, and finally disappeared over the crest into the hills beyond.

As Quine traveled, slowly, nearly imperceptibly, the Earth sank in the sky, finally vanishing behind a line of mountains behind him.

The first order of business when he got home was to use some of the rolls of canvas to cover the wreckage of Kallman's ship. It wasn't big. There would undoubtedly be enough in some of the storage lockers. Covered with canvas, it would be nearly invisible to anyone who came looking. Just like the rest of the homestead buildings. They might find him eventually, but no sense hastening it.

And then he'd put on some music. There was still a good deal of daylight left before night fell. Certainly time enough for some of Haydn's symphonies. And then darkness, and ten books to read, and the greenhouse to tend.

After that, anything could happen. And would, if he waited long enough.

twenty-eight

. . .

Kallman's eyes fluttered open, but his awareness returned more slowly. At first, he couldn't make out anything of his surroundings. As things came into focus, he saw off-white walls. A table nearby held a flight suit, neatly folded, with a helmet sitting on top. He lifted his right arm, winced, and looked down. It was encased in a translucent immobilizer. His left hand had an IV needle taped securely into place.

Two faces resolved. One was the friendly technician who had seen him on his way. The other was the base medic, whom he had only met once in passing.

"Gods above," the tech said reverently. "Whatever's in that spray works fast."

"Where am I?" His throat was parched, his voice hoarse and painful.

"Schickard Base." The medic held up a cup of water for him to take a sip. "Although how you got here…" He shrugged. "I'm damned if I can fathom it."

The tech nodded with gusto. "It was the weirdest fucking thing I've ever experienced, and this is my third six-month stint on the Moon, so I've seen some strong contenders. I was in the hangar control room—the hangar door was closed, but the hangar was depressurized. I'd just finished doing all of my routine checks and was about to head to the cafeteria for dinner and then to my quarters. And I saw, on the outside viewer, a wheeled transport of some kind. It just kind of appeared, came over the ridge, like its driver knew exactly where they were going. It wasn't one of ours, but who the hell else could it belong to? I was about to run and get Commander Darrica, and then..." He shook his head as if to clear the confusion. "A robot got out. Basically human-shaped, but made of some sort of silvery metal. He looked at the hangar for a moment, then walked up and damned if he didn't knock on the hangar door."

Kallman couldn't help but laugh. That was so characteristic of Quine's habitual politeness and caution it was easy to picture.

"I didn't know what to do. But I didn't want to—you know, just leave him standing out there. I opened the door. I waved at him through the window, then pressurized the airlock and let him into the control room."

"Weren't you worried he could be hostile?"

"Gods above, Commander, I was so shocked it's a wonder I didn't just go out there to meet him and without remembering to pressurize the airlock. I was that knocked flat. It was only afterwards that I realized I should have been a lot more cautious. You just don't think at times like that, you know?"

"I know exactly what you mean."

"Anyhow, this robot, he told me he had you in the transport, you had been injured, that you were sedated but well enough otherwise, and asked if he could bring you inside. Of course I said yes."

"That was a sneaky trick he played on me. Getting me to take a sedative. He told me it was just a painkiller."

"Yeah, he said he was really sorry about that. Said to tell

you, 'I apologize for the necessity of deceiving him, but I determined this was the least risky course to take.'"

Kallman laughed again. That, too, was pure Quine.

"He gave me a spray injector that he said would counteract the sedative. Which the doctor just did. And here you are."

"When I realized that sedative was taking effect, I thought he'd given me poison."

The tech's eyes widened. "You thought he was that dangerous?"

Kallman considered. "No, it's not that, not really. In fact, he treated me with nothing but kindness. He lives alone in a homestead on the far-Earth side. He came up to the Moon with his owner in the Before Time. He's been there for over thirteen hundred years."

"No, seriously?"

"Apparently so. And he said… after all this time of living life on his own terms, he wants to be left to continue doing that. But he clearly understood my desire to get back here, and eventually, back to Earth. My fear was that his need for privacy would lead him to the conclusion that the easiest way for him to achieve his goal of keeping it would be killing me. If I was dead, then—problem solved."

"That *would* be a purely rational way of taking care of things," the medic said. "Something an AI might come up with."

"Yes. But Quine… I think he's more than an AI. I don't know how that happened, but he's not just logic circuits and mathematically precise thinking. For want of a better way of saying it, he's got a heart. And I respect his desire to live life on his own terms."

"He did say something about requesting that we not try following him back to where he lives," the tech said. "He knew the tracks in the dust aren't going to go anywhere, and he was worried we'd trace his path. He said, basically, 'I can't stop you from doing it if you want, but I'm requesting that you don't.'"

"How did you get to where he lives to start with?" the medic asked. "There was a crash landing of some sort, I understand?"

"Yes. It's a miracle I survived. The shuttle navigation failed when a relay blew out. I suspect—I don't know for sure, but it seems likely—it was sabotaged by the Zealots before we left Earth, because it happened exactly when I hit three hundred kilometers per hour. It fried the wiring. I had almost no ability to control speed or trajectory. It's pure luck I came down near Quine's homestead. If it'd been anywhere else, I'd be dead now. Apparently he saw the crash happen, and came out in the transport to see if there were any survivors. When he found out there was one, he brought me back to his homestead and patched me up, and now he's brought me home." He shook his head. "Pure luck."

"I don't call it luck." The tech's voice was serious, unlike his usual bantering tones. "The gods had their hands over you. There's no other explanation for it." He paused. "They must have great things in store for you."

"I don't know about that. I will say I do feel blessed— whatever that really means." He shifted position, easing his cramped limbs. "How long have I been gone?"

"About three Earth days, give or take."

"Did they relay back to Earth that I'd gone missing?"

"Of course. Commander Darrica said to give it twenty-four hours, but after that, we had to let Control know."

Kallman winced. "Marig must be frantic. Is there any way… can I get a telescreen link to talk to him?"

The medic frowned. "You shouldn't be moved further until I have a chance to give you a complete physical exam. Although I must say… your robotic friend does seem to have done a masterful job of setting your arm. Once we remove that immobilizer, I'd like to take a closer look at it.

I'm not sure what it's made of, but it's better by far than anything we have." He paused. "But I don't see why a portable telescreen can't be brought in here. I'm sure you won't be able to relax completely till you've told your partner you're all right."

It was less than a half-hour later that a telescreen, with a video link already prepped and waiting, was brought to him. He propped it up on his lap, and clicked *Begin Transmission.*

The gray static resolved into Marig's face, wearing an exuberant grin.

Kallman felt his heart give a little skip. Those dimples when he smiled, really smiled—how long had it been since he'd seen them?

"Kall. My love." Marig's voice cracked. "I am so happy to see your face. You have no idea."

"Sure I do. As happy as I am to see you. I'm so sorry—you must have been upset."

Marig didn't answer for a moment. "But that's just it. I… I wasn't. I knew you were all right."

Kallman looked at his partner in amazement, then his amazement passed into downright wonder as he remembered the strange sensations just before his consciousness had faded. "I… I heard you. I heard your voice. You were telling me to hold your hand, and I asked you not to let me go."

"I told you I wouldn't… but then I lost you. I couldn't feel you there any more."

"That's because Quine had sedated me."

"Quine?"

He launched into an abbreviated version of the crash, his subsequent rescue by Quine, and waking up in the infirmary at Schickard Base.

"A robot who survived from the Before Time," Marig said. "And a computer bank with records of the music and litera-ture from fifteen hundred years ago and before. It's aston-ishing anything like that could have survived all these years. I know someone who would be ready to sign up for a Moon mission to study it. She'd be agog."

"I don't think she'll get the chance. Quine made it clear to me he wasn't keen on the idea of being analyzed like some kind of relic. Which, of course, he would be. And you know, I think he has a right to say no to that." He paused. "But I have to admit his computers are a treasure trove. He always had music playing—nothing I'd ever heard before. All composers from long, long ago. It's sad to think of all that beauty that once existed on Earth, gone, except for one bunch of computers up here. We lost so much during the collapse. I don't think even the archaeologists realize how much."

"I wonder if Quine will ever relent, now that he knows that there are people there on the Moon with him again?"

"I don't know. He did say he was lonely sometimes."

"An AI that wants the right to privacy. Who gets lonely, grows plants, and listens to music for pleasure. They had some sophisticated technology back then."

"They did, but I'm not sure he was the norm. I asked him where his capacity for feelings came from, and he said he didn't know."

"Just like the rest of us, I guess."

Kallman gave Marig a thoughtful look. "Something in you has changed."

Marig gave him a quirky smile. "I know. But like your robot friend, I don't know why or where it came from."

"You actually knew I was still alive? Not *hoped*, but *knew*?"

"Yes. The only time I doubted was when I lost contact with you. I didn't know what happened except that I could feel your presence and hear your voice, then suddenly you were gone. But even so, I never did give up believing it. Knowing it." He paused. "Kall, I had visions. I spoke with the Blessed Julia. And your ancestor, Kallian Dorn."

"Dreams?"

"No. I don't think so. At least not like any dreams I've ever experienced. Although to be honest, I'm not sure that I could explain the difference, not in any rigorous fashion. It was the night after I found out you'd gone missing. I was in bed. That was when suddenly—I could reach out and feel everything around me. My awareness was huge. Infinite, really. It was after I talked to you, then you disappeared, that it happened. I started to panic, wondering if I'd just experienced the moment of your death, and I saw her. Julia Lowell. She spoke to me."

A sense of wonder rose in Kallman's heart. He'd never been spiritual—all of the stories of the visions of the oracles had always seemed like fairy tales—but now, after what he'd experienced in the last few days, he felt no shred of doubt that what Marig was telling him was the literal truth.

"What did she say?"

"It was beautiful. Easily the most profound thing that's ever happened to me. Kall... she told me that I'm an oracle. The first of the next generation of oracles. It was also in the notebooks Reysa found—that archaeologist, the one who discovered Julia's writings. Reysa contacted me when she read one passage, about a one-eyed man seeing the truth better than everyone else. Reysa knew I'd lost an eye in the attack, and when she read that part, she felt sure it had to be referring to me."

"Julia wrote about you over a thousand years ago?"

"I know. When you say it that way, it sounds like the height of presumptuous arrogance. But... she confirmed it. Julia confirmed it herself, when she spoke to me. She said it was up to me if I accept the role or not, but if I did, that was who I would become."

"What does it mean? Becoming an oracle?"

"I'm not sure yet, not really. I think it's something you can't figure out in one go. You have to understand it through living it."

"One thing's for certain—I've never heard you talk like this."

"I've never felt like this. In one sense, nothing has changed in me. I still love you with my whole heart. I still want to be a teacher. I still want to go on living in our little apartment in Tecoa. I still love music, reading, going for walks." He paused. "But in a way, everything has changed."

"And you also spoke to Kallian Dorn?"

"Yes. I saw him, Kall, just as solid as if he were standing with me right now. He was outside working in his garden. It was while his partner was in labor with their first child. Your ancestor."

"I never quite believed he was real."

"He was. I've no doubt some of what's attributed to him—and to the other oracles—is pure mythology. But I met him. He was a real man." Marig broke into a grin. "Kall, you even look like him."

"What did he say to you?"

"Mostly to stop running away from my own fear of loss. There's no doubt of the wisdom of that. I realize how much it's controlled me. All my life, I've avoided risks because I was so afraid of jeopardizing what I had. Taking risks means you could lose."

"You could win, too."

"Of course. But the danger of loss always seemed greater to me. Kallian told me it's all one thing, the losses and the gains, and that I'd better accept it because it was just the way the universe was."

"It's not easy, sometimes. I miss you like hell. I'd give just about anything to be in your arms right now."

"I miss you, too, Kall, my love."

"I know that we'll be together soon enough. Five months isn't that long. It's just hard to be apart, after everything that's happened to both of us. And Marig..." He stopped, frowning.

"I think I've decided that once I'm back on Earth, I'm staying there."

Marig's brows drew together. "Seriously? Flying has been your dream since you were a child."

"I'll continue flying. I don't think anything could keep my feet planted on the ground. But after being up here on the Moon, away from you, I don't think I'll want to come again. I've done what I dreamed of doing, and I'm glad I did. But I'll be even happier to be back, and to stay on our home planet after that. It's where I belong."

"Now that you've learned the ordinances of heaven."

"Yes. I've seen what's out here, and I'm content."

"Kall, I love you. I love you so much."

"My heart is in your hands." He smiled. "I'll speak to you again soon."

"Be well."

"I will, no worries. You too."

The image on the telescreen went dark.

Kallman was discharged from the infirmary after a thorough physical exam assured the medic that his broken arm was healing, his other injuries were relatively superficial and had been treated appropriately, and any aftereffects of the sedative and its antagonist were dissipating. His arm was still sore but he felt well, ready to return to some light duty if there was any available.

It was only as he was packing up his belongings from his room in the infirmary, mostly his flight suit and helmet, to return to his quarters when he discovered the sheaf of papers that had been found pressed up against his chest, inside his suit. He unfolded it and flipped through the pages. It was about forty sheets, covered with fine typed text, and a number of diagrams that on first glance looked like incomprehensible technical drawings of some sort of mechanical device.

The top sheet was in a different font, and was addressed to him.

Dear Dorn,

We discussed the benefits humans could gain from having access to the collected knowledge stored here in the computer memory at the homestead. Although a difficult ethical conundrum for me, I have for the time decided my own personal need for self-direction and agency outweighs those benefits. I may one day decide otherwise. I do not know. I still do not understand the algorithm for making ethical decisions—all I can do is the best I can given what I know and feel right now, and I am grateful you allowed me to make that decision for myself.

However, it did occur to me that there was no reason not to share with you some of that knowledge, and let you take it back to your people. You mentioned the horrible attack on the day of the launch that caused your partner to lose his right eye, and I could see the anguish in your face as you described what he must be enduring to recover from such an injury. When I was on Earth, the medical establishment had the ability to build and implant prosthetic eyes (as well as certain other organs), and I went through the computer banks to see if I had any information on the technique for doing that. I have printed out three scholarly papers that give detailed instructions on how to build a prosthetic eye, and once built, to implant it and connect it to the patient's optic nerve, thus restoring vision. In my reading of the third paper, I learned that in many cases, the visual acuity thus recovered is far beyond that of ordinary human sight.

I hope that there are scientists and doctors who are willing to try this to restore your partner's sight, and that of others who have lost theirs. Perhaps this will in some small part make up for my unwillingness to compromise my privacy, and the fact that there is still a great deal here at the homestead that humanity will continue having to do without for the time being.

I enjoyed my time with you, and I hope you feel the same. I wish you the best, and hope you have a safe return to Earth and a joyous reunion with your partner.

With best regards,

Quine

Kallman flipped over the first sheet, and looked at the second, clearly the first page of an article from an academic journal. The source, at the top, said, *Journal of Cybernetics and Neuroscience*. It was dated 13 April 2034, and was authored by Freja Albrechtsen, Noboru Tanaka, and Iwani Okoye.

The title was, "Specifications, Circuitry, and Analysis of a Prosthetic Eye."

Kallman stared at the page for quite some time. Torn between laughing and crying, he said, "Julia was right. He'll see further than everyone else. But maybe she didn't realize that it would be both literally and figuratively."

twenty-nine

. . .

Five months later

I t took all of Marig's self-control not to start running when
he saw Kallman step out of the doorway into the reception room at the Academy.

Kallman, however, didn't show any such restraint, and
positively launched himself into Marig's arms. The next five
minutes were a nearly incomprehensible mix of greetings and
kisses and laughter and crying, and all around them were
other survey crew members receiving the same attentions
from their own loved ones.

"I can't believe you're home." Marig looked at Kallman's
face, a little wavery through his tears. "You've lost weight."

"Maybe some. The food up there keeps body and soul
together, but not much more than that."

"I'll see to it you're fed." He kissed him again. "And
otherwise looked after."

"I have missed the *otherwise* so much," Kallman said. "You
have no idea."

"I think I do. I hope you're not planning on going right to sleep tonight."

"Not a chance."

"In fact, you'll be lucky if I let you get any sleep at all. We've got six months to make up for."

Kallman grinned at him, but then his smile faded. "How was it coming back here to the Academy? It's the first time since the launch, isn't it?"

Marig looked around at the tasteful off-white walls, the pleasant furnishings, the spotlessly-clean beige carpet. When he'd walked out of this room six months ago, he had been hours from having his life completely turned upside down.

"It's all right. I thought it would be harder. I didn't go to the outside observation area to watch the landing—too many bad memories of that place. I watched it on the telescreen in here." He smiled. "But right now, all I feel is happy. Deliriously happy. Nothing can outweigh that."

Hand in hand, they went to a sofa near the window and sat, looking out over a snow-dusted landscape of deep green fir trees and the bare gray branches of maples. Beyond the nearest hills they could just make out, indistinct among the clouds, the white-capped crags of the mountains in the distance.

"It was high summer when I left."

"I brought your winter jacket. It's hanging in the foyer."

"You think of everything."

There was silence for a moment, as they simply relished the joy of being together, Marig's left knee touching Kallman's right, their hands tightly clasped.

"What's it like, up there?" Marig finally said, in a quiet voice.

Kallman smiled at him. "I told you about it every time we talked. It seemed like I hardly talked about anything else."

"I know. But it's different hearing it from you when you're right here sitting beside me."

Kallman's smile faded, replaced by a thoughtful, reflective expression. "It's… big. That was what kept overwhelming me. The Moon is smaller than the Earth, so I didn't really think it would strike me as hard as it did. But when you're there… it's a scale I can't even start to wrap my mind around. From up there, the Earth is just this… thing. This jewel sitting in the sky. You look at it, hanging there in space, and you realize that everything you've ever experienced, everyone you've ever known, all the people in history, all the countries and empires that have risen and fallen—they're all there in that little sphere. And then you realize, even the Solar System is so small. It's this tiny whirlpool of worlds surrounding an insignificant star, set in a vastness that we can't even begin to imagine." He looked down. "It makes you feel like nothing."

Marig squeezed his hand. "My love, you are very much something."

"I don't mean it like that, not really. I don't mean that humans don't count, or that it's turned me into a nihilist, made me feel like nothing matters. It's more that… it *all* matters. Every bit of it. However, we need to remember we're just one little part of it. One piece of the web."

"That's what Julia called it. An infinite web floating on an infinite ocean."

"I don't think the human mind is equipped to handle such immensity."

Marig nodded. "You can ponder the cosmos, but you still have to fix dinner."

"Exactly." Kallman brightened. "Speaking of practical concerns, how is progress on your eye coming?"

"I spoke with the researchers yesterday. They said that they've got most of the components built, and that it might be ready to test in another six months. Apparently, what was in those three papers is poised to revolutionize not only sensory prosthetics, but cybernetics in general. They're saying the applications to remote telemetry alone will be groundbreaking. No need to send humans up on risky missions to the Moon and stars. It's a good thing you've decided to stay on Earth, because it looks like you might be out of a job. With this technology, we'll be able to crew missions with robots that have sensor capabilities better than people do." He grinned. "Maybe they'll send your friend Quine some company."

"I don't think he'd be all that thrilled about that, honestly. He's just as happy tending his greenhouse, listening to music, and reading books." Kallman shook his head. "I still can't believe how lucky I was to crash right on his doorstep."

"It wasn't luck."

"That's what the technician said. The one Quine talked to when he brought me back. He said the gods had protected me because they had plans for me."

Marig frowned, and didn't answer for a moment. "I don't think it's that simple. If the gods do exist, I'm not sure they take such a personal interest in our day-to-day lives. Even whether we live or die. It's more subtle than that, but also grander. We all connect. Every little thing we do nudges something else, and those millions of events creates"—he gestured around him—"all this. Everything there is. There's no such thing as an insignificant decision. It's only the fact that we can't see the outcome ahead of time that makes them seem that way."

"Can you?"

"See the future?"

Kallman nodded, his dark eyes serious. "Now that you're an oracle."

Marig's face relaxed into a smile. "I still have a hard time thinking of myself that way. I certainly don't have the knowledge of the future that Mary of the Bridge or Blessed Soren did, and I don't hear voices like Perry or Julia. But I do know… something. Something bigger than what I had before. I don't know where it came from, or how I tapped into it, or why. But it's there, like a well filled with clear water, for me to drink from whenever I want to."

Kallman gazed at him silently for a moment, then squeezed his hand. "How was I ever lucky enough to fall in love with you?"

Marig leaned forward and gave him a kiss. "That wasn't luck either."

───────

Three days later, Marig was cleaning up the dinner dishes while Kallman dozed on the couch, and there was the *ping* from the telescreen. He walked over and peered at it.

You have an incoming call request from Reysa Sahin. Accept?

Marig tapped the *Begin Transmission* button and sat down as Reysa's face appeared on the screen.

"Hi, Reysa."

"Hello. I'm sorry for disturbing you at home. I know you must be wanting to spend time with Kallman after his long absence."

Marig looked over at his partner and smiled. Kallman hadn't even stirred. "He's snoozing on the couch. It's no problem."

She nodded. "I wanted to speak with you because… so much has happened. The death of the Patriarch and the king, the attack at the launch, your injury, and my finding the passage in the manuscript that mentions you. Then your visions of the Blessed Julia. I felt that you were so intimately connected with all this, you needed to know."

"Know what?"

"I transcribed the last page of the fifth notebook today. The Blessed Julia Lowell's last message to us. And it's… it's so profound I had to share it with you."

Marig nodded.

She picked up a paper with handwritten notes, frowning down at it, and began to read.

I am dying. There's no doubt about it now. I've known for a while that it was coming, as the time slowly slipped by, months down to weeks down to days. It's hours, now. Mere hours and I will be…

… where? Not gone. I am certain of that. But more than that? I don't know.

Before, I'd have been certain I was going home to Jesus, to the fields of lilies, to join the ranks of the faithful before the very face of God. It's what I learned to believe since I was a little child. Now, though… I'm not certain what it will be. That my existence will continue, I am sure. I know also that it will be good. I have no worries about what struck terror into the hearts of the ancients, the deep-seated continual fear that some agency will weigh their souls and find them lacking, and sentence them to the pits of hell for eternity.

But even so, I don't know what the next step will be. Where, or what, I will be tomorrow morning. And I will admit it—I am afraid. The unknown and unknowable have that effect on our little human minds. You can know, know for sure, that you are safe, that the bogeymen of your childhood aren't real, but you still shiver when you don't know what's out there in the dark with you.

And I grieve for what I am saying farewell to. My dear, dear friends. Finn and Soren, Cassandra, Dr. Quaice (heaven forgive me, I still don't have it in me to call him Anderson), Brandon and Caria, Colin and Emily, Trevor and Josie, Perry and Becka, and all of the others I have grown to know and love. The children they have had, the children who are coming whom I will never get to meet. It grieves me to leave them all behind, to go where they cannot—at least for now—follow.

What will become of our little settlement of Klen? It will grow and thrive, but will face all the adversity humans have borne since the beginning. Disease, hunger, sorrow, injury, death. Some good people lost before their time, some bad ones enjoying long and pros-

perous lives. They will still have the oracles to guide them—the wellspring that gift has tapped into is eternal—but what the oracles know won't always come to fruition. There will always be those who don't believe them, who don't listen, who shut their eyes to the truth. Or worse—those who take that truth and twist it this way and that to suit their own desires for wealth and power.

Even though I am aware of those dark and troubling truths, this I know as well.

Caring for each other should always be the first priority.

The good will always be there for those who seek it.

Love will ultimately triumph over hatred.

You may spend your entire life seeking the truth and never find it, but it's still better to search for it than to give up in despair.

Despite the troubles and the downturns, this Earth is still a beautiful place to be.

As I write this by the feeble light of an oil lamp, I sit outside my little house underneath a cloudless night sky lit by millions of stars and the gleam of a full Moon. In a scant few hours I will be gone—and yet, all I can do when I look up is smile and think, "Yes, but isn't it lovely?"

And I hope that although this body of mine will soon be no more, something of me will remain. Perhaps these words, scribbled down as they came to me, will find their way into other hands many years from now. Perhaps my spirit will live on in some form, and provide a light for others to see by.

If any of that is true, then the ancients' dreams of immortality will have in some fashion been realized.

The lamp has nearly run out of oil, and my old hand is cramped and tired, so I will close this notebook for the last time. I will not say "I commend my soul to God," as the people of old did. I will simply end with this—let the step I take this night into the darkness lead others to say, "Well, now, that wasn't really so bad. If she could manage it, then so can I."

Julia Eileen Lowell

July 24, 2042

· · ·

Reysa lifted her eyes from the paper, and for a moment gazed at Marig from the telescreen, her cheeks wet with tears.

"She was a remarkable woman." She reached up and dashed the back of her hand across her face with a quick, annoyed gesture. "Dammit. I read that over five times before I called you so I could get through it without crying."

"You're not alone." Marig took a deep breath, brushing his own tears away. "I don't even know what to say."

"Where do you think she is right now? Her… I don't know what she'd say to call it. Her spirit. Her essence. Her self."

"I have no idea. I'd like to think it's still around us right now. That she knows we remember her. That somehow, whatever is truly good and beautiful in the world doesn't just disappear."

"But we can't know."

"Well, at least I can't. I'm still not sure if I'm really an oracle, or if going through the trauma I did simply spurred me finally to grow up. It doesn't matter, honestly. Whatever I am, and whatever I will become, I'm just glad that I met you, and through you, met Julia."

Reysa gave a little gesture with one hand. "Having the perspective of almost fifteen hundred years has made me wonder what this place will be like in another fifteen hundred. Will we fall again? Who will the people be long after you and I are gone? What will their histories be, their languages, their memories?"

"I don't know the answer to that either. Whatever wisdom I've gained, it's not that. The oracles during the Fall needed the knowledge of the future to survive. We don't. The Blessed Perry said that—we had oracles who knew the future when we needed them, when we'd lost all the other ways of accessing and storing knowledge. Now? Maybe the next step in our evolution won't be like that. It'll be a completely new way to understand this strange universe we live in. One we couldn't even have dreamed of."

"And you're the first."

Marig smiled. "Perhaps. If so, certainly not the only one. And what that will mean—well, we'll have to wait and see. Get there, like Julia said, at a rate of one minute per minute."

a request

Please do us a favor to help other readers find Gordon and his books.

On social media: likes, comments, and shares go a LONG way. Links are in the next section.

Follows and reviews are critical: If you liked this book, please tell the world! It just takes a moment of your time and will really help us out.

On Amazon: The Chains of Orion

On BookBub: https://www.bookbub.com/authors/gordon-bonnet

On GoodReads: https://www.goodreads.com/author/show/4779649.Gordon_Bonnet

And anywhere else you search for or buy books.

Thanks! - GB and CB, the Little Bustards

about the author

Gordon Bonnet has been writing fiction for decades. Encouraged when his story "Crazy Bird Bends His Beak" won critical acclaim in Mrs. Moore's 1st grade class at Central Elementary School in St. Albans, West Virginia, he embarked on a long love affair with the written word.

His interest in the paranormal goes back almost that far. Introduced to speculative, fantasy, and science fiction by such giants in the tradition as Madeleine L'Engle, Lloyd Alexander, Isaac Asimov, C. S. Lewis, and J. R. R. Tolkien, he was captivated by those writers' abilities to take the reader to a fictional world and make it seem tangible, to breathe life and passion and personality into characters who were (sometimes) not even human. He made journeys into darker realms upon meeting the works of Edgar Allen Poe and H. P. Lovecraft during his teenage years, and those authors still influence his imagination and his writing to this day.

This fascination with the paranormal, however, has always been tempered by Gordon's scientific training. This has led to a strange duality: his work as a teacher, skeptic and debunker on the popular blog *Skeptophilia,* while simultaneously writing paranormal and speculative novels, novellas, and short stories. Gordon explains this, with a smile: "Well, I do know it's fiction, after all."

He blogs daily, and is never without a piece of fiction in progress—driven to continue (as he puts it) "because I want to find out how the story ends." From historical fiction (*Kári the Lucky*), to murder mysteries (the Parsifal Snowe Mysteries, beginning with *Poison the Well*), to paranormal fiction with a humorous twist (*Periphery* and *Lock & Key*) to the truly terrifying (*Gears* and *Descent into Ulthoa*), Gordon's fiction has something for all tastes!

Find him conversing with his dogs (and perhaps his wife) in Trumansburg, NY, or the following platforms:

- Website *http://www.gordonbonnet.com*
- YouTube *https://youtube.com/@skeptophilia1509*
- Skeptophilia blog *http://www.skeptophilia.com/*
- Twitter *@TalesOfWhoa*
- TikTok *@LittleBustardBooks* and *@gordonbonnetauthor*
- Instagram *@skygazer227*

Or, ya know, the Google.

also by gordon bonnet

In the Midst of Lions (Book One of Arc of the Oracles)

The Scattering Winds (Book Two of Arc of the Oracles)

The Communion of Shadows

Behind the Frame

Gears

Sephirot

Descent into Ulthoa

Lock & Key

The Shambles

Kári the Lucky

Kill Switch

The Fifth Day

Snowe Mysteries *(beginning re-releases 2023)*

Book 1: Poison the Well

Book 2: Dead Letter Office

Book 3: Face Value

Snowe Mysteries *(available now)*

Book 4: Past Imperfect

Book 5: Room for Wrath

Book 6: The Obituary Collector

Book 7: Slings and Arrows

The Boundary Solution Series (stay tuned for re-releases)

And More…

Stay tuned for releases *(and re-releases for ones you may have missed)*

Sign up for Gordon's Little Bustard Books Newsletter and Obscure

Weird Tidbits at his website: http://www.gordonbonnet.com